IN THIS CITY

AUSTIN CLARKE

Introduction by
DAVID CHARIANDY

Exile Editions

Publishers of singular
Fiction, Poetry, Drama, Non-fiction and Graphic Books
2008

Library and Archives Canada Cataloguing in Publication

Clarke, Austin, 1934-
    In this city / Austin Clarke ; introduction by David Chariandy.

(Exile classics 10)
ISBN 978-1-55096-106-5

    I. Title. II. Series.

PS8505.L38I5 2008   C813'.54   C2008-906128-4

Design and Composition by KellEnK Styleset
Cover Photograph by Joanna Ellenwood
Typeset in Garamond at the Moons of Jupiter Studios
Printed in Canada by Gauvin Imprimerie

The publisher would like to acknowledge the financial assistance of
The Canada Council for the Arts, and the Ontario Arts Council—which is
an agency of the Government of Ontario.

 Conseil des Arts **Canada Council**
du Canada for the Arts  ONTARIO ARTS COUNCIL
CONSEIL DES ARTS DE L'ONTARIO

Published in Canada in 2008 by Exile Editions Ltd.
144483 Southgate Road 14
General Delivery
Holstein, Ontario, N0G 2A0
info@exileeditions.com
www.ExileEditions.com

Canadian Sales Distribution: U.S. Sales Distribution:
McArthur & Company   Independent Publishers Group
c/o Harper Collins   814 North Franklin Street
1995 Markham Road   Chicago, IL 60610
Toronto, ON M1B 5M8   www.ipgbook.com
toll free: 1 800 387 0117   toll free: 1 800 888 4741

CONTENTS

INTRODUCTION

Austin Clarke has earned much critical acclaim for his novels, especially *The Polished Hoe*, which won the Giller Prize in 2002, and the International Commonwealth Writer's Prize in 2003. But Clarke is also a lifelong and demonstratively accomplished author of short fiction, a fact that might too easily be overlooked. Admittedly, several of Clarke's stories, such as "When He Was Free and Used to Wear Silks" and "Canadian Experience," continue to be anthologized and discussed to this day; and an anthology of Clarke's stories, selected from throughout his forty-five-year career as a writer, has now been published. However, until this very moment, each of Clarke's five short story collections have been out of print, denying readers, old and new, the rewarding experience of encountering Clarke's stories in their original arrangements and historical moments. Exile's re-release of *In This City* – indisputably one of Clarke's finest collections – is thus a very timely and happy event. For here, in peculiarly intense prose forms, we can find all of the wit, formal innovation, and trenchant social criticism that have made Clarke one of the most important writers of Canada and the Caribbean.

Austin Clarke was born in 1934 in Barbados. Although he came from a poor and single-parent household, Clarke managed to find his way into academic institutions that, historically, had been unwelcoming both openly and systematically to people of his background. He won a scholarship to study at the prestigious Harrison College in Barbados, and, thereafter, a scholarship to study economics at Trinity College in Toronto. Clarke arrived in Canada in 1955, and since has lived a life that the words "hectic" and "productive" can only begin to evoke. From 1965-73, he worked as a journalist and broadcaster covering social issues, especially the civil rights movement. From 1968-74, he served as visiting professor at Yale, Brandeis, Williams, Wellesley, Duke, and the universities of Texas and Indiana while assisting in the development of Black studies programs at Yale and Harvard. In 1974, he became cultural attaché of the Barbadian Embassy in Washington, and, from 1975-77, he served as general manager of the Caribbean Broadcasting Corporation in Barbados. From 1973-76, he served as advisor to the Prime Minister of Barbados, and, from 1989-94, he was a member of the Immigration and Refugee Board of Canada. Clarke has been writer-in-residence at several libraries and universities in Canada, and, in 1992, he was honoured with a Toronto Arts Award for Lifetime Achievement in Literature. In 1997, Frontier College in Toronto also granted him a Lifetime Achievement Award. In 1998, he received the inaugural Rogers Communication Writers Trust Prize for Fiction and, in the same year, he was invested with the Order of Canada. In 1999, he was awarded Canada's W.O. Mitchell Prize for producing an outstanding body of work, as well as the United State's Martin Luther King Junior Award for Excellence in Writing. He has received four honorary doctorates and numerous honours for his individual works. He has also, of course, managed to do a bit of writing: no less than 11 novels, five short-story collections, four non-fiction books, and a plethora of shorter prose works. At 75 this year, Clarke shows no sign of slowing. The publication of his 11th novel, most appropriately entitled *More*, has just been released.

Clarke is a writer of international importance, and contextualizing his work is no easy task. The challenge mounts when one recognizes that Clarke is one of those rare writers who have done much to create the very fields in which their work is now commonly placed. Perhaps the first thing that ought to be noted is that Clarke is one of the last major and actively practicing members of the "first wave" of contemporary Anglo-Caribbean writers, which included such formidable talents as V.S. Naipaul, George Lamming, and the late Sam Selvon (Clarke's personal friend). These writers rose to prominence in the 1950s and 1960s amidst major shifts in the social and cultural fabric of the English-speaking world. At the time, almost all of the "first wave" writers were based in London, England, then the indisputable capital of Anglo-Caribbean writing. But Clarke, of course, was based in Toronto, Canada; and he has contributed more than any other prose writer to the possibility, recently articulated by the late E.A. Markham, that the global capital of Anglo-Caribbean writing (outside of the Caribbean itself) has shifted now to Toronto.[1] Another thing that ought to be noted is that Clarke has had a deep and sustained engagement with Afro-American cultural debates as they have shifted through civil rights, Black Power, and more contemporary iterations or "moments" – a fact that can readily be observed both through a perusal of Clarke's writings and his extensive professional experience in the U.S. But *In This City*, as well as a great many of Clarke's other books, makes clear the fact that Clarke has always been particularly attentive to the challenges faced by West Indian immigrants and their descendants in Canada and especially Toronto. Here again the sheer scope of Clarke's life-experience is

---

[1] Markham makes this claim in his introduction to *The Penguin Book of Caribbean Short Stories*. He refers to "the huge colony of Caribbean writers in Canada" (xv), including Dionne Brand, the late Louise Bennett-Coverley ('Ms. Lou'), the late Sam Selvon, Cecil Foster, Ramabai Espinet, Claire Harris, Makeda Silvera, Olive Senior, M. NourbeSe Philip, Rabindranath Maharaj, Dany Laferriere, Rachel Manley, and Lorna Goodison, to name only a few. Markham explicitly suggests that "outside the Caribbean, the 'West Indian Literary Capital' has shifted from London to Canada" (*Penguin Book Caribbean Short Stories* footnote xliv).

important to grasp. When Clarke first arrived in Toronto in 1955, it was more than a decade before the revised Immigration Act of 1967, which, for the first time in Canadian history, allowed qualifying non-whites relatively unrestricted entry into Canada. In other words, Clarke first arrived in an urban space that was multicultural (as it always had been), but not nearly as "racially" diverse as it is now. Clarke's first major prose accomplishment, the novels comprising the Toronto Trilogy (*The Meeting Point*, *Storm of Fortune*, and *The Bigger Light*), were all originally published between the years of 1967 and 1975, and they focused on the experiences of working-class West Indian immigrants in the lonely and occasionally hostile contexts of a largely white city. But by the time Clarke had published *In This City* (in 1992), Toronto's black and Caribbean populations had grown immensely. Indeed, it is most telling that the first story of *In This City*, "Gift-Wrapped," concerns a young woman from the small town of Timmins who comes to Toronto and cannot help but notice the parade of "West Indians," although she ultimately finds this phenomenon, perhaps as an indicator of city life writ large, "too new, too rich, too diverse in colours and in rhythm for her to dare to be closer to it." (7)

"Gift-Wrapped" is both an attractive and unusual way to open *In This City*. In many respects, the story exhibits themes and circumstances that have fascinated Clarke for decades: an individual arrives in a big city dreaming of success and of escape from the past, but soon experiences social isolation and learns how, for many, the goals of urban happiness and security are inaccessible. But "Gift-Wrapped" is also striking in that there is strong if not absolutely conclusive evidence that the protagonist is white, or, at the very least, most unlikely of Caribbean background. "Gift-Wrapped" reminds us that people of very different backgrounds – even the dominant group – can experience the anomie of the city,[1] and that Clarke intends his fiction, even when focusing on people of African-Caribbean descent, to speak to broader social issues and experiences. However, it is also clear that most of the stories in *In This City* focus on Afro-Caribbeans (and particularly immigrant Barbadians) as they negotiate their lives and aspirations with others. "Gift-Wrapped" is immediately followed by "Initiation," in which a relatively conservative "university professor" of Barbadian background encounters youths living in Toronto's notably "black" Jane and Finch corridor, but using the language of black power "as if [they were] in Harlem and not Toronto" (30). Clarke's depiction of the youths is largely satirical, of course; and this echoes Clarke's own lifelong interest in, but also critical detachment from, American black nationalism (see, for instance, his famous interview of Malcolm X). But it would be a mistake to interpret "Initiation" as reflecting a dismissive attitude, on the part of Clarke, towards those youths (or even more experienced folk) who have identified, to greater and lesser degrees, with the theories, postures, and aesthetics of black pride. It is perhaps no irrelevant matter that, today, at 75, the occasionally self-proclaimed "conservative" Dr. Clarke appears able to sport both cuff-links *and* dreadlocks, sip martinis *and* reverently prepare pigs' tails and breadfruit, with magisterial confidence and no apparent sense of contradiction.

---

[1] Note, however, that the obvious counterpart to "Gift-Wrapped" is Clarke's "Canadian Experience," which was first published in the collection *Nine Men Who Laughed*. Like "Gift-Wrapped," "Canadian Experience" features someone who migrates from rural and relatively 'unsophisticated' circumstances to the city. The protagonist in "Canadian Experience" also hopes to become an executive in a downtown business. However, unlike "Gift-Wrapped," the protagonist in "Canadian Experience" comes from Barbados; and, in the end, he neither lands a job nor gets reunited with his family, but dies as a result of suicidal despair or a fatal moment of disorientation.

In fact, each of the stories in *In This City* resists hasty "answers" or summations, as good fiction always does. However, a few more points might be ventured. In "A Short Drive," Clarke offers his learned Toronto-dwelling West Indian protagonist a direct and highly palpable encounter with American blackness and race relations. But the protagonist soon learns much more than he might have anticipated about the "dualism" of identity in general. Of course, many of Clarke's other stories in *In This City* are very clearly about the immigrant experience. In "Letter of the Law of Black," Clarke explores the sorts of thoughts and emotions – the textual "care packages" and "remittances" – that can be sent and received by close relatives living apart. Here, a father advises his son, who is studying in Canada, to take heed of the "virtual potpourri of nationalities" that the nation now exhibits, but also to beware the dangers "of sponsors, fools and liberals" – advice that is instantly familiar to anyone with conservative Caribbean-born parents (56, 60). In "I'm Running for My Life," Clarke returns to one of his oldest themes, the complex and sometimes perilous circumstances that can be faced by female domestic workers in Canada (see, for instance, his novel *The Meeting Point*); and in "Trying to Kill Herself" and "Naked," Clarke delves deep, once again, into the sometimes grim interiority of Black immigrant life. But in "Sometimes a Motherless Child," Clarke pairs, for one of the first truly notable times, his life-ong interest in West Indian immigrants with his effort to understand the *children* of these immigrants, and their own complicated identities and aspirations. "Sometimes" joins a handful of texts by other Caribbean-Canadian writers that have begun to explore, with greater depth, the urgencies of "second-generation" immigrant life, and the particular stories and psychologies that emerge when one is born "in this city," but remains marked as "other." Once again, Clarke proves himself to be engaged most passionately with the latest shifts in

Canada's social and cultural fabric, and "Sometimes" ends up being one of Clarke's fiercest articulations of protest against "this city's" – any city's – violent wasting of its youth.[1] As such, the final story of *In This City* serves as an indispensable introduction to Clarke's ambitious depiction of youth culture and generational rifts among Caribbean immigrants in his latest novel *More.*

David Chariandy
September 2008

David Chariandy lives in Vancouver and teaches in the department of English at Simon Fraser University. His first novel, *Soucouyant*, was nominated for ten awards of regional, national, and international scope. His second novel, *Brother*, is forthcoming.

---

[1] It is most important to know that the two principal characters in Clarke's latest novel, entitled *More*, are a youth named "BJ" and his mother, who are wrestling with circumstances very similar to those first addressed in "Sometimes a Motherless Child."

GIFT-WRAPPED

When she went to look at the apartment, the sun was shining in the pools of water left back by the street-cleaning van. The street looked like slate or like slag that came out of mines and was piled into banks of snow all during the winter, and later into small hills of grey. And the pink impatiens in the stone boxes at the ornate front door of the building, one on each side and sitting squat and solid in front of the sheet of glass that gave each square of stone its imposing reflection so that it appeared to her as if they were four boxes of the pink flowers instead of two, and when she turned the corner from Bay Street, taking in the untidy, noisy garage of buses at the Gray Coach Terminal that went all over the country, and walked up the imitation granite slabs in the walkway to Midtown Mansions, she felt a little sick to her stomach. She was on her lunch hour, a break of forty-five minutes from the office where she worked in the heart of that section of the city she heard them call the Financial District; her first job following university in London, Ontario. And when she turned her glance to hear the announcement of departing buses, starting and stopping and puffing smoke and causing small congestions of traffic, with the West Indian taxi drivers refusing to move and give up their places in the unmoving queue and who would not accommodate the huge buses trying to turn, she remembered it was two months ago that she had arrived, excited, into this city, fatigued and ragged from the midnight Toronto express journey that began in Timmins, her home town.

When she had stepped out of the cool bus and onto the dirty tarred road in the Gray Coach Terminal, amongst the renovating clutter of planks and bulldozers, the smell of cigarette butts and of oil and gas fumes, and the humidity in the air that hugged her, she was dizzy and had the same nausea in her stomach. She was dizzy on that Saturday night also, from the success of her escape from the small, friendly town of Timmins. Now, on this Monday afternoon, her dizziness turned to agitation, and was caused by her indecision about taking the apartment, and by the imposing appearance of the apartment building itself. Midtown Mansions. In Timmins, she had for all those twenty-five years, except summers for the three she had spent at the University of Western Ontario, lived in a small house on McKelvie Avenue, smack in the trough of snow piled higher than the two-storey clap-board house, with father, a miner at the Hollinger Mines; mother, nurse's aide at the Timmins General Hospital; brother, now seventeen; brother, number two, fifteen; and sister, thirteen, all in high school, there in the three-bedroom house.

The advertisement proclaimed that she was going to inspect a bachelor's suite, and it said that it was suitable for a young career executive; male or female; in the heart of Toronto, with downtown luxury living, close to everything; no car needed and no parking problems as a result, or to suffer through, for the TTC was there and ran all night; close to the Eaton Centre, Massey Hall, the Thomson Hall, within sight of the CN Tower, and "from your window, you can see Sky Dome." She grasped the copy of *Chatelaine* so tightly in her hand, making it smaller, into a tube, that the print came off in her palm. Her palm was hot. She fixed the long strap of her black shiny handbag in the crux of her shoulder, and tried deliberately not to let her heels strike the walkway like bullets. She stopped and passed her hand, that with the tube of *Chatelaine* in it, over the pleats in her cream summer frock. She saw herself in the glass, reflected smaller than her five feet two inches, made small in the mirrored portrait framed by the huge entranceway.

"Eight hundred a month," the man said. "Of course, you pay two months in advance, and so on and so on." He seemed as if he had other things to attend to. When she walked with him to the door of his apartment, the door was ajar, and amongst the furniture which was too much for the room, an easy-boy sprawled with nobody in it; a large low coffee table piled with newspapers; and the television set, the largest piece in the room, bright and loud and with the natural colours of summer in it, she could see a million faces laughing and countless eyes looking up to heaven, while a voice said, "Oh boy, oh boy! It's hit-a-ton! *There* she goes! A home run for George Bell!" The announcer said how many home runs he had hit, but she missed that. Slowly, the man was moving towards her now, all the time looking back at the stream of faces; and then he closed the door.

And in truth, she could see the tall spire of the CN Tower, and the top of Sky Dome, and the haze-like thin clouds in the distance; and the lake and some sails like white pages of paper tacking in the steady breeze on the lake, and the buildings high in the sky, glistening in the sharp, blinding light. She looked at her watch: fifteen minutes more before she was due back at her desk in one of those tall buildings that were surrounding her, as she stood tantalized by the beauty of Toronto, and in two minds about the cost of the rent.

She had been living with a girlfriend, also from Timmins, in a one-bedroom apartment in a basement in the Annex, a stone's throw from the university where her friend was doing graduate work in library science. They had got along well: had been friends since high school; had gone on double dates to dances at the Schumacher Legion Hall; but now in this city, she found herself spending from Friday night until Sunday in the dark basement which sweated, and whose walls harboured little things that crawled and moved imperceptibly slow, so slow that at times she thought it was the movement of ideas in her head that caused her to imagine that there were bugs crawling in the apartment. The books that her friend brought from the three libraries on campus were scattered throughout the small one-bedroom apartment and printed her friend's life with a more important intellectual effect and priority, and she was left to sleep on the couch in the living room. She could almost follow the books, marked at pages with ballpoint pens, facing downwards like collapsed tents, and imagine them as the tracks she would follow each moose-hunting season in the bush just outside Timmins, as she walked scared beside her father, gun in hand, gathering meat for the long burying winter. And the basement seemed to her to be too similar to that dimness beneath the tall trees in the bush, and too similar to that smell of damp decaying leaves and shrub, that even the smell of cigarettes her friend smoked, and the incense that she bought outside the Eaton Centre from a black man dressed in white, in a robe that looked like her grandmother's nightgown, nothing could eradicate the fragrance of the ground, of being buried, the smell of fresh mould in a grave just prepared.

The feeling of power that came with the height at which she was now standing, looking towards the lake, and the exhilaration of the seventeenth floor, and the clean smell of the silk wallpaper on three sides with its pattern of spring flowers she had never seen, the large expanse of glass in her three windows, since she has this corner apartment, so clear, so transparent that standing before all this glass, the city came right up to her and she felt she was suspended, cut off from the people in her past. The glass was so clean from the Windex the man had used on it that there seemed to be no glass at all, as if it was not there to prevent her from the fall seventeen flights down to the hard granite in the walkway, so far in her drop on the two white boxes of crusted stone, like coral, the size from this height, of two shoe boxes. In Timmins, all through grade three, she kept her dolls in two shoeboxes.

It was exhilarating. She looked down, and in the seconds her gaze took to reach the pink impatiens, she imagined what it would be like to fall.

Her hand trembled as she held the pen and guided it over the paper of the contract; it was recycled; and over the blue cheque, and in the small space in the short line where she recorded all her charges and credits that affected her chequing account. Above the line she was writing now was $139.50 for her Visa; and above that, two days earlier, she had recorded "the Bay (dress), $80.00." At the end of the line, in the column for her balance, she had made the calculation, $13.85. But she did not write it in. When she was finished she had $13.84 – a slight mistake with a penny – left in her account. Her next payday was eleven days to come.

But the skies were blue all of July; and the two stone boxes were multiplied by five, as impatiens, mums and geraniums blossomed and transformed the entrance to her building, into an English garden; and she would walk along Yonge Street in the early weekend evenings and feel safe, before the tough, noisy teenagers who occupied the strip between Wellesley and Dundas; and she reproduced in her apartment a portion of the ebullience in the boxes she passed at least two times a day. And she would stand at her window that pointed to the lake, in the full smell of her pink geraniums, in two green plastic pots; and more flowers at peace and in bloom in the containers from Chinese dinners of chow mein. As she passed the five closed doors from her own door, on her way along the red-patterned carpet that muffled the clip of her heels, one of these five doors would be ajar, and a quick glance showed her the ferns and palms and cut flowers and the brass and the glass in the living room of her unknown, unseen neighbour. A large colour television flicked and switched the faces of dolls that were speaking like small children; or she would see the thousand cheering faces, and hear the scream, "There she goes!" She had never seen this neighbour since she moved in.

But she wanted to live like this. And she learned to tell the styles and designs that young men and young women wore and she could tell the stores they shopped in, along Yorkville and Cumberland; and she could call the names of all the boutiques in the Eaton Centre, knew the names by their fragrance, of the scents and perfumes they used; and she could pick them out on the exact page of *Vanity Fair* and of *Vogue*. She had cancelled her subscription to *Chatelaine,* and had mailed the old ones to her mother, in Timmins. In these evenings filled with the dying romance of August, she would walk along Yorkville, after a visit to her former roommate who still lived in the Annex in the basement with her books and bugs; and after coffee and cakes at the Other Café, and dinner at a pizza place on Bloor, or chicken at the Chalet, and with an ice cream cone in her left hand, for she was left-handed, walk and wonder; walk and dream; walk and was excited in her new -formed independence.

She was right to have made the excuse, tell the lie to her friend, and not go with her to Montreal. She was wise to have made the excuse, tell the little lie, and escape going with her last March break to Florida. And her friend's pestering urges to shop with her in the second-hand stores in the Village and along Queen Street West and the money she could save in those incense-filled, darkened boutiques did not make her change her mind. She wanted to be her own woman. She knew she had not spent three years at the University of Western Ontario for nothing.

Her apartment was spartan. But she had no social demands upon her time or upon the single mattress that lay on the floor, against a wall, with pillows propped against the wall, to make it into a settee by day, and a bed during the long, sometimes sleepless nights. One modern plastic chair, Art Deco, a few pots and pans, two dinner plates bought from Ashley's at a 70 percent discount sale, three large posters of her favourite rock stars, Police, U2 and Springsteen, and one of a landscape of snow powdering trees, in a place that could be Timmins, she had no money put aside for social things. She had just put a small rebuilt stereo and an alarm clock radio on her Visa card. And the payday following her second rent cheque, she had put five records on the card. So, she licked the melting ice cream cone clean, licked her fingers, and walked and looked at the sports cars and the Jaguars and Mercedes-Benz that flowed past her, almost touching the sidewalk, noiseless as the chocolate chip that had melted on her hand and turned her fingers into the colour of the bodies of some of the women tanned in a hue that made her think of that afternoon in early August.

The pulsing beat of calypso music had come right through the thick-paned glass, and she looked over the roof of the bus station, through the haze of exhausts, and heard that starting and stopping noise of the buses, and saw the West Indian taxi drivers lolling in their cabs, using the drivers' seats for beds, and then the riot of the colours and the noise. The parade of drums and music and the rainbow in the colours and clothes of the thousands of men and women, and the sequins glistening like stars on the costumes, held her tapping her feet to this new blood-coursing sound, tied to her window most of that August Saturday afternoon. It was too new, too rich, too diverse in colours and in rhythm for her to dare to be closer to it. Its richness frightened her.

That day passed. The ten boxes of colour at the entrance wilted part of the day; the watering van cleansed the roads, and sometimes when the stalks of the impatiens stood erect, she thought the summer was coming back. September now, and longer walks alone, on Bloor to Creeds and Holt Renfrew, and to Coles where she bought the magazines that told her about fashions and how to dress, what fabrics to wear; was she a winter or a summer, or a fall; how to make a gourmet dinner without meat, and how a young woman like she should present herself to the world, in the masculine brown panelling of her office; and without going home to change, how she could be sexy and fresh and still professional, in case she was taken amongst the indoor plants at Fenton's, on the high stools of Vines, or amongst the thick white linen cloths and dim lamps of the Prince Arthur Room. A young woman of her office took her one Thursday night to a symphony at the Thomson Hall, and afterwards to the King Edward Hotel to dinner, and after that to her apartment on Lascelles Boulevard, where she lived on the ninth floor, to sit and just talk and maybe we could sit on the balcony and watch the subway trains come into the Davisville Station, "I am attracted to you." She left her at the corner of King and Yonge, and the next day in the office she did not see her, but her body was shivering as if her veins were filled with ice water. It was the first time this had happened to her, although in the office they said this woman, who walked with a bounce and wore her hair cut like some men in Timmins would, was so. "I don't know, I really can't say it's so, but I am damn sure!" they said about this woman, in the office.

She warmed things up in bright-coloured waterproof packages in her stove; and five days a week, slipped out alone at noon and ate her apple and cheese sandwich on a park bench in front of City Hall; and as the weather cooled she went shopping though she could shop only with her eyes, and purchase in her mind clothes two other women in her office wore, as if they were going to weddings every day of the week, conscious that her longing eyes and imagination were larger than her balance at the bank. But most of all, she liked to finger the clothes and the shoes at Holt Renfrew, which she came to call Holts, at Creeds and in the boutiques on Cumberland, touching the silk and the crocodile leather in bags and shoes and leaving piles unbought behind her. She liked to push her dainty feet, size five, into shoes that smelled so differently from her own, even when they were new. And the attendants, dressed like the models in *Vogue* and *Vanity Fair*, got to know her, and smiled, and after a time moved away from her, leaving their smiles behind to make her comfortable and not too self-conscious. "You may take your time," they would say. "Just take your time and look. If you want help, just . . ." And so, she was left to live in this world of graciousness and richness and fantasy, and of clothes that came alive and jumped on her body, from the pages of *Vogue* and *Vanity Fair*.

A man in the office smiled at her on Wednesday afternoon beside the coffee machine. That Friday, he asked her for a drink. She took a glass of white wine as she sat on a stool at Vines, elevated from the other men and women laughing into their glasses. The second glass almost made her topple. He saved her fall, and he held her, light and respectful, at her waist. She climbed back onto the stool with his help. And Nancy, the tall woman who served the wine, became three giggling women. She saw the large bright band of gold, bright as an alarm, as two golden warnings on his left wedding finger. "Yes," he said when she asked the question, brave now and tipsy and talkative from the wine. "For six years now. With two kids. But I was thinking of taking you home." The wine was wearing off. He stood beside her, silent in the ascent to the seventeenth floor, her thoughts of his conquest whirring in her head, her trepidation at this confinement making her soberer still, until they walked along the red-patterned carpet, until they reached her door, when the neighbour opened her door, with two plastic bags in her hands. "Thanks for bringing me home," she said to the man. He bowed and smiled and left. He never smiled at her after that, that way. But the work she had to do for him increased.

Darkness came earlier now. She left for work when it seemed night had not yet ended, and when she returned, passing the ten stone boxes covered in light snow, as if the mound around the geraniums was coated white, it was already dark. She lived in almost total darkness now. Her friend, the graduate student, went to Montreal for the September term. The man in the office passed her desk these days and called her "Miss"; and the woman who lived on Lascelles Boulevard, in her short skirts and red leotards, wore her hair even shorter now; and the glass in her windows became panes of frost, and the definition of things and people below on Bay Street, and the CN Tower and the other buildings were illustrated now only through the countless lights that burned in them. The lights never slept. Perhaps the woman who had taken her to the symphony, and the man who used to smile at her, were working late together. The woman was the niece of the president. The president lived in Miami every year after October. She had never seen the president. She had seen this man with the large gold ring smile with the president's niece, felt relieved from both of them and concluded he was now after *her*.

The lights around her remained on, beacons on the secrets and the enjoyment that surrounded her in a powerful, unknown, enviable voltage. Next door, the music was loud on weekends; and, alone in the apartment, she moved her body on the mattress on the floor, and had difficulty retrieving the slipping futon to her cold body, clothes in flannel pyjamas that had a pattern of scattering daisies, as she imagines the crystal glasses and the ferns, the rice biscuits and the paté, and caviar; the white wines and the imported beer, and their bodies clenched together, whenever the music is no longer loud; and the lights being put out, one by one, when magic and assumed love make their legs refuse to follow even the soft slowness of a waltz; and there is the promise of two filled bodies collapsing on a bed, by agreement from the wine. She cannot find the futon. She cannot tell which is its long side from its short. So, she sits up and stretches out her hand, and feels the table lamp which has no table, and it falls over, and its noise helps her locate the switch. In the darkness she was listening. There is soft laughter beside her. She hears their intimate footsteps and their whispers and their laughter again, passing her door. She turns the lamp on. Its shade had fallen off.

On her table, assembled one Saturday afternoon after she had picked it up from IKEA, were Christmas cards bought from Coles, with angels holding candles; and some from a fancy shop on Front Street, from England, for her father and mother, her brothers and little sister, her former roommate and the young woman who had taken her to the symphony. Hers was the first card she had received, signed "I still love you." One of these fancy cards, when they were addressed, would go to her high-school English teacher, and others to her friends back in Timmins; and as she sat looking at the cards, she listened to the laughter next door. As the door opened, she could hear the music clearer. Reggae. She recognized the beat. That was the beat that rang in her ears, part of that glorious August afternoon, on University Avenue. Everyone she had met in the few months in the city would get a Christmas card. She was determined to build a network of cards and friends. But the moment she sat down to address them, she changed her mind. She would send one only: to her high-school English teacher.

She went to the fridge for a drink. The half-empty bottle of Perrier water stood in front, the light of the efficiency fridge pouring through its bottle glass, reminding her of the purity of the water in the lakes she had fished with her father. On the same shelf with the Perrier were yogurt, mild cheddar cheese, tomato ketchup and orange juice. The wire shelves and the strong bulb in the refrigerator made it look empty. This must have crossed her mind, for with the Perrier bottle in her hand she opened the door to the freezing compartment, and looked at the accumulated frost which had almost buried the two ice trays that were empty, and the two flat packages of frozen dinners. The fact that there were two reminded her that it was Wednesday night.

The cold draught touched her face and the awakened sensation sent her back to Timmins, in this time of year when her father's car would be buried in the snow, the day he parked it; and it would remain buried, an uninhabited igloo, or a sentry box painted white, before the front gate; it sent her back, back to the warm house on McKelvie Avenue swimming in the smells of Christmas, to the sap of the tree stolen from the reforestation field owned by the Ministry of Natural Resources; to the subtle, sensual smells of the cloth for their Christmas church; and to the oil applied to the sewing machine pedalled by her mother, religiously for graduations, Easters, dances and for weddings which broke out like an epidemic of pure love, and those that were quiet, to save the face in sudden pregnancies, and for Christmases. The preserves and the fruits; and the red wine her father made in the basement; and the high smell of meat not bought in the supermarket but shot in the bush, and therefore wild, but made less tough from the generous doses of red wine in which her father, Mr. Petrochuck to the entire street, became an expert; both in its tasting and in its illegal manufacture. She could see the living room floor covered with the pieces of cloth, dresses and shirts, in sections pinned on to tissue paper with markings of directions on them; and common pins onto which she had stepped and had got small dots of blood on her heels, lying undisturbed against the tramping of feet and the stomping of boots. The dress patterns always looked to her like sections of carcasses left to dry. Her Christmas dress, with its complicated front and back, lay on the green indoor-outdoor carpeting, like two sides of a large cow. Yes, the activity and the laughter and the enduring patience of her mother, working into the night that approached dawn, when the horn from the nearby mine sounded; and how she used to raise her tired, company-keeping young body from the couch beside her mother and stare into those eyes, grey with colour and with age, and see her anxiety and measure the beat of her heart in the meaning of the mine horn, and the possible result of that summons; her mother sitting erect now, though deadened in her chair by the labour of peering at the thread which had become invisible, and feeling the muscles in her legs, her calves, which could still summon her tired husband to bed; even after eight hours buried underground like an animal, searching for gold. She would sit and watch her mother, and feel the volume of her silence, follow the imperception of the day getting older, and wonder if she too, in whatever house, in whatever marriage, in whatever social status of this community of miners, would some day have to sit and wait in this heavy silence for footsteps at the door, when the horn sounded. It was that living through eternity, thirty minutes long, that made her vow, in grade twelve, that she would leave Timmins. To escape the fate in the friendly town, in that familiar, greeting town, so healthy to grow up in, so easy to swallow you in order to seek a better life in Toronto.

This is her first Christmas in this city. This is her first Christmas living alone. This is her first Christmas as her own woman. This is the first time she does not have to lend her hand in the preparation of cakes, of cookies, of dressing for the turkey, in making popcorn to dress the stolen Christmas tree.

The tree in her house in Timmins stood almost seven feet, in its stolen splendour and illegal majesty, and packed tight under its bottom branches with gifts, one for each child, in boxes wrapped in cheap green and red paper, stuck together with brown Scotch tape. The mine was on strike all of December that last year.

This Christmas, she has chosen for herself wrapping paper of silver and gold. Silver and gold and blue ribbon. She has no tree. But she has seen the one she likes, leaning in these cold nights, in piles at street corners, and in cold parking lots. Maitland and

Church. Dundonald and Church. Isabella and Church. Charles and Church. And brown expensive wrappings from Creeds.

At the office Christmas party, held two days before the 25th, she marvelled at the beauty and the glitter and the waste of drinks and food, and at the fragrance of the cut flowers; at the cheeses, the patés, and the smell of rum punch in its huge crystal bowl, like a crater of ice raised above the ground. All this overwhelmed her. The ground was the boardroom table, and at one end was a pile of gifts, two for each employee, chosen by lot; most of them wrapped to look like bars of gold and silver. The silver boxes were tied with blue ribbon. Some boxes were covered in paper so rich, it looked like brocade, or like rich fabric, with Chinese pagodas, reindeer stranded on a hill, and one was shining black paper, rich as onyx. She wondered what her mother would do, to see her here, merry around her friends of work; what she would say when she learned that she was not coming home for Christmas, that she was now accustomed to this different world, this urban sophistication, and these people, complete strangers five months before; strict colleagues for all that, until one day ago, each person conscious of rank and of salary, and now laughing loud with the janitor and singing carols in voices with too much punch in them; and kissing in corners; and the place of a hand on a knee and five fingers on the raised hem of a silk dress; and seeing the man who had taken her to Vines, for the first time without his vest on, holding a cigar as long as a ruler, drooped at the right corner of his mouth, and with spit on it. He holds his thumbs at his red suspenders, stretching them outwards as if he is measuring girth and mirth to be as formidable as Santa Claus, and slapping the president who came for the party on his back. No, she won't be going home to Timmins this Christmas. The young woman who took her to the symphony came up to her, and placed her hands on her shoulders and kissed her on her mouth, and she could feel her tongue as it slid over her lips and feel her fingers move up to her breast. And as quick as it started, it ended. And she realized she was holding a silver-wrapped box as large as a shoebox in her hands. Her hands were trembling. Her vision was blurred by tears. But in the next second her ears were filled with "Here We Come A-wassailing" and the woman's voice, rich as a baritone, was barrelling the tune, joined in by all the secretaries. When they reached the end of the first stanza, she joined in too.

"And where are you going to be this Christmas?" the woman shouted across the table with the gifts.

"In town," he said. When her tears cleared, she saw it was the man who had taken her to Vines. Beside him was a woman. She was not a member of the firm.

"We're staying right here," the woman said.

"Bill and you'll be coming to the cottage Boxing Day, though!"

"Uncle's flying me to Miami tomorrow. We'll fly back on Christmas Day, and drive straight to the cottage."

It was at this moment she thought of buying food for Christmas. She had done no shopping. But she assumed there would be turkey, because she always had it at home. She remembered this now, as if with the shock of almost having forgotten, that she had not called home to say she would not be there. How would she choose the words? It's not the flight, no, Mom. I know there's the train, yes, Mom; if not the train, yes, I know, there is Grey Coach, yes Mom.

"I'm really have a good time here."

"Are you happy?"

"I'm really happy here, Mom."

"All right," her mother said, not convinced.

"I really am."

"Long's you're with friends."

If her conversation could go like that . . .

Here in the chatter of talk and greeting, she picked out that almost everyone was leaving the city at Christmas. She had forgotten to think of a turkey. Her former roommate, Jill, was in Montreal. And of drinks. Even though she seldom drank, she had to have something in for Christmas. Wish I knew how to make punch like this! Perhaps a liqueur. Perhaps some sherry. Grand Marnier, perhaps. But a smaller bottle than these on this mahogany boardroom table. And some Sandeman like these on this table. I wonder if they sell small bottles? Her rent was due in two days. Her Visa card was strained by the record albums of Sans Saens and Berlioz she had bought. And she had bought no gifts for anyone yet. But for whom would she buy them? For whom? Mom? Dad? Johnnie and Pat, her brothers? And for her sister, Sue? For Jill, her former roommate? And for . . . *No!*

"Bill, the gifts! Can your wife draw for the tickets to Thomson Hall? She's impartial."

"Honey," he said, holding his wife by the arm, her body big with their third child. "Meet our latest addition to the staff. This is Miss Belle. Miss Belle, Patricia, my wife."

"Oh! Timmins!" the wife said, with a smile that came to her lips like lipstick applied; and was wiped off straightaway, without saying another word. Bill shrugged his shoulders in defeat and in surrender, and smiled the way he smiled the night he took her home from the Vines bar. That night, he had hardly spoken with her as they sat for the two hours drinking.

"Where're you spending yours? Here? Or back home with your family?"

"With friends," she lied.

"Good. Nobody should be alone at Christmas."

"I'll be home with family and friends," she lied again.

"Bill?" It was his wife, calling him as if she was asking a question. She was beside him now. "Oh, I forgot to wish you Merry

Christmas. Would you be in town for the holidays? Or heading back to Timmins? You do have family in Timmins?"

"With my friends, in Timmins or, maybe, Toronto."

'Nobody, but nobody, remains in Toronto for Christmas!" Bill said.

The nativity scene in the show window of the Simpson's store tied her interest to its cold glass, and her face became the same as the temperature of the night. She had walked to this spot, the five cold blocks from the office Christmas party. In her hand, without a glove, were her gifts: one from the woman who took her to the symphony, and the other two from the office draw. All three were wrapped in silver paper and tied with blue ribbon. Her body was warm. She did not notice the cold. It was below zero. And with a wind. Children ripped their hands out of their parents' protection and ran to the moving scenes and pushed themselves in front of the adults, and stood against the cold window and recited the names of the animals, and named the reindeer and Santa's village, and the names of the gifts brought to Jesus by the Wise Men, and hummed along with the carol played on bells. The three Wise Men were all white. She walked on, heartened by the children's cries, some of whom were the same age as her brothers and sister, in the deep slush under the trees of gold, under the lights strung overhead; passing windows of ready-wrapped gifts in colours of red and green. And she stopped for a while to listen to five men and a woman dressed in black, begging for money and playing carols off key, and loud. A man was drunk on the sidewalk. He wiped his mouth after the thick greyish slush erupted from his bowels. He stood where he was, wobbled a bit, and then stepped into the acrid gruel at his feet, and began to conduct the five men and one woman of the Salvation Army Band in "God Rest Ye Merry

Gentlemen" played in lugubrious mood and in *lentissimo*. Music for Christmas, from many cultures and songs played in a rhythm that made them sound like rhythm and blues, blared on to the mushy sidewalk from record stores. A man begged her for spare change. And another, for a quarter to buy coffee. Other men stood in doorways, as if they were frozen into the pattern of the concrete pillars. She left these sounds of Christmas behind and headed home, turning off Yonge Street into the darker street where her apartment building was located. The ten stone boxes had turned to stubby snowbanks. Frost was sprinkled by hand, like writing, onto the glass of the front door, in shapes of Christmas trees, with the message, *Merry Christmas*. She was cold now. Her body was shivering. The three gifts were like blocks of ice in her hand as she entered the lobby, as she paused by the soft warm hiss of the vent, and could barely hear the voice of Perry Como coming from the superintendent's suite. "I'll Be Home for Christmas." In Timmins, she and her brothers and sister sang this song, and were accompanied in it by the old Seabreeze record player, until the grooves were broad and Perry Como sang with more slurs than his style intended.

Going up the elevator with her was a woman dressed in a black mink coat, black kid gloves, and a black fur hat. "Merry Christmas, dear," she said, with a foreign accent. She had heard this accent in the North. Her own mother had this accent, after forty years in Canada. It made her feel warm. And happy "All this rush for one day. Just *one* day! We spend what we don't got." The woman carried three large shopping bags. *Creeds* was written on one of them; but she could not place the blue boxes in the plastic bag.

On the street earlier, most of the people carried bags, some persons had three, and she joked with herself that they were most likely intent upon purchasing all they needed, all that was available, before the last-minute rush started, and as if each shopper were intent upon emptying the stores herself.

The elevator stopped at the fourteenth floor. There was no thirteenth. And she heard "Jingle Bells," piped through an unseen hole in the ceiling, for the rest of the climb.

The lights in her apartment remained off for a long time. Across the hall, she could hear voices and laughter. She got up from the mattress on the floor and went to the window, facing the street. The man she saw slumped beside the red mailbox when she came home was still there. She stood watching him until her eyes glazed over, until her body and the cold of the glass were almost the same temperature. The man had not moved when, hours later, she put on her flannel pyjamas, and sank into the mattress on the floor. In the darkness, the red digits of her clock radio said 3:00. And she thought of the man, wondering if he was still by the red mailbox. But she did not move. She had still not opened her three gifts.

In the crisp, early morning, Christmas Eve, as she stepped through the glass front door, the cold dampness hugged her round her waist; she checked in her mind that she was properly, warmly dressed; and she looked at the ten boxes which had held the pink, yellow and red blooms, and felt sad that they were now mounds of white, buried beneath the snow, like her father's car in Timmins, obliterated out of commission, beside the road. She glanced across the street. The man was not beside the mailbox. Perhaps he had died standing up. Perhaps he got warm and thawed enough to move. Perhaps a police cruiser took him to jail. Or to a shelter. Or to a morgue. She wondered where he was now. Did he die standing up, frozen like the trees in the tall circle of iron protectors? Did she actually see a man last night? Or was it her imagination? The cold, and the coldness of this city, brought a numbness to her spirits, and she could feel the hair in her nostrils and the hair of her eyebrows turn to bristle.

At the glass counter of the women's department at Holts, where most of the women looked like the one in the elevator, she bought pantyhose for herself, and asked for a gift box; and she bought a white lace handkerchief, for herself, and asked for a gift box; and she bought a pair of hair combs, for herself, and asked for a gift box; and before she left the store, charging these purchases to her Visa card, she asked for some silver wrapping paper and a large shopping bag. In Creeds, she asked for two gift boxes, without making a purchase. The attendant noticed the Holt Renfrew bag in her hand, assumed that she was a woman of means, and smiled, and gave them to her. She placed her handbag into the shopping bag; changed her mind; took out the handbag, and checked her shopping list. The items on her list were turkey, sherry, liqueur, one shawl for the woman who took her to the symphony, one tie, cigars – for Bill – incense, men's socks and nail polish. She bought only the nail polish, and the ladies' shawl.

The trees were like golden diadems. They hung in the middle of Bloor Street, suspended high above her head; and the trees in the large stone boxes sprouted fruits of sparkling gold; and some had silver leaves; and the men and women in the store windows dressed for display, from the pages of the latest expensive fashions, remained in the same arrogant pose and posture, not having moved or batted an eye in all the days she had been passing them. And men and women with large parcels walked, slipping on the sidewalk as if they were dancing to the dirge played by a group of musicians dressed in the uniform of the Army of Salvation, who serenaded the shoppers. It took her a while to recognize the carol they were playing. The street was full and joyful and everyone she passed said "Merry Christmas." And she was smiling. Her jaws were becoming tight. And her lips were cracked. And her eyebrows were like bristle. A man asked her, "Spare any change?" And she gave him a Loonie. He blessed her three times, and told her "Happy Christmas, dear" once.

And then, almost all of a sudden, the street was empty. The people had vanished. It was just after six o'clock, Christmas Eve. The people had all passed away, as if the snow, which was now blowing, had swept them into the sewers beneath the street. Steam was rising through the circular grates, along the side of the street, and that was the only sign of breathing, and of life.

It was over. All the fuss.

She laid her things on the IKEA table. She placed the bottle of Sandeman sherry on the kitchen counter. She emptied the boxes from Creeds and from Holts on the table. She had bought no Christmas ribbon. The cards she had bought three weeks before Christmas, at Coles where they were cheap, remained in their boxes, unopened, unaddressed, unnoticed. The pink geranium plant in the windowsill needed water. She took the coffee mug with *I Love Toronto* written in fat round letters round its girth, and with a large red heart, filled it with water, and walked to the window. As she poured, as the plant remained unaffected by its sudden nourishment, she peered through the frost on the pane to see if she could see the man, Her vision was clouded. With her left hand index finger, all the while pouring the water into the green plastic flowerpot, watering the geranium to its certain drowning death, she marked *X* on the glass. Then *M*. Then *A*. Then *S*. And around these letters, she drew an uneven circle. It became the outline of a face. She drew the curve of its mouth turned downwards. Through an eye in the face, she saw a man; the same man, leaning against the red mailbox. She watched him until she heard the water hitting the floor in drops.

She moved from the window. She walked around the small apartment, immaculate and tidy except for the scatter of boxes and purchases on the table. No sound came from the people on her right. No voice from the woman who lived on her left. Everything was still. Softly her clock radio was playing carols, the same carols, over and over, the same tiring carols she had learned in kindergarten. She had listened to "Wish You a Merry Christmas" four times already. She opened the bottle of Sandeman Sherry. And poured a drink in the *I Love Toronto* mug. She took the drink to the mattress, spread a blanket over her legs, and sat and watched the darkened sky and listened to the silence. The window was closed. No life came from below. Just like the silence she and her mother listened to, for those thirty minutes after the mine horn summoned the end of one shift of life, spent in the bowels of the earth. In the northern silence, the wait and the silence gave birth, at its maturation, thank God, to the stomping of her father's feet on the side-door steps. All those miles from here, on this holy night, her own wait is merely silence. The silence of expectation and of fertility; a woman waiting for a birth, to deliver her from labour.

Carols the radio was playing, having for a long time now, become an unending drone, like the sound of the horn of the mine. The silence of the darkness is heavier with the drone. And still she sits and waits, with the untouched expensive mug of sherry beside her. Her mind goes back to those sleepless Christmas Eve nights tramping down the wooden stairs, just as dawn was about to break and the light of morning was similar to the colour of the sky she saw on the Christmas cards, and like the sky she saw in the window of Simpson's nativity; creeping in her flannel pyjamas, the kind she was wearing now; the hand of each brother in each hand; feeling the stickiness of her palms, as if they had gone to bed with chewing gum in their mouths and in their excitement, too; crawling under the seven-foot Christmas tree, higher than any tree in the forest before it was stolen, like two wise men and a female angel; and opening their presents, countless as the stars, before it is time. And one Christmas Eve, she had to open ten large boxes, wrapped in red or in green tissue paper, before she could assemble and make sense of her gift: earmuffs, scar, pin for the scarf, tam-o'-shanter, mittens, inner gloves for the mittens. On the floor, these gifts of limbs were finally skeletoned into one body, when she ripped open the green box that held the thick, green, flesh-crawling, acrylic leo-tards. And they would sneak back over the skeletons, having walked over the trunks of one dress her mother could not finish. And the smells, more than any other reminiscence, of the untidy Christmas morning house.

The apartment is spic-and-span; clean and immaculate. She sits and waits, and then her waiting and the silence are broken by the heavy breathing of her slumber. The blue Christmas-card light comes through the window, which she does not see. The clock-radio is awake and wishing "Merry Christmas" to its listeners; and it says that the day will be cold, and there will be no snow, and that Bing Crosby will sing "White Christmas;" and there is a church service, and talk of turkeys and presents . . .

"How many did you get?"

"Hundreds."

"How many, stupid"

"Five."

"Me, I got ten."

"Ten?"

"I opened ten presents to finally find all the pieces of one lousy new outfit!"

"I wish I had brothers and sisters."

. . . and mince pie and pudding and funny hats hidden inside bright crackers, and more carols sung by a choir of boys in a cathe-dral somewhere in England.

She is sitting at her father's table and he has just plunged the hunting knife into the turkey where its kidneys would be, if a turkey has any kidneys; and the smoke is just clearing from the log forced into the cast-iron stove and the meat of the moose is still tough and red, as if the gallon of wine in which it has been soaked for days is its own blood; and the galvanized pipe is red, and the sparks fly, in wrong directions . . .

"Get a bag! Wet it! Wet it!"

. . . and she can hear, between sleeping and waking, emerging from that netherworld, twigs crackling like an anxious voice. And the crackling in the stove becomes the sound of her name being called out, which pulls her from her sleep, which pulls her from the mattress on the floor; and in this state, fluid and unpunctuated as a sleepwalker's, she goes to the door and opens it, a thing she has not done before, in this city with all its creeps and men abusing women.

It was when she looked into the man's eyes, and ran her eyes over the apparition of his body, trousers of green plaid, red woollen shirt thick as a lumberjack's, and red sweater, dressed as if he is going into the busy, did she look at herself, to see that the top of her grey pyjamas is unbuttoned, for three buttons from the top, and the pants on which the white daisies are more numerous and visible on the rumpled material, and always bought too large, even from childhood and for economy, have sagged down her hips. But the man was not examining her body.

"Get dressed," he said, looking at her feet. "Get dressed! Patricia and the kids're downstairs, waiting in the car."

INITIATION

Click! Click! Click! Click! Click! Five bolts and locks, and pieces of light artillery, machinery and equipment made this sound of entry. It was like heavy equipment clanging on the Toronto waterfront, or on a construction site. Five anxieties that meant, in this section of the city, protection and safety and secrecy for whatever was going on, "was going down" behind the red-painted glossy door, was not to be exposed to any and every visitor, and certainly not to the man.

"My man!"

The door was open.

"Hey, brother!"

"What's happenin?"

"Ain't nothing happenin, brother."

"What's happenin is happenin!'

"Right on!"

"This here's my main man!"

He introduced me.

"Right on!" And he burst out laughing.

"This be a cool motherfucker! This motherfucker be West Indian-English, brother!"

"So, what's happenin, mah man?"

"I'm cool. Things cool. Every thang's cool!"

"How's everything, bro?"

"Right on!"

"Yeah!" Barrington said. "Meet my main man!"

I was introduced a second time.

"Is this brother *into* the revolution?"

"Prof at the university."

"Motherfucker! Shee-it! Ain't this a motherfucker! Prof, eh? The Ivy Leagues, eh? Gimme five, my man! Revolution needs some heavy brothers, professors and shit! *Heavy!*"

The full, strong, powerful and deep tone of the saxophone, which I recognized as John Coltrane's, came like a wave of rescue and destruction over the room. The music was like a thick layer of nurturing blood. It was as if the music was a synopsis of all I had been exposed to outside on the street in this section of the city, Jane and Finch; and a summary of what was going on in this room. A synopsis of the smell, the hope, the fear, the joy, the liquor I had drunk, and the women, and the power of the city itself.

"Yeah, my man! What's happenin on Bay Street and downtown? Yeah!"

"Ripped off these magazines for you, bro."

"Right on! Revolution *needs* documentation, brother. Power to the people! Yeah!"

"Got a little surprise for you. Outside. Some wheels."

"Right on! *Vinceremos*, brother, *vinceremos!*"

"Some serious shit!"

"Where's the brother from?"

"York."

"Where's he *from*? Where's the brother's aesthetic-cultural roots, man? The South?"

He looked at my American army fatigue bought on Jarvis and Queen, and worn while I was teaching a summer course in Black Literature, and I wasn't sure whether his strong gaze suggested astonishment or complete dismissal. He was the size of Mohammed Ali, with the same lightish complexion, and his eyes were grey and piercing. They went right through me, and this determination of gaze made him more powerful, and me, withered against his disapproval. He was dressed in skin-fitting blue jeans and a long black robe that reached to his knees, with three embroidered lines round the collarless neck. Red, black and green. I had just arrived from New York and my student, who was now standing uncertain between the two of us, had picked me up at Pearson International Airport. Barrington's arrival in a maroon late-modelled Mercedes-Benz was as incongruous as my introduction to this man in this apartment in the heart of Jane and Finch was uncomfortable. Barrington wore blue jeans at York, with holes at the knees and in the seat; and he gave me the impression for the first semester I was his professor in Black Literature that he was a neglected, indigent, fatherless and motherless product of Jane and Finch. "Product of the ghetto" is the phrase he always used to describe himself, to me and to the other black students. But they seemed to have known the truth. I was accepting his definition of himself, romanticizing that definition and making my friendship with Barrington and my own understanding of him more easy to swallow. I was going to spend a few hours with Barrington, meet his aunt, he said he had no mother, and check out the scenes in this section of the city, and visit the places which I had read about in the *Star* newspaper and in magazines, and which I had lectured about in Barrington's class. This stop was not on the tour. And I was not moved by the investigative introduction I was being put through: for my mind was on the booze can and a chicken-and-waffles place and the barbecued fish and jerked chicken I had been reading about. I loved my outfit. When I arrived in New York in early June, I was wearing a three-piece suit, college tie of Trinity College, and brown suede shoes.

"Where's the brother's roots?"

"The islands."

"West Indies?"

"The brother's a Carbean man."

"Yeah!"

The tall man, who looked more and more like Mohammed Ali the longer he stood before me, was rocking on his heels as I had seen Texans do, as they stood at the bar in the restaurant where I went once to have southern-fried chicken at Chicken Box Number One. "Gimme five, brother! *Afro-West Indian.* Yeah! Gimme some skin! Yeah! Marcus Garvey. Yeah! Padmore. Yeah! Peace and love, brother!" With each "yeah" he shook my hand stronger. "Paul Lawrence Dunbar! Dunbar. Yeah! *If I should die, let me nobly die.*"

As we stepped farther inside the room, I saw that it was haze with blue smoke. And I could remember, in that instant, waking in the early mornings in Barbados, when the mornings were the same colour, and I could not tell whether it was the wind blowing the dying gasps of a cane-fire that had raged during the night, whose smoke was now fanning us into our unexpected safety, after a night of unknown disaster. Not really sure whether the morning light was married with the blue low clouds, taking in the colour of the canes themselves and the sea a few miles down the hill. And there was a smell to the haziness of the atmosphere. I did not see nor notice any lamps burning. When we came up in the elevator, it was late afternoon outside. Early September.

And like the morning haze which moves slowly towards you, and envelops you in its harmless embrace, so too did the room of this strange man take me into its arms. John Coltrane went into a roaring, untamed straining and screaming, making his instrument sound like the voice of a lion taken out of its veldt and placed against that tradition transported out of the jungle and put into a cage for eyes to see; and the iron in the cage; and against the restriction of chords laid down by gamekeepers and by tradition and others who said that those chords could not be broken I began to think of the shouts of black power which I had been hearing around me, at York, and that time in Texas, two improvisations on the original theme, and here in Jane and Finch so different from where I lived in this same city; still the same words, shouted at me as if the men shouting them felt that I was as unbeliever, a West Indian man and not one of them. But I kept coming back to the shouts and the meaning I got from the shouts when they were not too confused by the spit of their own violence. And I began to wonder if this is the meaning, the quintessence, of the new blackness taking root in this city. I was beginning to feel I was in Harlem.

"This is some heavy shit," Barrington said, using a language and gesture I had not heard nor seen in months at York. He was searching for a place to sit down.

"Trane's heavy shit. *Let me nobly die!*" the host said, screaming the words out, as if he too was a musician with an instrument, accompanying the sounds erupting from the speakers. He made his voice seem like the instrument, as he repeated the words, *Let me nobly die!*

"We got a deal?" Barrington said. I was beginning to doubt that I knew this young man who had come to my office and my downtown home so often to discuss his assignments which were always late, but which, when finished, were of exceptional insight and solid intellectual organization; this young man whom I had pitied because of his deprived background in a small apartment somewhere in this section of the city, beaten down by reams of features in the *Toronto Star* and by second-year sociology students, inquiring to understand this black community where we were now, without father and mother, and occupied by strangers who came to visit his aunt, whom he said, apologetically, "was involved in some mean things, motherfucker." I did not know him at all, as he stood bargaining with this tough, heavyweight champion of a man, whom I could see fitting as easily in the Kingston Pen or the Don, as I was seeing him now in this gloomy, lampless apartment whose windows were closed against the life outside on the September street, filled with colour and life and noise and large automobiles which blared the latest in reggae and dancehall, blowing their horns when even an ant came into their shined, slow-moving path.

"Do we have a deal, brother?" Barrington said.

"Baby, you come into my crib," the man said, speaking a different language, as if he was in Harlem and not Toronto, "and with a brother who's *into* the revolution, being a brother from the Ivy Leagues, and you ask *me* if we have a deal? Shit, baby, we been dealing . . ." He did not finish his thought. He put something to his lips, the room was darker now; and closed his eyes, and the steely grey eyes disappeared; and he inhaled deeply, and in an instant of exhaling the room became bluer. He started to cough. Something was caught in his throat. "Shit, baby, we got a deal! Check this out," he said, handing Barrington the thing held between his thumb and index finger. "Try some o' this shit, my Afro-Westindian brother!" There was a large X, in gold, on the cap he wore.

Barrington acted for me, and spoke for me.

"Whoooooo!" he said. He returned the thing the same way the host handed it to him.

"Vinceremos, compadre! Vinceremos!"

"Latinamericano," Barrington said, with a Spanish accent.

I did not know Spanish.

"Fidel!" the man screamed.

"Fidelito!" Barrington said, as if he was in Cuba.

"Castro."

Barrington passed the cigarette to me. I panicked. But I knew that the etiquette and the protocol of this room demanded that I take it. I had never smoked a cigarette like this before. Although I did not know what it really was, I still knew what it was. It was

30

thicker than any I had seen for the past few months, hand-rolled by the old men in the streets of Harlem, who sat on wooden benches under the canopies of old, almost derelict stores, or on the park benches which seemed to be placed everywhere, every three steps that an old man could take, in the hot, never-ending New York humidity. This one was wrapped in brown leaf.

I wanted to be accepted, and regarded as cool, so I accepted it. I did not exactly know what to do with it, and how to use it with the same coolness Barrington had employed.

"Castro!" I said too loudly to be cool, which I wanted to be, and in a voice I knew had embarrassed my student, and was suspicious to my host. But they ignored me. I had heard my own voice come out like a bellow as I spoke. And I knew that it jarred their sensibilities; and was inconsistent with the candles which I now saw for the first time; and the incense which made the place seem like an altar in a church of the holy spiritual Baptists. The incense and the candles gave off a blue haze. The room was mysterious, like a mission-house for brotherhood, like a church.

"Owwwwwwww!" Barrington said. As he exhaled and as his voice came out with the exhaled breath, he sounded as if was a dog.

"Ain't this a bitch?" the host said.

I could make out a colour photograph on a wall. Through the haze, I could barely make out a man in the uniform of the Canadian armed forces. The man in the photograph was holding a gun.

"Brothers in Latinamerica sure have their shit together!"

The haze from the candles and the incense and the thing we were smoking made us all soft in the room; and made the room itself smaller than it was; and clothed us in a peace which took away the dilapidation, the noise, the fatigue I was feeling, the anger and the loneliness I had seen and had felt on the faces of the people below in the street.

"How much for the wheels?"

"Four bills."

"Shit, baby, this is colonialism!"

"Four bills."

"I got to get the motherfucker off my hands in two days!" His manner was not complaining. It was boastful, informing me of his prowess in the transaction. I still did not know what was going on.

"Three bills then, motherfucker."

The man took a roll of bills from his pocket, round and the size of a coffee mug, and rolled off the amount. Without counting, Barrington pushed the notes into his jacket pocket. The suit was silk with narrow shoulders, and expensive. It was the first time I had seen him dressed like this, like a junior stockbroker. But I remembered his summer job was on Bay Street. He did not look at me while the transaction was being made. I was not supposed to see, or know. John Coltrane was now playing as if he himself had witnessed this, and was approving it, and was blowing a benediction. I could think of nothing to cause me to be so contemplative. And I was thinking if, as a party to this deal, I was entitled to a cut; and I was thinking that if it was a deal, an illegal deal, and my student was caught, or the man had second thoughts about the deal and went to the police, if I would be involved as a witness, and as an accessory. And seeing all this money, and being in Jane and Finch which I had read about, where money grew on trees, and had lectured about; this area, with all this bigness and strangeness and mystery and excitement, whether I should not demand my cut. And then these thoughts went from my mind, and nothing else seemed to be of meaning, seemed to exist, nothing but the smell and the twirling, the small fragile vulnerable rise of the smoke from the incense and the candles. Nothing else in the room seemed to exist. There was nothing else. This room was nowhere. And still, it was in this city. But it could be anywhere. It was wholesome nevertheless because what was being done, could be done. And it was ugly because of what was being done, in my presence. And I was the witness. But I no longer wanted to be a witness. I had been placed on this threshold since I came to Jane and Finch, and I wanted no longer to be left out. But I knew I could not be a part of this Toronto. This room was Toronto: good and bad. And in the way we were being defined, not that I felt that Barrington and the man were aware and concerned about this. I was now relaxed. I came close to being a part of things. The weight of my journey from New York came off my shoulders, and I was light; and the hunger that had gnawed at me, anticipating the chicken and the jerked pork from the barbecues of the booze cans on Oakwood and on Vaughan, was now abated; and the distance at which I had stood from my student and from this man was squeezed into the closeness of brothers. I continued to look around the small room, trying to find some object which might give me balance, a context, and be able to place myself in this room. I was not offended by what was going on, and I did not feel that initiating me into this, by my student, was an offence. And I began to feel as if I was a black man born deep in Harlem in America, and was no longer West Indian, as they had painted me at the door by their intro-duction. I was beginning to feel like a brother. And I must have become one, for just as I accepted this image of myself, I began to see what was happening around me. There were three other men in the room with us. They had been there all the time. They were sit-ting in a far corner, on couches low to the floor, like Japanese fur-niture. And they looked that way, because the couches had no legs. They were sawed off. There was another colour photograph of the man, my host, in uniform, hugging a woman whose face looked Chinese or Japanese. The darkness in the room made the distinc-tion impossible. I studied the woman's face and decided she was Vietnamese. I found the context of the room, and the place. We were four men.

Coltrane was finished.

"This is a Man's World" came on next. But it had really been playing for some time. And this is how I might have got the analogy with the men. But is this what the singer had in mind? Strong men? And whose world was he singing about? I had looked throughout my three months in New York at the men and the world those men controlled. Were the men in this room, and their world, of four different sizes and complexions, the men James Brown was singing about? They had one thing in common, these men. Barrington and I stood out from them. But they had one thing in common, common to them all. Their image. Their dress. And their behaviour. Not their behaviour, because it was not behaviour. It was posture. Their posture. Their trousers fitting them like an extra skin, to their thighs. They wore brown leather boots. They were all dressed in various patterns and designs of Afro shirts. Dashikis. Round their necks were necklaces of cured, lacquered vegetables and beans, and peas. But more than this powerful image they had taken on, was the smell of the room. It fascinated me, the smell of their perfume. It was Youth Dew by Estée Lauder. It was a smell I had come to know musicians wear. And that other smell. The slow-working, insistent smell of the gift from the revolutionary brothers in Latin America.

I knew I was conspicuous among these men. I knew I stood out, in my army outfit which was nothing more to me than a summer costume; a costume like their own costume which was manufactured to make them look more African and tie them into an international black brotherhood. And Barrington, straight out of the pages of fashion and *Esquire* magazines, in his "Harry Rosen and Hazelton Lanes syndrome," as he liked to refer to his style. But I was not embarrassed by my outfit because, as Barrington himself said, "It ain't nothing, brother." This was the first time he called me brother.

His former self-assurance, his buoyancy, his blackness and style were now dulled in the haze of the two blue smokes rising, the menthol of Salem cigarettes and the Colombian grass. Coltrane was on again. It did not take much for his saxophone to make me forget James Brown: and his mellowed melody to "Acknowledgement" was like a statement of joy mixed with anger, and I felt that he was saying to all of us that if the joy in our lives might be lost, then we could always revert to our black anger. The other men in the room wore caps with Xs on them.

There was a round table in the middle of the room. The host had pulled back the deep, rich crimson velour blind at the window facing the street, and the light poured in, and made me feel I was waking from a dream. This table in the middle of the room had once been taller. It had been a dining table. Someone had cut its legs off. In the middle of the pullout couch which had no legs, and where I was now sitting, there were large grease stains on the back. And on the cushion beside me were many other stains almost circular. I pondered on the mysteriousness and origin of these smaller stains. The couch was well used. One of my legs was under the cut-down dining table. I was becoming impatient for the business to be transacted. I was beginning to feel uncomfortable. The other men in the room had not said a word to me, and they sat staring at the wall before them, waiting and staring. And not moving. Every day during my time in New York, I was reading in the newspapers about raids, and of black men being manacled and thrown into paddy wagons; and the newspapers carried photographs of the men; and one showed the house from which the men were taken. It could have been this room. I was impatient; but I did not understand the full etiquette of these kinds of transactions.

"Let me lay some o' this tea on you, brother, before you split. This tea's like gold. From the famous Colombian Aztec mines, where the brothers labour under the lash of the whip. Yeah! *Let me nobly die,* yeah!" I was becoming a little confused by this man's sense of history and of geography.

"This is my main man," Barrington said. I could not understand why he had to offer that stamp of approval for my presence. "My *main* man."

I gave up. I could feel that the night was going to be long. In all this time, I had no idea of how many hours had passed; and I was not certain which day it was. It was as if we had spent days and nights rolled into one, as it used to be at a poker table. I had spoken one sentence in all this time. Barrington's talk and the other man's banter were like snowflakes on my head. I was thinking of home. But the snowflakes were covering my head, and making me chilly, making me hunch my shoulders as if I were outside in the snow. Toronto is *cold* at this time of year. And while they were making preparations to smoke the Colombian Aztec gold, and were fixing a tube out of a piece of Reynolds Wrap, and were no longer talking, their own words which had been like the snow, melted. And the skies were clear again. Light was coming through the window. They were all sitting round the chopped-down table now. I had grown accustomed, acclimatized to this room; and in one corner I saw another table. There was another table, large, oval-shaped, and made of mahogany. In the little space left over from the piles of books, it was polished to a high sheen. All the books were about the black race, stretching from Africa and ending in America. *Dutchman & Slave: Famous Men of Color; Up from Slavery, The Autobiography of Malcolm X* and *Wretched of the Earth* were among them. Standing on *Wretched of the Earth* was a colour photograph of a man, in uniform, walking under a ceremonial roof of swords. Beside the man was a woman in a wedding dress. She was showing all her teeth in a grin of achievement, so it looked. Her teeth were even and beautiful and white. The two of them in the photograph seemed in a hurry to get out of the rain.

The woman had a Chinese face. There was no rain falling in the photograph.

Barrington loosened his tie. I knew that night, perhaps midnight, would catch us here. In my resignation, as when your impatience gives way and the hour against which you had gauged your departure has come and gone, and you plan for the next day, I looked round the room, making the most of this situation that time has no meaning, "time is money!" And I saw with some shock that the walls were lined with books, and above the bookshelves were more photographs and paintings, all of black people. I could be in Harlem, or Africa. All the books dealt with the black race. I did not know that there were so many words written about this black race, in these times, in the North and in this city, when black men, and the educated ones, were cursing and screaming and making speeches about the lack of history and things written about black people and wanting to go "home" to Africa, and calling themselves African Canadians, without the hyphen.

They were not interested in me, had ignored my presence, as they gathered in a tight knot round the Reynolds Wrap and the gold from the Aztecs. So I moved round the walls, as if I was in an art gallery, as I had promised to do and had done when I was taken to the Schomburg Collection in Harlem, which was nearby to the city college where I had been teaching; and I read the titles of these books, history, sociology, anthropology, science, literature, biographies of musicians, waiting to find one that had a subject matter not about blacks. In the shelves on the first wall, the books packed neatly name by name, in alphabetical order, as if the room was in a library, I came across titles I had never seen. They all dealt with black people, with coloured people, with men of colour, with niggers, with Afro-Americans, with Negroes, and with African Americans and black Canadians. I saw leather-bound copies of *Othello* and *The Tempest*.

"Shakespeare?" I said. The discovery of this error made the word explode with the gratification of finding that your lover is a liar.

"He's a brother," the host said.

I had heard talk by some radicals at York and by some professors about the *Sonnets*, and a dark lady; and I was sure that the epithet referred to the velour that ladies wore at fifteenth-century dinner parties. The second wall of books was monolithically black and did not divulge the inconsistency of the first wall. Barrington unbuttoned two of the three buttons on his Harry Rosen jacket and relaxed completely, sitting on his back, slouching. "Yeah," he said. The other men said "Yeah," with profound contentment. I move on to the third wall. Someone behind me got up and adjusted a reel-to-reel tape player, and a voice came out, talking as if it was singing. Singing as if the voice was an instrument. And then there was a scream from the voice. I did not know what was going on. But I wished I knew more about black American music, and about black Canadians. It was not the blues. I knew the blues. And it was not gospel. I listened to gospel every Sunday morning on a University of Toronto radio station that beamed it in from the South, and when I was home in downtown Toronto I could barely get the blues from Buffalo. This solo, this chanting of words, was like nothing I had heard before. But I strained my ears and my attention, and tried to concentrate. And then I knew what it was. I knew it. It was a poem. But the way the poem was being read was like jazz being played. I wished I knew more about black American music and about black Canadian style. And I wanted to do something about it the moment I escaped from this blue-hazed, turning room, the moment I escaped from this Toronto version of Harlem, back into my condominium in Rosedale Valley Road.

"Yeah," the host said.

"Yeah!" another man said.

"Chuck the brother out," the host said. "Right on!"

I was too buried in the lyricism of the voice; too much was happening for me to recognize the poet. Some of the brothers, for I had begun to regard them as brothers, began to snap their fingers in rhythm, and this made me feel that I had heard the poem before.

"*This* is what's *happenin*, brother," the host said.

"Brother's into some heavy shit."

"Roi!" Barrington shouted.

His voice scared me.

"The Imam," the host said, as if he was introducing me to the poet who was in the room with us. "The Imam."

"*. . . no love poems written*
until love can exist
freely and cleanly."

"Check it out," one of them said.

"*. . . Let Black People Understand*
that they are the lovers and the sons of lovers and
warriors Are poems and poets and
all the loveliness here in the world."

A drum was beating an African rhythm in the background. It was not a professional drumming. It was someone's hands on the chopped-off table. I know drums. But it was adequate and appropriate. The voice in the tape player was screaming now. It was in the room with us.

"*. . . We want a black poem. And a*
Black world.
Let the world be a Black Poem
And let all Black People speak this poem Silently
or LOUD."

At this final word, the voice has risen to a chilling scream. The drums rolled. Fingers on the oval-shaped mahogany table were like bongos joining in a rolling crescendo. And then, just as suddenly as the voice had screamed from the tape, so suddenly, too, did the voice disappear. The light was coming in from the street. And the voices of all the men in the room went dead. All I could hear now was their breathing and an occasional "Yeah!" and the noise of the tape spinning and spitting off bits as it came to its end.

"Brother Roi is a bitch!"

I could not tell who said that.

"Have we ended our transaction amicably?" the host said.

"Deal," Barrington said.

"Gentlemen's agreement," the host said, a new man. "Let us shake."

"*Vinceremos.*"

"Who did you say this brother was?"

They had forgotten me again. I did not exist any longer, against their tight ritual and understanding.

"It's my main man."

Barrington said it with less conviction than when we had arrived.

But they had treated me as royalty, in silent adoration, all during the time they had been listening to the poem, and up till the conclusion to the transaction. Over and over, they had said, "My man, my main man." And sometime during that time, they had handed me the Reynolds Wrap, and I had done the obvious thing with a tube, never mind that that tube was made of foil. I had blown into it. Bubbles raged inside the glass pot, like one used for making coffee, like a storm off the rocky coast of Bathseba in Barbados. At that moment of torrent and torment, the men had fallen dead, mesmerized, in silence and bewilderment. Masks of shock and recrimination came to their faces. Profound unbelief. And a smile of compassion brought life into the masks.

"My main man."

I had tried a second time, taking their disapprobation to heart, and had blown harder, taking it in, with my eyes bulging against the intake of breath and water and fumes, against the storm of bubbles, and the hurricane about to erupt inside me.

Barrington had become serene with approval.

"Yeah!" the men said. It was a chorus of joy and of initiation.

"My main man," Barrington had said, aware of his value now in this circle of brothers, who seemed on the point of murdering him for bringing an interloper into this circle of brotherhood and stealth and danger; uncertain of what he had been shouting to me every day last semester at York, about "his racial credibility." "Yeah! Like you breathe it in . . ." He had ended his advice in the way you would ask a question, with your voice raised.

I had smoked my pipe. Smoking my Reynolds Wrap pipe, and trying to follow the blue wisps of smoke from the bowl that looked like a coffee percolator, I had never experienced such peace and exhilaration; and I had begun to talk; and as I talked, I had had no feeling for the words which tumbled out of my mouth; and I could not hear my own words as I had talked; and I had begun to see them as if they had been suspended between the shelves of the bookcases, marked in large characters, plain enough for a dunce to follow, like it had been back in Barbados in Standard Two, when I was first taught how to hold a pen and dip it into the inkwell, and write the ABCs and *the cat sat on the mat*; and I was back in the island, and was talking with my words multiplying; and the ideas I was expressing became thick and entangled themselves in my mouth like saliva, like molasses, like syrup from the sugar cane; and some of the words dropped off the lines in the copybook and were stuck onto the lines gouged into the blackboard with a nail by the headmaster's practised hand, just as my infant's handwriting used to climb mountains away from the guiding lines on my black borderless slate; and I had got up from the couch that had no legs, and I had used my fingers to get the words back between the double lines, back into place, subservient to my desire; back into objectivity; back into clear apprehension; but my words had remained suspended, like the writing of a man who never learned to write when he was a child.

On the wall facing me, as I had turned to get balance, was a large map of Africa, in outline, painted green, black and red, in alternating lines round its border. It was drawn by a hand that knew more about symbols of nationalism and black power than about geography. So, Africa had become in the hands of the cartographer, the shape of a cutlass, or a bill. But I had known, even before I had pulled on the tube of Reynolds Wrap and had got my perceiving fuzzed by the power of the gold from Colombia, that I had been in the midst of fierce, black beliefs; and that one of these beliefs was an acclamation of Africa as voluble as the screams in the poem. So, if it was indeed Africa that was being represented, I knew that I had not smoked too much of that shit not to have known that it did not matter that the cartographer had not used the child's prank of tracing reality with a piece of tissue paper, and that what had been drawn from the myth of memory did not require the technical and geographical authenticity as if the black map-drawer was trying to prove that the world is round. I knew drums. So, I knew something about Africa, and about African sculpture; and how African artists had fucked up proportion and perspective and people like Picasso and other Frenchmen with their *égalité, humanité* and *democraté* shit, had used the tracing paper, thrown out the original and called it "cubism." "Them African brothers are some mean motherfuckers, proportion-wise, and perspective-wise." I think it was I who said that, some time, in some seminar, at York University.

This man of Africa on the wall, facing me, "who's the fairest of them all?" has no rivers, and no mountains, and no lakes, and no faults, and no waterfalls, and no towns, and no townships, and no cities. "Where Timbuktu is, brother?" and no borders and no neighbouring lands with no neighbouring unneighbourly tribes. Africa stands alone. And the black cartographer has made Africa his new home. "Carry me back to ole Virginnie? You be crazy, nigger? Bereft of people, bereft of vegetation, so there ain't no motherfucking Tar-zan, Jack!"

Africa stood alone. It was the same thing with the piece of silver attached to a strong string of leather, hanging from the neck of the man who had spent the whole day in African time, doing a deal with Barrington, for a car he was reselling. His name, Barrington had told me afterwards, when we were eating chicken and ribs in a West Indian restaurant at the corner of Bloor and Sherbourne Street, Stingray's, where the air was fresh; Barrington told me his name is Ali Kamal All Kadir Sudan.

"Ali Kamal All Kadir Sudan?" I had asked. "Like the country? Sudan?"

"Motherfucker was *born* Terrence Washington Jefferson Lincoln Lucas, the *Third!*"

His mother was a new Democrat?"

"Father, too!"

"Named after three American presidents."

"Motherfucker left York, with two BA's and a PhD!"

"One for each president?"

Africa stood alone.

"You was rapping like a motherfucker, Jack! You got into some heavy Black Muslim shit, too!"

"I can't remember."

"That they can't be Black Muslim 'cause ontologically, you say, there can't be white Muslims and black Muslims. Shit like that. You laid some heavy shit on those revolutionary brothers!"

"I don't remember."

"My man! My main man!"

"I can't remember that."

"Gimme five, brother. You talked like a bitch, and you was so hip that that made the brother, Mr. Ali Kadir Sudan, lay *two* more bills on me! I be in good company with the right revolutionary rhetoric, and shit like that."

"I don't remember."

"And we went into two booze cans. After we checked out the strip joints."

"Nor that."

The night was heavy. The night was swirling round me. The night was a dream. In beauty and in the images that wound themselves around me. And even in that half-consciousness, that disorientation, I still did not remember. I could not remember anything.

"We took a taxi to my place. You told my aunt what a brilliant student I am, that you wished I was your brother. I changed cars at home. My old aunt was pissed off that I took her Benz. I am driving *my* car now. The Mustang. The one I'm selling to Ali Kadir Sudan."

"I can't."

But I was trying to recall, through the haze of my dream, watching a small black man standing at a door of the entrance to some place that was full of men and women; and the man standing at the door was wearing an army uniform; and I remember hearing something bad said about Korea and Vietnam; and then the music began to pour out of the humid place; and when I went in, or was led in by Barrington, I saw smoke, smoke was the only thing I remember clearly, smoke was the only thing I was seeing with clarity of definition; so when I was led in, I saw a man at the mike, standing like a king from some part of the outline map of Africa, a chieftain or something; and he was singing *"I'd rather drink muddy water, than . . ."* And I knew I had heard this song before, in Harlem; and thinking about that got me thinking of the number of hours and days I had been resurrected from the clutches of Harlem and New York. I was trying to remember.

"Silver Dollar," Barrington said. "This is where it all started, my man."

I had not been sober enough, nor clear-headed enough to see what had been going on around me, but I did see, through a haze of disorientation, the face of the man, the singer, the chieftain, turning slowly around in time with the blues he was singing; and I had tried to follow the revolving of the man's face, as if I was testing my eyesight and my power of concentration, like reading the name of a song printed on a gramophone record turning at thirty-three and a third revolutions a minute; so the blues singer was turning his face, and then all of the faces in the packed, smoked room were turning, as if they were faces painted on to the label of the 78; and suddenly the room was out of control.

"You talked like a motherfucker! You put down some heavy shit on the brothers. And brothers who fought in the Korean War and were still fighting in the Vietnam War. Some heavy shit. I really don't understand why the goddamn staff sergeant, with his chest full o' ribbons, didn't whip your ass for calling him an unpatriotic Canadian, and didn't whip mine, for standing beside you. Shee-it!"

"What's the time?" I asked. There were clocks on stores, clocks that were turned into running illuminated numbers, running from one end of a sign to the next, like a child's train set. There was time all round me, and still I asked the time.

"This is Spadina Avenue!" Barrington said, giving me the time. "The heart of the city!"

"Yes."

"Man, you are six servings of raw oysters. Six. You're freaky!"

"What time is it?"

"We went to a booze can. You been talking about booze cans all the time. So we went and heard a Garveyite nationalist speak, 'cause you said you gonna hold a seminar on the nationalists when we get back to York, so we went to hear one. But the Silver Dollar was something else again. I never seen a man vomit such shit all over a Spadina Avenue jazz club before. You vomited like you was ripping out your goddamn guts!"

"I vomited in the Silver Dollar?"

"I washed you off in the men's room, shit!"

^In the men's room at the Silver Dollar?"

"Those oysters had castor oil in them."

"Did I get the impression that your parents came from Barbados?"

"You remember all that shit about the highest literacy rate in the world, and how it doesn't surprise you that I'm at York, and my old aunt got into that elitist shit, segregating me from the brothers in Jane-Finch and on the street?" You remember that? You really don't remember any of this shit, do you?" Barrington shook his head, disbelieving. "If York could see you now!"

"Fuck York!"

"Right on!"

"Fuck it!"

The woman in the Red Rooster bar, in Harlem, had come into my mind. She had talked like this. Tough like this. It was the first time I had heard a woman, a lady, talk so tough. I picked it up from her. This tough shit-talk. I must open her gift. It was still wrapped in the gold paper, tied with a blue ribbon, in my briefcase. And I must track down that other woman. But I couldn't remember if I had met that other woman in Harlem or at the New York City College.

"Where did you pick up this heavy shit about revolution and revolutionaries? Man, I can't believe that you, a West Indian academic, saved my ass from a stomping by that staff sergeant with his chest full o' combat ribbons? Where did you study this black revolutionary shit? All this shit about Harlem, and shit? Your intellectualism on the revolution caused the brother, Ali Kadir, to lay two more bills on me for this beat-up Mustang. Shit! *Harlem!*"

"Spadina!" I said, wishing it was Harlem.

And here we are. In spirit and in wish. There are hundreds of people, mostly men, in the road. Cars are parked three deep on either side. As Barrington slows down, I can read the names on stores and shops. The House of Proper Propaganda covers the width of a bookstore. And more people are going in and coming out of it than the audience at the Apollo. This name I can see clearly above the heads of the crowd. No one in this crowd is moving. It is a sea at rest, calm, but tense, as if the winds that shall turn into a hurricane are still on the horizon. I can remember it now; and I can see the tip of the long broomstick that holds the Flag. Barrington parked the Mustang beside Young Lok's Chinese restaurant. He makes it four deep now, in the crowded road. The closer I get to the crowd, the more frightened I become. The wind off the horizon is getting angrier. There are two many people. I feel nervous. There is tension and a kind of anger in the crowd, as if it is a crowd standing before a man hiring people, and the crowd is ten times the size of the number the man can hire, and after those lucky ones are led in through the wicket gate, hell breaks loose; there is tension and a kind of anger, as if the man on the two-tier platform, made from two boxes, is going to tell this crowd things they know and things they hate to know. Behind me, I can remember this now, is the Theresa Hotel; "Castro stayed there when he came to America, the week after he kicked Baptista's ass, the 26th of July, 19-something, *vente-seis Julio*": which happens to be my birthday; I know the Theresa Hotel; and close by, the Apollo Theatre. Even back in Barbados, when my mother said I was "knee-high to a grasshopper," before I was old enough to identify a grasshopper, although there were thousand hopping around in the bush near our house, I had heard of the Apollo, for Miss Ella Fitzgerald was singing on Re-diffusion Radio every evening at six, *"Evening shadows make me blue . . ."* and forty-nine listeners had requested that song the evening I first heard her sing it; and from that grasshopping time, I had linked the two names, Apollo and Ella Fitzgerald, just as later on I would link Jekyll and Hyde, Abbott and Costello, Jesse Owens and Adolph Hitler, chalk and cheese, meat and potatoes, cou-cou and salt fish, and jerk pork and festival.

"When Castro stayed at the Theresa," the Harlem woman had told me, drinking bourbon and Coke; and she had been talking about Castro and the Theresa a long time before I paid attention, "when Fidel drove up to the Theresa, niggers in Harlem went crazy. Niggers who could hardly speak American-English was brabba-rabba-ing in 'spaniol. Cats who only smoke Salems and the weed was walking on 125th, chomping the biggest goddamn cigars you'd ever seen. And for a long time after that, every black man in Harlem was pro-Castro, and anti-American and talking Spanish. Marxist-Leninists like motherfuckers! The House of Proper Propaganda sold Spanish dictionaries to cats who couldn't even read the writing on a numbers' ticket, or the words off a goddamn traffic ticket! It was a motherfucking beautiful time, Jack."

"Yeah," I said, trying to be cool, and claiming book knowledge about these things. "The Harlem Renaissance happened right here where we are sitting in the Red Rooster, all round here. Countee Cullen, Dunbar, Langston Hughes and *if I should die, let me nobly die."*

"Right on!"

"If I should die."

"When I grew up around here."

"I respect you for that. Roots."

Wasn't shit!" Venom in her words.

"You're on sacred ground. The Harlem Renaissance, poets, artists, painters, playwrights and novelists. Sacred ground."

"It's a motherfucking slum, honey. A ghetto, and . . ."

"Ghetto with a difference."

"*A ghetto*. Harlem ain't no Renaissance, sugar. You only read that shit in books written by Carl Van Vetchun."

By the time we reached the edge of the crowd, I was steeped in a revision of the history of these streets. The Southern leather of my boots, my cowboy boots, not quite cured and accustomed to my kind of feet, was making my corns rebel. The crowd is moving in to the man on the box with the Flag fluttering, as if his words are a magnet, or is the sucking wind blowing in from the horizon.

"He's on this same soap box every Sunday. Been hearing this shit every Sunday since I was ten. It's like a blue number, or a Billie Holiday solo. Lasts for hours. It's for the tourists, honey."

"I am a tourist."

"Not that I'm putting down the brother. But it's all for the tourists. How can you be a serious black nationalist rapping this revolutionary shit, standing on a soapbox with the American Flag beside you? At least you taught me to see the lack of logic in those symbols."

"College is college. And there's logic and there's logic. This is Harlem. The Harlem revolution."

"The Harlem Renaissance, sugar."

We are close enough to see the man on the box, and his eyes, and traces of saliva that spit with his anger from his mouth. He is dressed in a black suit. It looks like the one Barrington was wearing, but this is Brooks Brothers with narrow shoulders and three buttons, and lined in silk. I turn my head to see if the dream is enduring, to see that Barrington has changed into his campus uniform; blue jeans, army surplus jacket with three stripes turned down, a sergeant; and brown expensive leather boots. The man on the box has a military bearing. Perhaps he too was in Korea and Vietnam. Perhaps the Second World War. His hair is short, reminding me of U.S. Marines and the Canadian army sergeant, and his body has gone through the rigour of that kind of boot camp, and is as lithe as that of a tennis player.

". . . so, we're living in troubled times, brothers and sisters. We're living at a time when *anything* can happen."

"Teach!" a man shouts.

"Brothers and sisters, a couple years ago it couldn't happen unless Uncle Sam said so. Or Khrushchev said so. Or DeGaulle said so. But now, it can happen *any* time." I wonder where I am: in Harlem, or in this city?

"Right on!" the crowd agrees.

"The man also knows that the only way we're gonna do it is through unity. Through unity. So, they *create* another trap. Every effort we make to unite among ourselves, on the basis of what we are, they label it *what?*"

"Racism!" the crowd answered in a unified shout.

The wind from the horizon was coming in.

"Yes, racism. If we say that we want to form something that's based on black people getting together, the white man calls that racism. Mind you, that is right. And you have some o' these Negroes in Harlem, these white-minded Negroes running round here saying, 'That's racism.' I don't want to belong to anything that is all-black."

"Say it! Say it!"

"The worst trick the man played on us is when he named us Negro, and called us Negro. And when we call ourselves Negro, we end up tricking ourselves. Whenever you see somebody who calls himself a Negro, he's a product of Western civilization . . . not only Western civilization, but Western crime. One of the main reasons we're called Negro is so we won't know who we really are. 'Long as you call yourself a Negro, nothing is yours. And nothing is you. No language. You *can't* lay claim to no language, not even English. You already messed that up! You can't lay claim to any name. Any type o' name that identifies you as something you should be. You can't lay claim to any culture, as long as you use the word Negro to define yourself. And you can't lay claim to any *land*, 'cause them ain't no country named Negro-*land!*"

When he said this, confusion broke out. The rest of his words were drowned in the angry rushing of the wind over the waves. Comments that sprung up like small whirlwinds, from the truth in his words, and the shame buried in those words, and applied to the crowd, made the crowd become one voice of protest.

"They listen to this shit every Sunday," the woman said.

One voice of frustration. And one tremulous voice of unful-filled dreams.

"Dream deferred," someone shouts.

"Burn, baby, burn!" the crowd screams.

But no one in the crowd of rustled waves moves an inch from the man on the box. And the man on the box does not take a pack of matches from his Brooks Brothers three-buttoned suit to show it to his audience's rage, in a gesture if only that, of fruitless sym-bolism. The crowd waits. It is like waiting for the full blast of the wind from the horizon to come in and smash the fishing boats and the schooners at anchor. The crowd waits, and takes the remaining punishment in the words of the man on the soapbox, standing mil-itary, and noble, and proud, and black, beside the Stars and Stripes. The eagle, on the tip of the broomstick that held the Flag as upright as its age could do, was tarnished and a piece of one wing had been chipped off.

". . . and you could walk around here calling yourselves Demo-crats, and voting for Democratic presidents . . . ?" The tide was rising. "Well, a Democrat is nothing but a Dixiecrat without his sheet."

"We better split," the woman had said. "We better split." This time I heard the words from Barrington, anxiety in his manner. "Gotta get back to York in time for dinner."

We were already beside the old Mustang. I could still hear the crowd so far from here chanting, "Burn, baby, burn." But we were the only two waves, the only two undulations in the powerless swelling tide on Spadina Avenue, which remained as if the wind from the lake had added no tide, and no fuel, to this great black vastness of three-laned road.

Verrrooommmm! Verrooooommm! Verroooommm! Verroooommm! The voices of the crowd, even from that stationary distance, almost drowned out the stuttering automobile, while Barrington said, "Motherfucker, motherfucker," over and over. *Verrooommmm!* At last it started. It had taken five attempts to move me from this threatening avalanche of remembered words. I wished Barrington had already delivered this Mustang jalopy to Ali Kamal All Kadir Sudan; and I wished that his Barbadian-born aunt did not need the Benz to drive to Florida with her husband. And I wished that it was still summer, and that we could . . .

We got out of Spadina Avenue heading north. The trees were in their first change of colours, and I could see autumn in the yellow and the gold of their leaves; and I could see oranges piled in undisturbed anticipation for the women walking with small dogs in furs, and the men in black suits walking with alligators in the workmanship of their briefcase; and the avenue became wider and only one line of cars, like Barrington's aunt's, was parked in the lazy wealth and safety of Avenue Road; and we ducked under a bridge and came out, on the wrong side, through the campus, Queen's Park, and turned left and came to the Park Plaza Hotel; and I saw, along Avenue Road, all the mangoes and golden-apples; avocado pears and paw-paws; green peas in shells, sweet potatoes and fish still wriggling in bins as if they had forgotten they were no longer in the deep blue sea; and men selling, impervious and resentful of the change of weather, wearing shorts and shirts the colour of the horizon when a storm is coming, or when the sun is setting. And then we were in Forest Hill Village. Barrington stopped the old Mustang, now running like a charm now that we were out of Harlem's harm and Spadina's crowd, and we were inside this bar, which had nine circles drawn in its hanging advertisement; and I went back to the car, parked like the others, in one line, and took my overnight bag, with which I had travelled to New York and stayed for three months.

"I'm having bourbon and Coke," Barrington said.

"Scotch," I said, going to the men's room with my flight bag. "And soda."

When I came out, Barrington was ordering another bourbon and Coke.

"Shee-it!" he said, motioning the waiter to place another scotch and soda beside my untouched drink, and observing my change of dress. "Cavalry-twill trousers, button-down blue shirt, hacking jacket and suede boots? Shee-it! Where's the camouflage army out-fit?"

"Left it for a chap I saw in the men's room."

"You and he had a conversation?"

"He was writing a poem."

"In the men's room?"

"Now, when we get back to York . . ."

LETTER OF THE LAW
OF BLACK

"Edgehill House"
Edgehill Lane
Edgehill Tenantry
BARBADOS

I am writing this letter to you now, at this rather late time, because when you left the island to go away to Toronto, there was too much emotion in the air, and talk was impossible and talking did not make sense. Most of the things that was said was what I call emotion; all that emotion was good for someone as young as you, taking up a journey in life, to another country which is strange to you, although you may forget that you were born there.

The emotion itself was not complete though, was not real emotion, and it rang a bit empty to me, because I am too old for emotion and passion, and because the one person who could have made the rafters ring for joy, that you her only child, was going to a place where she had so many happy years, and tragic years, was not there. Then, was not the time. Then, was not the occasion to bring back memories, whose only meaning and point in bringing them up would have demanded the bringing up also of the tragedy which define those memories. Your mother.

I waited all these year also, because I wanted to be sure and certain that you got through your first year in Toronto. They tell me, and I am referring to the lawyer-fellow and the vicar who live beside me, that the first year of studying the things you are studying is the most hardest of the four years proscribed for studying. The first year is the hardest and saddest. That is what the lawyer-fellow say. The vicar say that being in the first year, you are free from whatever spiritual responsibilities being at home here, assumes you should carry with you; and you are alone in a new kind of freedom, and that very often you will need somebody with experience and affection, to help you confine yourself within that very freedom. It was the vicar, I think, who used the words "inner spiritualism," to make the point that I am now making to you, using a summary of his words as I do so. To me, it is a more simple thing. I call it knowing and understanding what freedom really stands for.

And if I remember correctly from my own days in that country while I was on a two-year farm labourers' scheme working on farms in Southern Ontario, Chatham and London and Windsor, before I forgot to report to the man in charge of the conditions of the farm labourers, and took a leave without leave, as you may say and lost myself in Toronto until they tracked me down, and deported me, a man with my education at the best school in Barbados, and with all my years in the Civil Service here, things which you already know. Before they hounded me down as it was their duty to do, and send me back here, but not before I had amassed thousands of dollars for your maintenance and upkeep, I call to mind that the first year in that country, or in any other country where you are a stranger, demands your complete attention to little details which later turn out to be a damn complete waste of time.

You have to watch your allowance. And the allowance that the government people, and the man in charge of the farm labourers, used to give was nothing you could write home about. You have to watch your allowance, as if you are a banker or an economist. Or as if you are an investor. And the worse thing that happens is that you bound to become, and does, a hoarder and miser. God help you son, that you do not follow in my footsteps, as a stranger in that land, and have to be a hoarder.

For instance, being the son of my loins, you bound to love clothes and women, not necessarily in that order. But as to clothes, you may see a shirt for ten dollars, and you buy it because you think it is a saving. But the next day, you will pass another shop window and see the same shirt, on sale for half the price. And being new, you do not know, and would never think that you could take the ten-dollar shirt off your back, wrap it in a nice cellophane parcel, and return it, and get your money back. Canadians do it every day. They taught me never throw away a receipt, even a receipt for a French letter, if you see what I mean! So, never throw away a receipt from a store, not even a liquor store.

You could tell me if Stollery's Emporium for Men is still at the intersection of Bloor and Yonge Streets? I spent many dollars and more hours talking to the manager, and getting the wrong advice, and the proper fit from the male clerks. Their shirts are not bad. But the best ones I wore, and still have some of, after fifteen years, were obtained at the Annual Jewish sale of clothes in the Canadian National Exhibition, or at a second-hand establishment, named the Royal Ex-Toggery, near the Anglo-Saxon residential district of Rosedale. So, you see, I took the best, the best of the second-hand, from the best of both Toronto worlds, the two founding races, at the time. The Anglo-Saxons and the Jews. I am talking about the Fifties. Now, as I have been reading from the clippings you been sending down, and from chatting with the old tourist on the beach, the place is a virtual potpourri of nationalities, saddle with something called a new sense of nation, or multiculturalism.

The Jewish man dresses well and elegantly. It is small wonder that Hitler stole his clothes. The Jewish man who dresses, and I knew a few in my time whilst I worked illegally in their homes and in their stores, dresses in good clothes. You can learn something, this and more, from the Jewish gentleman. It is not fit for me, your father, from this distance, to utter to you what you can learn from the Jewish woman. But our own Hitler is here, wagging his tail, brushing out his fleas against my foot as I write this letter to you. Perhaps, I had said the name Hitler aloud as I wrote it, and he thought I was commending him for his companionship, and for guarding the old place and protecting me from the varmints we have down here as Barbadians, now that you away. If he could talk, and had the use of language, he would say hello to you, although if he did have that blessing of speech, years ago he would have blasted you in condemnation for your unmerciful treatment of him, and for your insistence that he lived nothing but a dog's life. "Dogs amongst doctors," I used to overhear you saying to him; and then Hitler would give out a yelp, as if trying, in his own way, to inform me that you had kicked that precept into him. A dog's life, indeed. How empty, and still how full. He is lapping up water from the blue enamel bowl in the kitchen, as I sit at the kitchen table, with the door open, writing you. The pullets have multiplied. The cocks crow and screw from sunrise to sunset. And still, I cannot find a blasted egg laid by these thirty-something hens that the two fowl-cocks master, for the thieving neighbour on my right, and the light-fingered bastard on my left. But God do not like ugly.

Nothing here has changed. I went into your room the other day and dusted off the cobwebs and the dried skeletons of scorpions and bugs off your books. The sea air and the salt in the wind, are the censors of books in the island. No wonder that people in these hot, tropical countries eat up the television programmes from North America, in preferences to the pages of a book, and in consequence do not know their head from their backside. The book, my son, is moth-eaten, just as the morality of politics in this country is decaying. And Mannigheim, our leader, is the biggest, fattest, and most bothersome moth to fly around the eyes, and sometimes to get into your mouth. He is either a moth or a stinging bee.

I happened to notice the titles of your small, but well-chosen library of books. I was pleased to see that although you have read the Classics at Harrison College, you still had time besides all that Latin and Greek, two of the deadest languages I can think of, for good literature. You should, while you are there, and during term breaks and March breaks, look at the Russians, especially Pushkin, the vicar say. You know, he was one of us! I nearly dropped dead when the lawyer-fellow told me so. He went to school in Amurica, and studied all this black thing that people about here now talking about. If you had stuck me with a pin, not one blasted drop of red blood would have oozed from my stunned body. Pushkin is one of us. By that, I mean, a colonial man, more than I mean the obvious namely that he was black. Even in your position of being in a minority, or as I read in the clippings you send down, a member of the visible minority – as if you could ever be invisible – being in a minority through colour, in a country like Canada, whose immigration policy was pearly *white* officially, up until 1950, and you can ask Don Moore, if he's still living, the fact of being a colonial, you young intellectuals would say, "post-colonial," or "neo-colonial," but I am old and old-fashioned, and the only university I went to was the University of Hard Knocks, and so I say *colonial*. The colonial is the fact that transcends blackness. Blackness may change when you are amongst all black students; or it may change when you are in the company of good white people. (Have you had the chance to look up Mr. Avrom Lampert yet, as I have asked you, and pay him my respects? He was extremely kind to me, and most helpful in renting me a basement. It was damp, but that was all right. Things used to crawl on the walls. I have eaten more bagels and latkees – do you spell it so? – in his home during my time in that city, hiding from the immigration, than I have eaten flying fish and peas and rice. I hope he is still in the flesh. I still owe him the fifty dollars he lent me, thirty years ago, to pay a bill. Shirts, I think. And you know, I lost the receipt! However, if you see him, do not mention the fifty dollars, though. Time heals all debts.)

You should browse through some Russian literature. In addition to Pushkin, I would think that Dotsoiefsky's *Crime and Punishment* would be worthwhile, as the vicar tell me. One winter, when I was flat on my back with fever, indisposed through heath and threatened with dismissal from my job of being a janitor, and laid up in a small attic room on College Street near where the Main Public Library used to be, where I took out and read *Crime and Punishment* in two days of delirium and high temperatures thinking it was a detective story, I got worse. They rushed me in an ambulance, with the sirens blaring, to the Toronto General Hospital. They, meaning the two Canadian students who rented rooms next to me that summer, and another Canadian who used to put me on my guard immigration-wise. Dr. Guild, the physician who saw me in the Casualty what they call the Emergency up there, just smiled and told me to get a bottle of Gordon's Dry Gin. I had told him of *Crime and Punishment*. I hope you would not have that kind of relapse when you seek to broaden your literary horizons. If you were to read *Das Kapital* or *The Communist Manifesto*, as the lawyer-fellow say, even though you are reading it for your degree in Economics and Political Science, if you read it outside your course, *they* will say you are a communist. You should, if you read those two ideologies, be careful enough to hide their tolerance under your academic gown. Or hide their colour under brown wrappers. But if you are seen on a streetcar or in the subway reading Pushkin or *Crime and Punishment* or Tolstoy, *they* will say you are an intellectual. Even if they call you a colonial intellectual, as they have a habit of doing, such as black writer, or black artist, or black doctor, it would be different. You would, by this intelligence, be more dangerous to them, and *they* would not be able to despise, or worse still, ignore your presence, and call you a visible minority.

Who are these *"they?" "They"* are all the unspeakable, invisible spies, the un-nameable people, people who watch you when you do not know, do not feel they are, or should, who take it upon themselves to be your sponsors. Beware of sponsors. Beware of liberals, too. Beware of patronage. Beware of fools. And beware of Gordon's Dry Gin.

The only ones you do not have to be wary of . . . I just had a silly thought, the musings of an old man. We can say, "beware of," and be splendidly and syntactically correct. But we dare not say, "those whom you should be beware of." English is such a blasted puzzle. Such like a young woman under thirty-three. A woman under thirty-three, who does not know how to make love when she says she is making love, is as unattractive as bad English. I do not know what that means. And I do not know why I said it. Do you? I am not, as you have guessed, talking about all thirty-three-year-old women, girls, up there in that city. I am talking about those who were born in working-class districts, in London, in England and in the East End of Toronto, of West Indian parents; those who grew up in the slums of Brixton, and do not tell you this, when luck or a football pool brings them to you, unprepared for Canada; and when they speak to you in their Bray-tish accent, which if you remember listening to on the BBC World Service radio news, and have been taught, as you were, by Englishmen at Harrison College here, you would readily see that their Bray-tish accent is nothing more refined than the cockney of a braying jackass. They are all lower class. Beware of the lower classes of all races. They spit on you because they grew up spitting on the ground. Spitting was the way of their lives. They were spitted on; and now, they spit on you.

Spitted, spat, spatted . . . spat on. *Haaawk! Cah-Chew!*

Did I ever tell you of Kay? Why would I have done so? You are, after all, still my son, and while you were here, you were still a little boy, and there was no way I could, or should, have spoiled you by these disclosures, and spilled my love life and escapades in that city of Toronto, to you. But now at twenty-two not quite yet, according to our customs and ethics and culture, at twenty-one, and therefore a man, not yet peeing a pee that foams the foam of manhood; nevertheless, at twenty-one and being away, abroad, overseas in that city which gives you a certain privilege, I shall bend the moral and disciplinary precepts you learned so well at Edgehill House, and tell you about Kay.

Kay dressed well in cheap clothes. She loved clothes, but didn't have the money for her tastes. Kay talked with a Bray-tish accent. Kay said, "I am not a Canadian. I was born in Bray-ton," meaning Britain. Kay looked intelligent. Kay was affianced to a Barbadian man of unknown social background; but who had some brains, some luck, and through the emergence of Black Power, the un-achieved importance of Eldridge Cleaver and Black Awareness, was given a scholarship to do graduate work at a university, in the Sociology of Violence. The Sociology of Violence! Did you ever hear anything like this? Beware of poor West Indians who, with changing times, find themselves in graduate schools, in second-rate universities, writing second-rate theses in second-rate disciplines. The Sociology of Violence! They are the worst kinds of socialists.

But to get back to Kay. Kay was courting this man, was to be married in the October, when I invited him in the September, to tea one afternoon, when he brought Kay along. She was the most beautiful black woman I had ever seen. I served tea and biscuits, grapes and cheese, and then wine. *Chateauneuf du Pape.* After tea, we had pickled pig's feet and scotch. She was very Bray-tish during tea. She held the teacup the wrong way. With both hands. Cupped.

And she said, three times, "I like this silver tea pot. These are lovely cups. Chinese? Bone cups? I like these Chinese bone cups. This is very civilized." We had been talking about West Indian immigration to Britain and to Canada. She said, "I am Bray-tish." It was the second time she had declared her ancestry. When it came time to eat the pig's feet, she put up her nose. Her nose is rather flat and broad for that kind of superciliousness. Years later, when I met her sister, and her "half-sister," as she called her, and her mother, all three noses were flat and broad. But those three flat broad noses understood the ancestral dignity of design. They understood pig's feet also. Not Kay. "I've never eaten pig's feet. I am Bray-tish," she said, when her fiancé, embarrassed by the stupidity of her airs, told her about souse, probably to take the reservation out of her palate and taste. He looked at me in one of those quick nervous glances. He was mortified, as mortification mortifies a man of low class, and he told her about his "primary proposition" and about the "point he is trying to make." Beware of "primary propositions" and "points people *try* to make." I had welcomed her because I saw only her beauty. Beware of beauty. I saw her good looks. Her appearance. Beware of appearance.

"Girl, don't be a stupid bitch, do," he told her, trying to make the point that he disapproved of her airs. "Woman, what British you talking 'bout? I am doing a Ph.D. in the Sociology of Violence as it affects the West Indian Diaspora in Britain. And I know. I know people like you been eating nothing but shit like fish and chips in Britain since 1950, when the first wave of immigrants washed-up at Southampton. Ackee and bad salt fish. Pig ears. Pig snout. Pig tail and rice. And kiss-me-ass fish and chips! Or weren't you brought up on Yorkshire pudding? Look, girl, eat the blasted trotters, do!"

That was the first sign I got about Kay's problem of positive or negative self-identity. She did not tell lies at those times. She allowed people, me and my friends, to make conclusion about her, and spread them, and in turn, believed them, and she kept silence, knowing all the time they were lies.

She graduated from McMaster in Business, we said. She was a trainee at a large commercial bank downtown, we said. She was born, as I have said, in Bray-ton, we said. She had a nanny, we said. She went to private school, we said. She called herself "a banker," we said.

She was, in fact, a teller. A junior teller. At a counter in a small bank. It was not even the main branch. And she was born in Jamaica. She went, however, to a girls' boarding school in Clarendon. One day, she called me. She was crying. Her fiancé had met a white Canadian woman, much older than she, much older than he, who had a child nine years old. He told his colleagues in the Sociology of Violence as it Affects department that he was going to marry this white Canadian girl. And he did. And he regretted afterwards. But never apologized to Kay. Never called. Never wrote a letter to save breach of promise proceedings. Never sent a message. Never sent back the three hundred dollars she borrowed on her credit card to buy his wedding suit from Stollery's store at Bloor and Yonge. Was not mortified by the mortification of the Breacher of Promise, or by the Sociological Violence wrecked on the jilter.

The church had been booked, she said. The reception, in a rec-room, what a doleful term! A rec, could it be a *wrecked* room, was booked for the reception, she said. Flowers were ordered, she said. Her girlfriends at the bank, all tellers, and of lies, presumably (not one of them a junior trainee), were invited, she said. They had bought their wedding dresses, she said. She had bought her wedding down, she said. White, she said. She had one child left back in England, he said. Everything was arranged, she said. The "wrecked" room was vacuumed twice by the superintendent of the apartment building, she said. It was situated in a dreary district in that city where there were five factories and one slaughterhouse, for cows and pigs. Do you think that's why she did not like pig's feet?

I found myself in the ticklish predicament and role of a father-figure giving fatherly advice to a young woman I wanted to take to bed. Young, because at that time I was twice her age, plus three. Her father left her mother when she was two, in Bray-ton. You were not born then. I saw myself as the main character in the movie made of the novel *Lolita*, the vicar told me about; about a novel about a dirty old man, and a dirty little girl of sixteen and of sexy disposition. I saw the inequality and the immorality in our relationship. She was a nymphomaniac. I was steadily on a diet of green bananas, prescribed by a woman once my age!

I found myself, after working ten hours six days a week, in a packing company as a packer's assistant, walking beside a person in blue jeans and white ankle socks; eating small plastic tubes that contained frozen ice of many colours, and artificial sugar. Holding on to a paper napkin, on a Sunday afternoon, to wipe every trace of dripping stickiness from the white hairs of my beard. (I grew a beard then, to help hide from the immigration people.) So, walking through Queen's Park in the dead cold of winter, and leaving conflicting, contradictory, unequal pairs of deep prints in the thick, indifferent snow. Deep, because we used to walk hand in hand, and slow, and talk. What do you talk to a woman half your age, plus three? And who likes *Chinese* bone tea cups, and does not eat pig's trotters.

"I didn't know you had a granddaughter so big, man," Rufus, a fellow who walk-away from being a farm labourer the same way I did, said to me. The son of a bitch! He had seen us necking on a bench whose colour I could not tell, the snow was so thick. He probably meant, by his salutation, that I should think of incest. Had he said, "robbing the cradle," I would have been happier.

Rufus is not more than five years younger than me. He had refused to grow a beard to camouflage his illegality at the time.

But she, Kay, twenty-two at the time, made me, by her sensuality, look and behave older than I was. And I, knowing my own age, seeing her look *and* behave like Lolita in the movie version, increased the eating of green bananas from only Saturdays, to Friday, Saturday *and* Sunday. And a Chinee man in a store down in the Kensington Market had pity on me, and gave me something Chinese to drink. My son, it was Sodom and Gomorrah, after that! Beware of twenty-two-year-old women. Lolita, as you would remember, from the book or the movie, was not the kind of person anyone could accuse of having brains. In the four years that we lived together in the town house, I never could accuse her of *that*. Of other things, maybe. And I accused her of many other things. But never of *that*. She was, however, infelicitous in other ways which I shall tell you about at another time; for at the moment, I have to boil some rice with lard-oil in it, and a few fish heads, for this growling dog, Hitler. Why did you ever christen this poor, unfortunate dog by the name of Hitler? Were you being intellectual? Symbolical? Or diabolical? Suppose Hitler had won the War? Don't you see that all this time now, Hitler would be one dog you could not kick?

The government of brown-skinned and red-skinned men that is governing this place (there is no woman in this cabinet!) has raised the price of propane, and since I am cooking for a dog – what a dog's life! – I have to prepare his vittles on a wood fire. The previous colonials who owned this house, before it passed into our family, through whoring and prostitution and piracy, in 18-something, were smart enough to build a solid iron grate, with a stone fireplace, so I shall be bending over a fire, blowing my guts out, to give it wind and make it burn, and cook the rice and red snapper heads, for Hitler.

It is only nine o'clock in the night here, on a Friday night. A good night. But it could be after midnight the blackness is so thick. Days in this part of the almost forgotten world are short. When they get short, and the nights long, the lawyer-fellow and the vicar and me would deal a few hands of five-card stud. Sometimes, we play "no limit": sometimes, ten dollars a raise: highest raise, fifty dollars and raise as much as your little heart desires. These last short days with the long nights, the vicar has been lucky. The layer-fellow had to tell him that the parishioners lucky too, because that demon's hands won't be in the collection plate! We three, old men, retired from life and from the tribulations of the young, with money in the bank and time to spare . . . what more – save health, praise God – do we want? But where you are, in that city, at this time of year, September and autumn, the days fade more gradually, more romantically, though faster, into night than they do in June, July and August.

So, before it gets blacker than that afternoon in 1910, with the May Dust, I still have to read the Good Book. I am reading from the front and going steadily to the back, with the help of some strong, stiff snaps of Mountgay rum and water.

Don't ever feel you are too much of an academic to read the Good Book. And do not let "blackness" or the colonial syndrome make you feel that the only people who get something mentally nourishing from the Good Book, is white people, racists and Jews. The Good Book is beyond culture. I don't know who wrote it. And I don't care. It is like the air, the skies, the wind and the blue sea. It is attainable. So, even if you have to wrap its cover in brown paper, and hide the title from some of the radicals and semi-atheists in Trinity College, in order not to be called unsophisticated and be called a fundamentalist . . . beware of fundamentalists, especially fundamentalist women under twenty-three . . . still do it. You can hide and read. You can't reap and hide. As a matter of truth, you should enter that kind of meditation, in the privacy of your conscience.

I have finished with Genesis again – not a bad piece of writing – the vicar told me so, and I have to agree with him – and am now moving through Exodus.

"Then Jacob gave Esau bread and pottage of lentil. And he did not eat and drink and rose up and went his way: thus Esau despised his birthright."

When I read these word in the evening, in this tropical part of the world, sitting under my mango tree, with Hitler beside me, and a rum and water on the beach beside me, with the stillness of the air, the smell of flowers and the smells of all these polluting fumes from cars and buses and lorries, with the crickets chirping and the mosquitoes humbugging me, I still can't help feeling that the meaning of these words is more immediate and precise in this circumstance of climate. I read the same passage once kneeling down in St. Paul's Anglican Church on Bloor Street just before you get to Jarvis, after you pass Church Street, one week before I was to face the immigration people with regards to deporting me, or letting me leave on my own oars, in case I wanted to creep back into Canada. And all I felt was that I was reading the Bible, praying for help, in order to understand in less than twenty-four hours, the economics of my situation and the versatility of my fabricating a story to impress the immigration officer with. I felt nothing more. It could have been like reading the *Telegram* newspaper, which was one of the best pieces of journalism ever sold in that city. But here in this island, with the vicar living beside me, with all the poverty, dead dogs and dead crappos in the road, untouched and unmoved for days, with all the poorness and poverty and political pillage by the government of the Brown-Skins and the Red-Skins, I feel that Moses or Mr. Genesis had just written the words for me personally to read, and had intended these words specifically for my ears.

I never got this feeling of recognition, this pointing out of respect, when I read this verse, that Sunday morning in St. Paul's Anglican Church. It was damn cold, too. Minus 20-something. It was January. It is 98 here.

And don't ever let me hear that you have become so modern that you have started to read the new edition of the Good Book, which reads like the constipated prose of that American writer, Ernest Hemingway. Read it in the King James Version, *not* the Oxford edition. Me and the vicar came to words, and nearly came to blows over this same argument. Christianity is contemporary, he say, as if he was talking to a child, or was talking about manners and deportment.

Listen to how beautiful these words are*: "And tarry with him a few days, until thy brother's fury turn away."* Where but in the King James would you hear language as pretty as that?

Only a person with Kay's understanding would want such language modernized, for easier comprehension. The infelicities of the young.

I don't know how and why I got started on Kay. But having begun, you should hear the end of that part of my life. I do intend, however, that the end of my life shall be slightly postponed. At seventy-one, I intend, as I have said, to begin at Genesis, and word-for-word, word by word, worm and work my way through, until I reach Revelations and Concordance. Another poetic word! I feel that I have reached concordance with you, my son, in the writing of this letter, at this stage, for after Hitler has been fed his rice and fish-heads, hoping that no bones are caught in hi swallow-pipe! and I have read a few chapters of Exodus, I shall retire for the night, and join you again, soon in a concordance of love and of deep nostalgia. I have to complete both: this letter, and the Good Book; and I wonder which of the three remaining duties of my remaining days shall have been dispatched first. The Good Book? This letter? Or my life?

The feelings which I have been expressing to you, and which I have been expressing particularly with more emotion and honesty than normal, are taking hold of me, because all of a sudden, you are not here; not here in the big old house, whose emptiness echoes as if it was a rock quarry and I myself dynamiting coral stone. It is an old house. And it is large, larger than for one man who spends almost every hour of the day and night inside it, except when I am next door with those two robbers, the vicar and the lawyer-fellow. But it is a happy house, a warm house, a museum of memories and events and things which have been ourselves and our past and our aspirations. Your absence gives me the joyful opportunity both to view these things and to rearrange them. Your absence, I hope, is merely temporary. Four years of study in that city which at this time of year must be forgetting the life and love of summer.

I was talking about feelings. Yes, these new feelings which I must be expressing in my letter to you with a vengeance you had not known before, are feelings more normal for a woman, a mother who follows her child into another land, with words of love and reminiscence, to express. And in the case of most women, this kind of love and reminiscence need not be pure love. It could be her transmitting the cord of birth, the maternal cord, the umbilical restriction that reminds the child, the daughter, that she owes an unpayable debt for being born. It is important that you do. I do not wish you to miscalculate my motives, even if they are devious.

I have, and I probably transmit feelings to you which state that I am not only your old irreverent father, but am behaving as if there is a piece of the woman, the mother, inside my advice and words. And I hope that as a wise man, with the blood of your dead mother's veins inside you, an Edgehill, that you will disregard all the advice I have been giving you, because I am speaking a different language, and breathing in a different air. Disregard it as a *modum vivendi*: but regard it as a piece of history, to be used as a

comparison. Having now absolved you from all filial encumbrances of the mind, let me now incarcerate you immediately, for
your choice of a philosophical position which is not valid, or tenable, precisely because as I have said earlier, you have assumed that
there was not a history before your time, and you made the mistake of calling it a political situation.

You said you wrote a paper on the British Constitution, and
that professor gave you a B. You showed your paper to a Canadian
friend, and he asked you to let him use it as his own submission. In
the same course, you said. To the same professor, you said. The
same length, you said. The identical paper, you said. The only
change in the paper, you said, was that your Canadian friend put
his name, a different name from yours, on the paper. You said all
these things. Those are the facts of the case. And your Canadian
friend got an A for the paper, you said. And you ask me now, if this
is not racial discrimination, or bigotry, or unfairness. It is not so
much your shock that it happened, and to you, but that there was
no explanation, no regret, no forgiveness from anyone when you
pointed it out to them.

I myself am shocked that you would have confronted the professor with his own bigotry. I am also shocked that you expected an
apology and did not get one from him. You seem to feel that all
these incidents of bad manners, all these expressions of a lower-class
peasant syndrome have only begun with your presence at Trinity
College, and that Trinity is above that rawness of disposition. Had
you an eye to history, to the realism and the logic that other black
men before you had passed through the portals of Trinity College,
you would not now be so smitten by your paltry experience.

You are, in spite of the black American, Ralph Ellison, who
would claim you are invisible, you are rather outstanding and conspicuous. An easy, unprotectable target of whims and of deliberation. You are also a conscience. And if you know anything about

consciences, then you should know that that part of our makeup, of our psyche, is hidden, is dark, is criminal, is Christian, is pure, is degenerate, and is beautiful as is Caliban.

There was a group of West Indian students at a place in Montreal, a second-rate place, called Sir George Williams. Montreal, as you know, and in spite of what you may be hearing these days amongst the Anglophones at Trinity, is essentially a French conscience. Why did I say this, when I am really speaking about the West Indies, and a bigoted professor of Biology; and not about the culture of a place? The West Indians protested. And the Administration at Sir George, which had become during these protests a most third-rate institution, ignored their pleas of protest. The West Indians held a demonstration. They held it in a room where there was a computer. I never could understand that computer. Why did they not demonstrate in the Department of Biology? Or at the professor's home? In my estimation, it would have been better tactics philosophically to have done one, or the other. However, the computer was damaged. Allegedly damaged by the West Indians, they said. The West Indians were arrested. All the newspapers said so. The West Indians were charged. The West Indians were later sentenced. To various prison terms. One of them is now a Senator down here. Another is a Senator up there. Does Trinity have a computer? Do you wish to be a Senator? Up there? Or down here?

These are not the sentiments I like to send to you, in a red, white and blue air-mail envelope, with a fifty-cent stamp on it, all the way from this island to you, up there in that city buried almost to your knees in snow, and in hostility.

I thank you for sending me the phonograph record by Lionel Richie, *Games People Play*. It was also the name of a book by a man named Tofler, lent to me by the lawyer-fellow. I could not understand why so much attention was given to Tofler's book, which I have not read, and so little to Lionel Richie's song. The *Third*

Symphony of Beethoven's arrived without a scratch or a warp. I wonder how many postmen or post office workers have put their paws on this masterpiece before it got to me? Pearls amongst postmen.

Unfortunately, there are no pearls in the music that the Government Radio in this place plays. The music is like the voices of the politicians: vulgar. *Games People Play,* which I remember dancing to with Kay, almost every Saturday night at a West Indian calypso club, the Tropics, fifty years ago, is still fresh and contemporary; and very sensual. Is it the same *Games People Play*? If Hitler was a woman, Hitler and I would take a few steps. It is the kind of music that makes me want to dance with a dog! Which never dies. Timeless. Incidentally, although I do not advocate that you become a Christian, I do insist that you find time to sit in a church, at least once a month. But preferably, in the Church of England. If you should stumble into a Catholic church, or if you are taken there, choose the best: the old cathedral at the corner of King and Church. Sit inside a church. Listen to the music. Pay less attention to the sermon. The sermon is not meant for you, for our people. But the liturgy and the ritual are artistically rewarding. And so is the liturgical music. So far as Trinity is concerned, and in case you are hung over, and desperate on Saturday nights, and cannot rise for breakfast before the dining hall closes, slip into the Chapel; take a seat near the rear; find the hymn; that shouldn't be a problem, you were a choirboy in the cathedral here; and sing loudly; but not as if you are the soloist. And before the worms in your unrepentant stomach growl you out of favour from amongst the "divines," the theological students as they are called by the vicar and the lawyer-fellow, and out of favour of the sincere worshippers, the latter of whom are there because of the breakfast that is served after the collection plate, you may find yourself amongst the blessed, meaning the hungry poor; for the rich would not rise so early on a Sunday morning; and when they do rise, instead of oranges, bran flakes, soft honey that is grey in colour, bran bread and bran toast, warm milk, bacon done too hard, and soft-boiled eggs, the rich would rather eat eggs Benedict.

If you were here at Edgehill House, you would be partaking *our* Sunday breakfast: crab backs, stuffed with pork and champagne. *(I found a bottle dated 1943. Dom-Pee.)* A pity it is, that I cannot put a crab back into this red, white, and blue envelope, and send it to you!

Games People Play! It is a song that keeps coming back to my ears, whose emotion will not let me forget the sadness of love spent in Toronto. But I have to begin to move my finger along thee lines of Exodus, and watch for the bones in Hitler's supper, and scratch the fleas from his back, after supper.

Hoping that the reaches of these few lines will find you in a perfect state of good health, as they leave me feeling fairly settled in concordance,

Your loving father,
Anthony Barrington St. Omer Edgehill

I'M RUNNING
FOR MY LIFE

She was in the bedroom when he touched the door, and did not enter. She had heard him come home earlier, had heard the front door open and close, and had panicked. She had thoughts of running downstairs. But she had changed her mind. He would see her, and catch her, and ask for explanations, even though he knew it was part of her job to clean the bedroom; and she knew she could not satisfy him with her explanations. She knew she would be fired. She feared being fired. She wanted to enrol in a night class at George Brown College, to do something to improve herself; and even though she had not, and could not decide which course she should take, she knew she had to do it, to upgrade her life in this city. And she wanted to buy Canada Savings Bonds, to invest in the future. And she wanted to take a trip to New York City with Gertrude, who liked plays and art galleries; while she, she knew, wanted to visit Harlem and Brooklyn where she had friends. And she wanted to bring her savings up to the figure when she could more easily face the bank manager; and afterwards arrange a loan for a down payment on a small house in the East End, although she hated the East End, but the East End was the only place in this city where a woman like she, living on her own, making next to nothing in wages, could afford to have a roof over her head that she owned, before, as she always said, "God ready to take me to my

grave, and the cold earth in this place become my roof everlasting!"
She feared being fired before she had made a woman of herself. She
wanted time. And he became sad to think that she could be fired
just like that: she, who had worked for him so long; too long; too
well; in dutiful, efficient, faithful service. She was like a member of
the household.

It was her guilt which built these thoughts into the mountain
of fear. Her guilt sometimes turned her into salt. Just like Lot. And
this is how she described it to herself, in her Christian way of thinking. She knew she was certainly breaking one of the Command-
ments. But her nervousness did not permit her to name the exact
one, in this moment of remorse. Was it the one about covetousness? Theft? Dishonouring?

When she first heard him, she was writing down a telephone
message for his wife; and standing beside their night table, she had
noticed the book, *The Joy of Sex,* and had wondered why it was
there, and if they needed it, and used it, and why they had to use
it; and she looked at the message she had written down for his wife,
and at the book whose message troubled her, and could not decide
if she should put the note on the cover of *The Joy of Sex,* and cover
up this suggestive book, or stick it in the telephone; and all this
time, he is at the door, and she in his bedroom.

She had stood frozen. The second touch of his hand on the
door reduced her to tears. Tears of guilt, of shame, of disobedience,
of conflicting loyalties, and in the face of God. The message was left
by a voice she had heard many times before. And it was only when
she heard his steps retreating over the muffling thick carpet, and
had already begun to picture him going down, with his hands dan-
gling at his sides, walking like an ape, with his head bending for-
wards and backwards, as if he was sniffing out a bone that was
buried and lost; picturing him with his feet which moved with no
energy, desultorily, like a spring that already unwound and lost its

liveliness, only then did she crawl from under the bed. Why did she hide when she knew he was going away from her? She was surprised that she did not bang her head against the iron bedstead. Did not get stuck in the space between the floor and the springs which caused the bed to sag, as if and she were lying in it, reading, most likely this book, *The Joy of Sex*. And she had struggled not to sneeze and disclose herself through the thick dust that rose to her nostrils, already clogged through hay fever, as it always was during December, January and February, and made worse by the coldness in the house whose temperature she always raised, no matter how high the thermostat was already set. She could not bear a cold house. And first thing every morning when she arrived, even before she turned on all the radios and all the lights in the house, she raised the temperature five degrees. She had been praying that the elongated, weightless and shapeless cottons of dust, silken and balled up, would not enter her nostrils.

What time is it? From the darkness under the bed, she can see the computer digits on the radio's face, telling her in red, that she has spent more than one hour in their bedroom. Before her escape under the bed, she had passed her hands through the deep-layered drawer that contained *her* silk underwear, panties, camisoles and slips. She had run her fingers over the designer dresses that filled one closet. She had touched, had opened, re-touched and had sampled more than three vials of perfumes and scents; and had played with a gold-painted atomizer that contained cologne, as if it was a water pistol. All of these vials were expensive, she knew; for she had seen them in the magazines which *she* read, in Creeds and Holt Renfrew where *she* shopped. She tried on the polka-dotted blue silk dress a second time, and was convinced that she looked much better in it than *her*. And with this she possessed it in her mind, felt that it belonged to her, because *she* had so many, some of which seemed to be the same dress with the same design, and also because she felt it was wrong for one woman to have so many dresses, while others, many many others, had none.

And even now, under the dark bed, with the dust tingling her sinuses, and the silken balls of thread and hair stifling her, one leg of her ashen-grey pantyhose was still on her left leg. It was the only covered leg. The pantyhose was marked from the heel to the bottom of the knee with a run that had walked sideways and lengthways at the same time. The delicate material of the pantyhose wrapped her in a tangle, and tangled her up, so desperate had she been not to be detected; and she felt as if she was handcuffed, just as they had done to poor Mr. Johnson before they shot him and blew his head apart like a watermelon falling into the road; and she was unable to extricate herself; and she could imagine how foolish she looked, tied by this silk, in case somebody, in case he came back into the bedroom, and looked down, and saw her, and discovered her. She had seen somewhere, perhaps in one of *her* glossy magazines, or it could have been while walking up the ravine one morning in the summer, a worm covered in this same thin silk; yes, it was while she was walking up the ravine to catch the streetcar, it was while she was walking, striding jauntily in the ravine, flowers and faces, lawns and dresses swaying in the wind and she herself was kissed by the redeeming freshness of warmth of life, that she had seen the worm, as if the worm was turning itself into silk right in front of her eyes, as if the silk was turning into a worm. The winter had been so long. She had smiled then, and had called it the wonders of the Lord. Now, in this mesh of the pantyhose, she did not smile. She did not think of birth, or of new life, or resurrection. She was thinking only of escape and of extrication.

She did not know how long she would have to remain in this ridiculous imprisonment. How long it would take before the coast was clear; before she could descend into the quiet house, like a tomb with its dead head within it; dead even when he and *her* were at home; how long before she could complete her domestic tasks of the day, and run down to George Brown to register? Or stop in on her friend, Gertrude, who worked at a book store on Yonge Street?

The roast beef looked ugly while she was washing it with lime juice and salt; and slapping it to season it with herbs he liked to taste in his food; strange for a man born where he was born and raised, that she secretly held the belief he was not white, entirely; and the potatoes which he wanted boiled and then baked until their edges were brown with a golden crispiness; this enticement for food that he had, and which made her mouth water at its appearance; and the green peas from a can, like beads from a string that had collapsed into a mound; and the rice. Plain Uncle Ben's long grain, which she was instructed to cook without salt, without parsley flakes; "I can't stand those damn green things!" *she* said one night when the white-and-green mound of steaming substance was placed before her, as *she* sat like a princess in her blue polka-dotted silk dress, the same one she had tried on in the bedroom a few minutes ago; and was on her way to the opera. How long ago? Months now, maybe. But it could be years. Time was playing such tricks with her memory since *she* had left; with overnight bag, all her credit cards, the joint chequing account empty; and the shining Mercedes-Benz, which he had just got washed on Davenport and Park Road; and *gone*.

The house was quiet. It had been quiet all the time. She listened in this silence for music, for the television noise, for movement in his room with all those books, and all she could hear, or all she thought she heard, was her own heart beating.

And then she did a strange thing. She tightened her grip on the house slipper she was wearing, and on the right leg of the pantyhose; and with the other hand on the hosed left leg she raised her head, in the same way she raised her head when she was in church, when she claimed she saw the face of God, daring, ambitious, secure and charged with Christian righteousness and arrogance, and she traipsed down the stairs, as if nothing had happened. And as she moved, she indeed wondered if anything had happened, and if it was not all her fruitful imagination. She made more noise going down than she had ever done. She made more noise than anyone who lived here had ever done. She ignored consequences and detection. She ignored termination. She forgot ambition and educational advancement. And she went down with arrogance, in innocence in her laughable impromptu attire.

When she reached the kitchen, the house was still empty; empty as it had been all day; empty as it is any day in August when they are away at the cottage.

She was safe now, and sinful; and she moved about the kitchen as if she owned the world. She had placed the pantyhose in her large hip pocket. She had passed the African comb through her hair that was like steel and was black. She had run cold water from the restroom off the dining room, all over her face. She was a new woman.

She served his dinner. There was no noise. *Her* place had been set. He did not ask for *her*. He did not look at the knives and forks, soup spoon and dessert spoon and fork, at the other end of the oval mahogany table. He sat about four feet, at his end, from the place setting. She did not hear his chewing. She did not hear his drinking, wine and water. She did not hear the chime, the tingle, the slight pat of glass, cutlery and napkin ring.

But she felt naked. His eyes moved with the rhythm of her body. She touched her bottom once when she returned to the kitchen, to make sure she had clothes under the housedress she wore when she served. She could feel in her tension, in her opposition to him, his hand on her waist. She could feel his fingers on her legs.

There was no noise. He made no noise when he ate. And he said nothing to her when he was in the house. Never. But she felt he was assaulting her, in this silence, with the roar and violence of his eyes.

He got up from the table, and threw one last glance in her direction, as she stood at the sink. He wished he could thank her for her efficiency, for her company, for looking after him now that he was alone. He looked at her, and straightaway his mind was on his work. In the small mirror above the two-basined sink, she saw his eyes, and then his face, as he moved along the carpet which did not reproduce his weight, or the thoughts which she felt were running through his body. He had already dismissed her from his mind.

She turned the lamps in the dining room off. She closed the door. She did not feel safe. She took the served dinner off the mahogany table. She scraped the roast beef, the potatoes, the green marbles of canned peas, everything into the large tin garbage pail. He did not approve of leftovers. She left the plates and knives and forks and crystal glasses of *her* place setting, on the rectangular mat that showed the buildings of Parliament painted on them in the colours of moss and brick and granite, where they were. And then she left, after locking the door two times, and she broke into tears. She sighed deeply, pulled herself together, and took the steady climb out of the ravine, on her way to the corner of Bloor and Yonge to take the subway going west to Bathurst Street.

Time was out of joint. She could feel the presence again the house. She could feel it heavy and plain and hiding somewhere inside the mansion. Perhaps, it was ghosts; or spirits. But she did not believe in ghosts. Not she, a Christian-minded woman as she was. But she was going to find it: find the cause, or the presence, and its hiding place; and if the cause was in the form of a living person, or a dead body, she was going to seek it out and then try to master it.

She went upstairs on the second floor, and looked into each room off the flight of the bannister that swung to her right in a wide, polished swath, walking slowly and with deliberate bravery, running her palm over the bannister, as if she was wiping and polishing with her yellow chamois cloth. On the third floor, inside the master bedroom, she looked around, trying to determine if anyone had entered it since she had left the evening before; trying to seek some clue to meet the heavy and oppressing presence she could not see, but which was following her even as she perused the house.

Everything was in order. Each item and article, clothes and lotions in vials, and books, including the *Joy of Sex*, had remained as she had left them, yesterday.

So, she retraced her steps, all the time finding company in the rhythm and blues on the three radios on the first floor. After turning on all the lights in the house, and raising the thermostat the moment she entered, she changed the stations on the three radios from classical music to her favourite Buffalo station. The rhythm and blues made her so happy and relaxed, and appeased her spirit and helped her face the long day of work, with peace and patience. Now, this music was adding to her anxiety and discomfiture. She turned each radio off.

The house was like death without music. She endured this silence. But she left all the lights on. She was safe and comfortable with all the lights on. The late winter sunlight which had no heat to it, was still bright; and the lights hardly added to the illumination in the rooms.

She went into the library to see if the Indian blanket she had thrown over his body, dead in sleep immediately after he had eaten the roast beef, was still there. Perhaps, it is this. This Indian blanket was taking on, and inhabiting all the spirits and the ghosts of those tribes. Those tribes, those men whom she saw standing at the corner of Bloor and Spadina, old men, some old before they are young; defeated warriors, with faces the same as she had looked at in her school books back in Barbados, identical in the fierceness which her history book in Standard Seven had shown her, but without their spears and tomahawks.

The Indian blanket was on the floor of the library. In a bundle. In a way that said it had been thrown off the body, during the night. In a way a child would toss its covering off its body, no longer cold. She took it up, and held it against her body, and folded it while holding it against her body; perhaps bear, or fox, or caribou, or seal. She didn't know much about these things. Her friend Gertrude would know. Gertrude worked in a bookstore. Gertrude read most of the books in the bookstore. The Indian blanket felt odd, as if the animal from which it was made was still alive.

She took up the crystal scotch glass, and the empty soda bottle. The decanter was empty. On her way to take these into the kitchen, she noticed the door to the basement ajar. And lights on. Terror gripped her. Someone was in the house. A man. An intruder. A brute-beast. One of those varmints roaming Toronto interfering with women. A thief, perhaps.

She tiptoes the rest of the crawling way to the kitchen, her blood hot with fear and with the violence she knows she could be facing. And she drops the blanket on the clean countertop, and was about to rest the crystal glass in the sink when it dropped. The shattering glass is like sirens. The sound is like a cry of rape. A cry against rape. She cannot move. Her mind is in a hurry, confused, filled with decisions, not one of which she can take. She listens for the crash of the crystal to end, as if she is about to count the number of pieces which the Stuart crystal will dissolve itself into; but the glass is not broken. And she thinks this is an omen. It is her imagination which told her it was broken. Still, the danger lurks. Still the presence, now transformed into a person, a rapist, a thief, remains.

She reached for the large iron saucepan on the peg-board above the stove. But this proves too heavy and unwieldy. She chooses the large frying pan. Also of iron. And she crosses herself two times. Gertrude had told her how to make the sign of the cross, as Catholics do. She thinks of calling Gertrude to alert her, but she does not. And she never, in spite of promise, got around to taking down the rape crisis telephone number. But why couldn't it be that it was she who had left the basement door open? And she creeps along the floor, making more noise than normal, suppressing what noise there is through her caution, no noise coming from the radio to distract her attention and her deadly intent and the deadly blow she is going to deliver, and not breathing, just in case. She should have called Gertrude. Is it 911? Or 767?

When she reached the open door to the basement, she moves her hand instinctively to the brass panel for the light switch. The switch answers her touch. And below her, through the agaped door, the entire basement is bathed in the pure whiteness of light. She stops at the head of the stairs. She inhales. She hefts the iron frying pan. She can deliver a deadly blow with it. And then she goes down. Step by step. For the first time, realizing how noisy these steps are. Somebody had forgotten, after all these years, to line them with broadloom. Soft creak after soft creak. And still no sound from below in the bright light which seems to blare and scream out her terror.

She reached the bottom step. She closed her eyes quickly; opened them again, quickly, to get accustomed to the fluorescence. Still, no sound.

And then, she saw it. The T-shaped form made by the light, on the floor. Coming from the same closet she had stumbled upon, last week. The faint yellow of the stroke from the left side of the door, going rightwards across the top of the door. She hefted the frying pan. She was holding it firmly; and by God, whoever it was, he got to come clean! The bastard going-have to kill me, or I kill he! The iron frying pan was weightless in her hand.

She crept silent, step after silent step, the frying pan raised and ready, her eyes staring, and seeing blood, her body and the pan and her steps in a tense synchronized oneness; staring at the weak light forcing itself out of the half-open door; and clearer now, brighter now in her control of the threat and how she is going to master it, she sees that the shape of the light from the closet is not a T, but an inverted L. And she moves as a yacht would move silent over swift water, and when she comes face to face with the door, she didn't know she could get there so fast and with such stealth; and she raises the iron frying pan ready, and at the same time, with her left hand, she flung the door inwards, and screams, "Bastard!"

She finds herself standing over her.

He is sitting on a box marked CONFIDENTIAL, his head in his hands, bent down in a stooped posture of complete dejection. He was facing her. But he was not looking at her. His eyes were not looking at her. His eyes were not open. But he was awake and alert. And then he opened his eyes, and remained sitting and staring at her, as if he was sleeping, dead to the world. And she stood there, full with her former pity for him, and with a new tormenting and strange desire, like a feeling of love for someone who has never known love, with the frying pan in her hand, but now at her side, her own eyes staring back in bewilderment and wonder. But most of all, with pity and with a great strange love.

She tried to control the shaking in her body with the emotions running through it: pity and love and a tinge of indecentness that she had robbed him of his privacy, even though she could not understand that he had sought to be private in the basement of his own mansion; she felt she had unsanctified the holiness of his retreat. Whatever was his problem, whatever was his misery; whatever had caused his heavy drinking and his apparent surrender even with a life of such success and wealth; whatever his misery that she had left him; and whatever *her* good reasons, it was his home, his mansion, his castle and his dignity that she had ruptured through her fears and fantasy and the reading of recent horrors beaten and slashed and driven into the flesh and psyche of women.

"My God, Mr. Moore, I could have killed you!"

"May," he said. "May." She could see that he wanted to say more.

"What're you doing here, Mr. Moore?"

"Oh, May."

She was holding him now, in an embrace. He had risen to reach her. And she could feel the weight of her body against his; and he could feel the weight of his head against her breasts; and the softness there, and the pulsating blood, such as he had tasted once when he was on holiday in the Bahamas and had danced in his wildness to the beat of calypso; and could feel, as he felt then, the flesh in her back as his arms tied the Bahamian woman too close to him, even for a dance; and she was frantic and affectionate; squeezing him, holding him to her, frightened and faithful: for he was her employer and she was a woman, overcome by her grief and her pity; and pure and un-sinning: she could feel her body for the first time in three years answering to the touch of a man's hands; and knowing that notwithstanding that dirty dream she had the night before, the thought that rushed to her head like blood itself, she knew she wanted him. She could feel his desire touch her *there*: plain, hard and honest; and she could feel her body give in . . . for the three cardboard boxes marked CONFIDENTIAL, PICTURES & PHOTOS, and TERM PAPERS were large enough for their two bodies; and were soft enough and adequate enough and supple enough; and so, she put him to lie on his back, flat against the ridges and edges of the three boxes, and he had more than space and comfort so he closed his eyes, for he could not look at nor witness what was happening to him, after she had eased the tight-fitting custom-made corduroy trousers below his waist, and had pulled them down along his legs to white that she was surprised; "You should be in the sun" passed through her mind; seeing that his legs were skinny, and she left one trouser leg on, since it was too much trouble in her rush of emotion getting both over his shoes; and she raised the light-blue cotton dress, her smock as she called it, her work dress; and she pulled this up, and sat on him. It was then that he saw the rich brown flesh, her belly with its slight bulge, and her breasts with their black circles round the nipples, and the thickness and silk of her hair betwixt her thighs. Such lusciousness he had not seen before. But deep down had always yearned for. It was when his eyes rested on her greatness that the sight was too much for him, and in shame, in surrender, he closed his eyes. He also closed his eyes because he was praying. Always before, in the years of his marriage to *her*, it was fear and doubt and trepidation and he always ended up feeling inadequate, for she wanted to do it by the book, and she wanted him to talk, and say precisely how he liked it, and if he liked it this way or that, and he had to spell out for her the positions into which she had taken him. This is why now, not being able at this point, to know if there was going to be any difference, he closed his eyes. The realism was too much for him. It was like closing his eyes, momentarily, when the car approaching him had its high beams on, to avoid temporary blindness. But he preferred it with his eyes closed, anyway. And how was he to know that this would be the experience, the moment, he had been waiting all his life to have; and at the same time, the time and the experience he had been running for his life, to avoid.

And when it happened, when he reached his manhood inside her, she closed her eyes and said something like a prayer. And he screamed, "Oh Jesus Christ!"

And like a ritual, like a cleaning up after, like the practised taking up of things and putting them back in their correct places, she put back on her brassiere and her light-blue smock, and left the room. He was too weak to move. He was too invigorated to want to move from the three boxes marked CONFIDENTIAL, PICTURES & PHOTOS and TERM PAPERS. But more than anything, it was the peace in which he lay. And was contented to remain lying. And wanting in that contentment, to take his own life. To die.

She was standing in front of the double sinks in the kitchen. Her hands were moving automatically. Her face was serene. She could feel a new kind of life in her body. As if her blood was being taken out and changed and poured back in. She was staring into the backyard . . . and the trees were white and the jewels of snow brightened by the bright powerless sun, took her wandering, walking, looking into the windows of shops along Bloor Street; and looking into the peaceful waves of the sea near Gravesend Beach where she lived in Barbados. Her hands moved over the crystal glass she was washing. And she realized she had been merely holding it, when the light took up the intricate working on the glass, and the sparkles jumped and had a life of their own, like stars in the darkest night of blue. Then, the full force of her act struck her. Her mind was no longer focused on the glass. What had she done? What had been done to her? But what had she done?

When she realized what she had done, she panicked. Tears poured down her cheeks, and she could feel the water and she did not feel her tears were warm, as people said. Her tears were cold. She felt cold all over. Terror gripped her, and she wondered what to do. What had she done? From her Bible it was clear what her act was. And her religion would chastise her; and she knew she would have to atone for it. She knew she would not wish away her act of adultery. And more than that, her sacred vow to herself, and to Gertrude that no man would ever violate her body, not even if she had, as before, given her body in love, or in a passionate act of lust. When she knew what she had done, she became irrepressibly depressed. The act and her entire body became one inexplicable lump, a large ball, some kind of encumbrance that was ugly and bad, blocking the way to her other thoughts about anything else she knew about herself, as if the act encompassed her entire being. She was now nothing more than adultery itself.

The tears continued to bathe her face. But she realized the feeling her body, and the newness there, and the love she had given. No one could erase that. No one could say it was not love, that it was not her gift, that it was his assault.

When she knew this, when this thought like the spirit she felt many Sunday nights in her church gripped her, when she knew this, and was this, she broke down.

She picked up her winter coat from the chair on which she had placed it, hours before, and threw it over her shoulders. And she rushed through the front door, not really knowing where she was going; ignoring her woollen hat, her scarf and her gloves; and she ran across the circular driveway, crushing the snow and leaving pointed marks where her speed had destroyed the firmness of her footprints; running in the thick snow without her winter boots; ignoring the treachery of the ice beneath the snow. She bounded into the bookstore, rushed up to Gertrude who held five books in her hand, a pencil in her mouth, with three customers standing beside her.

"Come! Come!" she said, and went behind the counter by the cash register, and grabbed Gertrude by the hand, and said, "Come!"

On the way through the door, she told Gertrude, "This is business. Woman talk."

"What about my job?" Gertrude said. They were in the middle of Yonge Street, with two lines of traffic in either direction bearing down upon them. May ignored the cars.

"In here!" she said.

"The Pilot Tavern?" Gertrude was aghast.

One week ago, May had scolded women drinking liquor so early in the day, calling them sinners. "To drink?"

"Something happened."

"Wait!" Gertrude screamed. "The traffic!" It was almost too late. Brakes screeched as the two lines of traffic in two directions came to a shouting, abusive and gesturing halt.

"They have to wait."

"Danger," Gertrude said.

They entered the bar. And walked past the line of stools on their right hand, and which stretched the length of the bar counter. On their left were small round, black-topped tables, shining and placed into the spaces left between the custom-built leather seats. She guided Gertrude to the rear of the room. It was darker here. She chose a seat near a door over which was marked EXIT in red.

"Gerts, what have I done?"

"You sure's hell cost me my job!"

"This is business, man. Woman talking to woman."

"I'm concerned about my job."

"I tried to call you."

"You just come me my job, May."

"To tell you."

"How *could* you?"

"All morning, beginning last night, I had this feeling, like a burden, you know? All the lights was left on. And the radio was on my favourite station."

"How'm I going to explain this to Mister—"

"It was as if I couldn't help myself, all morning I couldn't help myself. All morning I feeling this presence. And I went down in the basement. And there he was. There he was, Gertrude."

"God, May, how'm I going to explain this? What have you done to me, May?"

"And there he was, in a little room in the basement, sitting down on a box. Do you know what was marked on this damn box he was sitting on?"

"How can you do this to *me*, of all people?"

"CONFIDENTIAL! CONFIDENTIAL! was marked on that damn box, Gertrude. I could have killed him *dead*, when he surprised me so. Dead, dead, dead, I tell you, this afternoon, Gerts. What you want to drink?"

"Something soft. Perhaps a soda."

"A soda? A soda, Gertrude? Do you think I bring you in here to order a soda, in a crisis like this? Gerts, I have done something, and in this hour o' darkness, you want to drink a soda? How the hell can you listen to my burdens if I drinking something hard, and you drinking a blasted soda pop?"

The waiter was standing over them. He could not understand her speech. Her speech and the accent in which it was embedded were too strange for his Sicilian ear. He remained standing and waited.

"Bring her a brandy. And bring me one, too, please."

"Coming up," the waiter said, and left.

"You can't help me to understand this burden whilst you stay sober, and me walking in the valley of death. Girl, drink something strong."

"I left my purse in the store."

"I have money." And she placed her purse on the table.

"And my job, May. How *could* you?"

"The CONFIDENTIAL box, Gerts. And I with the iron frying pan in my hand. And I see him there. Like a baby. Like a child. And I don't know if it was the dream about the woman-lion that I had and had told you about, or the dream about the dog. As I stepped through that door this morning, my spirit wasn't itself. It was the blanket."

"What the hell does a blanket, pardon my French, have to do with my job? You compromised me in front of my customers."

"An Indian blanket, Gerts."

"Indian from the East?"

"Indian from *here!* The Indian blanket that I wrapped him in, yesterday. I told you about that. When I could hardly control the thought o' murder, remember? Well, I may not be able to explain it like you, but there was something in that blanket. I don't know anything about the cultures o' people, but Gerts, something was existing in that blanket. And for me, a Christian-minded person . . ."

"And drinking *this?*"

The waiter had placed the drinks before them.

"The cultures o' people and native people don't mean a damn thing to me, but I feel something was in that blanket. Some-damn-thing." In one sip, she drank half of her brandy. "Now, I am in the basement. He in the closet. Like a little boy. Put in a corner. And when I saw his eyes, and what was happening to him, concerning the wife, yuh know? Gerts, I don't know what I have done. It is terrible, Gerts." She was crying now.

Gertrude, still pale and wan from the sudden intrusion, sipped her brandy, and then feeling its power, drank it off in one gulp. She liked brandy.

"All the way up here to you, running like a damn madwoman, Gerts, and the tears pouring down my two cheeks in sadness and in confession over what took place in that little basement room."

"You killed him, at last? You killed the bastard, eventually? That's the trick you want me to believe, eh May, after you have gone and got me fired? 'Cause, I sure's hell can't go back there!" She drained her glass, already empty. "Is that what you want to make me believe you did? That you killed him?"

"I *had* him."

"You *what?*"

"Had him, Gerts. I had him. Mr. Moore."

"Waiter!" Gertrude said, and motioned for another brandy. "A double, please." And she remained silent for a while, while she tried to understand what she had just heard. "Had him? Like, had sex with him?"

"Fooped him, Gerts."

"You mean. You mean, don't tell me, but do you mean, *sex?*"

"Fucked him, Gerts!"

"You? And Mr. Moore! *Sex!*"

"Waiter?" Make that a double, please." She had, in her confusion, forgotten that she had ordered it already.

For a time, perhaps longer than either of them realized, or could count, it remained still, dead, and with a silence that spoke amazement.

And when it was broken, eventually, it was broken by Gertrude's laughter. She leaned back in the straight-back chair, and laughed, until something like tears came to her eyes. She took a lace handkerchief from the sleeve of her brown fitted dress, and passed it over her eyes, and dabbed her cheeks with it.

"And how do you *feel* about this?"

"Is that all you can ask me?"

"Who initiated it?"

"What you mean, who initiated it?"

"He assaulted you, didn't he?"

"I, a woman, and at my age, mixed up in fornication with the man I works for, and all you can ask me, after drinking-off two brandies, is how I feel? And who initiated the fornicating?"

"Listen to me. Take it easy. I know you are distressed by this. But who initiated it? You have to tell me. He came at you, didn't he?"

"How do I feel? How do I feel, Gerts? I feel like shit. I feel dirty. I feel like a sinner. I feel like a whore, and a robber, too. A woman who robbed a man. I feel also like a savior. I feel, in a funny way, good. Damn good. But scared."

"I know. I know. In these cases, the woman takes on a terrible guilt, and sees herself being the victim."

"And it is this that's worrying me, and I run to you, my only living friend in this city, in this country, to seek solace and a word of wisdom from you, and *all* you can tell me, after two drinks, is *how* I feel?"

"Sexual assault! That's what it is, May. I know you're in no condition to see this clearly. I understand that. It is an assault to your body. The *unfair, criminal* advances of a man with power, and wealth, over a poor woman like you. You have your rights. You have to do something about it. We have to do something about this. And if you don't, I sure's hell intend to!"

"Gerts, you realize what I done? You realize how my life has changed, plain and simple, by this one act? And I never planned it. I never even imagined myself in such a thing. And with the man I works for? In a room? In a basement? And me, a woman who you know detests basements? And going to church twice a Sunday, and two more times during the week? I planning to go to George Brown. Planning to buy a house. Planning to get my hands on some Canada Savings Bonds. And now look! Gerts, you're looking at a woman who believes in God."

"You have to tell me you don't love him."

"I can't answer that."

"That you feel hatred for him."

"Nor that."

"You don't know you do."

"I can't answer that, Gerts."

"Of course, you won't know. It's a matter of master and slave.

"*What?*"

"I didn't mean it that way."

"Slave? Well, Jesus Christ, woman!"

"Please, May."

"You said master and slave."

"I mean power imbalance. You *know* what I mean. We watched it on television together, for nights!"

"What the hell is this power imbalance, when I talking woman-to-woman about being close to a man. I fooped a man, Gerts. Can't you get that in your damn head!"

"I'm trying."

"Well, try harder."

"What're you going to do?"

"I thought you would know."

"You're *not* going back in that house."

"And why not? I have a business lunch to prepare for, tomorrow."

"After he raped you? Are you crazy? You're going to report this, this assault, to the police. That's what you're going to do. You are in no shape to, you're in no shape to, to, to . . .'"

"A sin, Gerts. A sin, yes. Fornication, yes. Perhaps, adultery. But not *that*, Gerts. I'm not any vic, what you call it, the *victim*. I'm no damn victim, Gerts."

"We'll see about *that*."

"I'm no victim, Gerts. Don't call me a victim."

"God, May."

"I don't know how it happened. And I don't know why."

"These things do happen," Gertrude said. "Everyday. On television. And in real life." She drained her glass. She took up her friend's handbag. And made ready to leave. "These things happen." And saying this, Gertrude made the first gesture of friendship since they had been sitting in the bar. She reached out her hands, and placed them over May's, and tapped May's hands with her own; and then started rubbing them, sideways, and upwards and downwards. May continued crying. The tears dropped at the edge of her glass; and when she saw that, she moved the glass to evade the water. But she had moved her face also, and one long drop kissed the surface of the rich brown liquid. The tears continued without effort, without her trying to stop them. And she did nothing to wipe them away. And they started to fall on Gertrude's fingers, and she too, caught up now, in the soft, sad, passion of the moment, allowed the tears to fall on her hands. "We're going to fix that fucking bastard!"

TRYING TO KILL HERSELF

The snow had buried every landmark and identification and clue she was accustomed to, that helped her to distinguish her rooming house from the other houses that lined her street. When the snow fell like this, and when it was night, she was lost in whiteness. The whiteness was the same thickness all along the short street. The tree in front of her house were covered with the same thickness of snow, like clotted paint, thick as that on the Christmas card that bore the tragic information.

She walked very carefully, very slowly in the misery of the deep snow. Why am I still in this city? Instinct or fear warned her to slow down her already cautious steps; and this second sense helped her to reach the three-storey rooming house where she had been living for five years. Every part of it, but for the six front windows, was covered in snow. No light came from the windows. And suppose, just suppose, I was a woman who drinks! She stood where she was, to make sure.

"Eh?" It was a man walking close behind her, ploughing into the holes she had left, thinking she was talking to him.

"God bless you, son," and she waited for him to pass, to be alone once more with her thoughts. She followed him in the deep channel of pounded snow, wide enough really for only one person to walk. Look at this blasted snow! And if I were a person who drinks, and coming home to this, how would I find my way home? She looked at the houses along the street, and saw no difference, no distinguishing mark in their character and build. Back home, we build each house different from all the others, to bring out the personality of the house *and* the owner. But up here, every house is made to look the same. Just like the people. Lord, look at this thing!

She crunched the snow, soft and unresisting under her heavy weight, thinking, as she descended into the darkened steps to her basement apartment, that she must get out soon, out of this underground living, this confining hole; and as her weight crushed the snow, she could not really know at that moment that she walking on wooden steps, so deep was the snow. Lord, don't let me die here, in this city, and to be buried in the snow! She stopped a moment under the eave which was not well built and which was not repaired properly by the landlord, for it kept out nothing, neither snow nor rain. And she made up her mind that first thing in the new year, first thing come the new year, I moving from this basement 'cause basements're where animals should live, not human beings, a place where you put distant cousins to sleep on a weekend. Lord, I can't figure out some of these recent rich West Indians with their big house-and-land up in the suburbs, furnished for a king, and when they invite you to a party, shove you *straight down* into the basement to dance and drink liquor with curry goat and rice, holding on to plastic cup and paper plate and plastic fork, all night long as the reggae music breaking your eardrums because your feet must not touch their broadlooms. She was determined to look for a better place.

The short sentence on the Christmas card, the terrible message, caused her to be nervous and agitated, and she had some difficulty getting the key into the hole. Everything was white. Even under the eaves, repaired three times so far for the year, by the landlord. She couldn't see, it was so white. But she could feel and guess at the opening.

The smell of the apartment, closed up all day, came at her with a rush of blood to the head. But it was a welcomed scent of life. Not like the extreme cleanliness, that smell and feeling the smell gave her, when she went to work at the hospital, and on the subway platform and the streetcars and buses. She always felt that the people who used them had no life. Not that she preferred the nastiness of places like New York and their subway. I must take a trip there, before I go to my grave. But why am I thinking about grave and death, even before I have lived a decent life in this city?

Incense which she burned before she left for work, placing it in the soft dirt in the green plastic pot of her favourite diefenbacias, and left burning like a spirit in her absence, and the incense she burned the moment she returned, to help kill the lingering smells of her profession, and especially too when she cooked curry chicken, the incense filled her nostrils. And there were other smells: the elbow grease and the thoroughness of the detergents and sprays that changed the smell of her cooking into the faint fragrance of heather. And of course, the scents from the green bottles on the water tank of the toilet, left with their mouths agape, their grey wicks like unhealthy tongues. And of Limacol she used to rub her arms and legs and her forehead, when she felt a touch of the flu coming on. And that of her perfume, which sometimes she left open, in her rush to be punctual. The smell of close acquaintance with a room, with a chair, with the floor which was not level and which was covered in linoleum, over which she had placed scatter rugs, and which leaned in two directions from the front door, all throughout the apartment to the bathroom at the back.

The first thing she did after lighting two sticks of incense she bought from a black man dressed like an African in white robes and a white skull cap, and who called her "Sister," and to whom she said, without a smile, "I'm old enough to be your damn mother, boy!" was to stand and inhale the rising wriggling smell of the line of smoke, and then sneeze loudly and violently. And then she took the Christmas card from her handbag. She placed it on the tall, unpainted walnut dresser in her bedroom. Her bedroom was cluttered. It was the area curtained from the rest of the large room, the living area, by a bellow-like cream screen made of leatherite. She closed this screen like a concertina, pulling it out, until it reached the latches which she locked religiously one time, and opened one more time, making certain her body was safe and could not be seen in the squeezed-off small congested room, from the window which was level with that of the neighbours. Too many oddballs roaming the streets, and for a woman like me . . . She leaned the Christmas card against a bottle of Limacol. Beside it were several bottles that contained creams and lotions, and bottles and vials of pills for headache, for blood pressure, and for the small woman's problem she suffered from, from time to time.

Back in the living area, she sat on the sagging couch. The couch was placed against the wall that she shared with the people on her left side, as she came through the door; the east side; the side that was her left, depending upon whether she was facing the couch, or had her back towards it. She turned her back towards the couch very often, in Christian disapproval, almost every Friday, Saturday and Sunday night, after eleven o'clock from the neighbours on her left side, "that blasted side," as she called it, when they turned up their stereo and played it full blast, and doused her in reggae and rap music, "that heathen music," as she called it, that they played and played and laughed and shouted to, and she knew they were drunk, and behaving as if they had not left the West Indies too long, and were now living amongst decent people. It played and played and pounded her body and mind with its unrelenting beat, and drove her mind to murderous thoughts. But she never complained to them. She was too much a Christian-minded person. Never knocked on the wall with a broomstick. Never refused to say,

"Good morning, my dear," to the father, or the mother, or the strapping sons and pregnant daughter when she met them in the early morning, stiffened against the cold in their thin clothes, dressed in the winter as if they were still back in Trinidad; or when she saw them bright and blazing in colours of the summer, as if they were going to a picnic in the Caribbean with all that noise, or marching in the Caribana parade.

Beside the couch, covered with a printed cloth down to the floor to hide the stain and the tear that ran to the floor, a cloth of frayed edges like tassels, over the deep green broadloom type scatter rugs and carpets, was a table covered by the same printed cloth. The cloth had a design of roses. Red roses. Roses of Sharon. She loved roses. And that was one reason why she was so drawn to the Christmas card and its message which dealt with a Mr. Johnson from Jamaica, who had himself been attending his roses in his backyard, and talking to them as any gardener would, when a neighbour who was not from Jamaica and did not know roses or gardeners or decent people, told the police there was a mad man in the backyard talking as if he was crazy, going mad over the bed of red roses. That is what happened to Mr. Johnson. That terrible thing. She looked at the Christmas card, and passed her hand over her Bible. A vase with more red roses, those artificial ones. And a book, *Women*, which a patient had given her, as a birthday gift last year, for being nice to her after an operation. A small panda, which she had bought for a child on the ward and had not remembered to take it to work. And a larger teddy bear, which her girlfriend had bought for her for Christmas, last Christmas. She slept with the teddy bear between her legs, to give her warmth and keep her company.

She opened her Bible.

She opened the heavy, dog-eared book at Hebrews, to chapter one. She passed her little finger on the right hand, a pointer for her weak eyes, over the first verse, over the second verse, mumbling the words in rapid speed to herself. When she passed her pointing finger over the third verse, it was what she wanted. She began to read aloud.

"*'. . . when he had himself purged our sins'* . . . Yes, Lord . . . *'sat down on the right hand of the Majesty on high'* . . . Praise his name . . . *'being made so much better than the angels, as he hath by inheritance obtained a more excellent name than they.'* Your precious word! *'For unto which of the angels said he at any time, Thou art my son, this day have I begotten thee'* . . . I am thy humble daughter. *'This day have I begotten thee?'* Lord, if only your word had said *forgiven*, instead of *begotten!*"

She closed the Bible. She went on questioning the use of *begotten* for *forgiven*, wondering if the man who wrote the passage could have made a mistake.

"Now, I am going on my two knees before you, Lord, to ask for forgiveness for what I've done. And to pray for Mr. Johnson and his wife, poor soul. Our Father who art in heaven, hallowed by Thy name, Thy kingdom come . . ."

When she rose, after lapsing into a longer impromptu prayer than could have been written in no Bible, or Prayer Book, she brushed the lint and grains of dust from her knees. But she was still in her winter coat. She began to feel the warmth in the room. For her, temperature was always was always like life, like warm blood. She left her thermostat always at eighty degrees Fahrenheit, from October until June, in all the five years she lived in this basement. Even if I was paying to heat this place outta my own pocket! And from July until September, she kept it at seventy.

It was now time for the telephone; and she reached over and got it. Living alone for so many years, loneliness never really touched her, and made her sad, not so long as she had her Bible and her white Solo telephone, with three extension cords added to the original curled length. She bought them one Saturday afternoon from an Indian discount store on Bay, and made them the topic of conversation that night with Millicent when she saw she could walk from the front door to the toilet bowl in the bathroom at the back of the basement.

"Girl, how you this evening?"

It was six. Millicent was on the other end, indulging with her, in their nightly conversation. She would put the world right to-night, as she did every night, discussing her work, the hospital, the doctors and nurses and the patients; Millicent's employers, life, things, and before the end of their conversation, which lasted some-times for two hours, while they cooked and sometimes burned the rice while talking, happy and laughing and swimming in the sweet-ness of gossip, the conversation would end, always, on themselves: women. Tonight, her voice was low and unhappy; her spirits damp-ened from the message on the Christmas card.

"Well, my dear, some thoughts passed through my head today, on account of what happened to Mr. Johnson, that I had to pros-trate myself before my Maker and ask Him what things coming to, in this damn city."

Seven-thirty came quickly. Millicent would be in her small kitchen, cooking peas from a can, mashing Irish potatoes which she liked, and which she ate every day, and frying steak which she also liked, round steak, and which she cooked with little or no salt and less pepper, "the pressure, you know," she explained; and smothered in ketchup, thick as mud. And a bottle of imported beer. Lowen-brau. And before bed, which was punctually at eleven, a glass of Hennessy brandy. Millicent had no time, and no guilt about not saying her prayers before she flopped into her bed.

"The snow today, eh? Deep enough to bury a man. And I haven't even taken off my winter coat since I got home. You still see-ing Percy? Percy talking marriage yet?"

She smiled and listened to her friend tell her about the three women Percy has, and how if Percy doesn't get his act together, "One o' these days I might have to kill that son of a bitch! I going with the same man six years, keeping myself clean for that man, and he not thinking marriage?"

She stopped talking and listened to Millicent's voice; and when Millicent stopped talking, she too remained silent, and listened to Millicent's breathing, gauging her anger, and her battle with Percy; and Mr. Johnson came into her own thoughts, and she held the Solo, and listened and thought and could utter no word, as if the weight of the words she wanted to speak but could not, were too heavy. Still, she did not speak. And still, she did not end the conversation. She could almost hear the distance from the centre of the city up to the suburbs where Millicent lived, in the noise of the silence the Solo was making. It was like this sometimes. When she just needed to know there was someone at the other end of the telephone, but incapable of continuing the conversation. Millicent called her crazy for doing this. Millicent asked her if she had something on her mind, when she did this. And she said, "I know it's bad manners to be like this, but I have nothing to say, child. Nothing do I have to say." It was some time before she realized that Millicent had had enough, and had hung up on her.

She unbuttoned the three buttons of her winter coat, and loosened the blue scarf round her neck; and pulled the deep blue woollen blouse out of her brown polyester slacks, making herself more comfortable; and after doing this, she was no more comfortable, for her tam-o'-shanter of green, red and black, which she had knitted herself, and had put a large round ball of blue wool in the middle of the skull, was still on her head. When she realized that the telephone was dead, she was cut off from the rest of the world, feeling as if she was cut off from a friend she had loved all her life, forsaken in the harsh decision of that kind of termination, and not being able to call, to hear the person's voice, but not to speak, just the desire to hear a human voice, but feeling the hurtful pain of being cut off, since there was a new number "at the customer's request, *unlisted*," she sighed. How could people be so cruel?

She dialed again. She kept all her telephone numbers in her head; and sometimes she dialed a number, not knowing at the outset whose it was, but recognizing the voice the moment it answered, and then the long inexhaustible talk; her work, the hospital, the doctors and nurses and the patients; and Lee's employers, life and things.

"But Lee, you didn't read in the *Star* that there was three bullets? *Three*. Not one, dear, but three. There was three bullets fired in that poor man's head. The first one missed. And hit the 'luminium lid clear off the pot 'o rice and peas his wife was cooking that Sunday. You know those strong, fat red beans Jamaicans cook in their peas-and-rice? What a crime, eh, girl! That thing 'bout the 'luminium lid off the saucepan o' food, is the first ounce o' truth I heard from all the things that I read and that come over the radio and on the television. When I sit down in here at night, and watch the *Journal* every night at ten o'clock, and see these things, I got to shake my head. I talked to everybody I know and still can't get the truth outta nobody. Until I received the Christmas card. No. No, I don't know who sent me the card. But until I got this card I was not an inch further to the truth. I would say that the police is guilty of 'ssassination, plain and simple. I had cooked some of this same rice-and-peas for you once, didn't I? Yes, man. We was watching the baseball game that Friday night, when George Bell hit the gran' slam. That same night the police fellow came on the television asking for more bigger guns to protect the police from criminals like Mr. Johnson. Criminals who threaten their lives with a *garden fork*? My dear, I bet you when the truth does come out, and it may take years before the truth come out, I bet you,

Lee muh-dear, that they confess and admit before some commission that all Mr. Johnson had in his hand was a lil spade, made outta tinning, before those two police gunned him down. This city turning into *Miami Vice*. Now, the very police asking the public to permit them to bear more bigger guns to bore more bigger holes in innocent people."

As she remained silent and angry in her silence, agitated while Lee answered her in words that came from afar, from another planet, strange even in the way they sounded, she felt as if she was being washed out into the sea. The silence on the line continued a little longer, as she listened to the voice she had known for so many years, telling her she was wrong, that the police, to a man, was there to "protect you and me." And it made her sad to know that this voice, and these words, were coming from perhaps the only person, woman or man, in this city, in this country, in the whole world, whom she ever trusted.

"It is pure and simple, a case of ordinary sinfulness, Lee."

"No, darling. It is merely law and order."

The telephone went silent. She could hear the heavy breathing coming through her ears. She could feel the hot breath of the breathing. She could even see Lee's eyes gone smaller, like slits, and see how her face became crimson. Lee's face went red whenever she was overjoyed, when her favourite baseball pitcher fired a shut-out; when she was embarrassed by a dirty joke; and when, she said, she had orgasm. She had confessed all these things.

She ignored Lee's sentiments, and tried to take her mind off the disappointment, splitting her attention between the breathing silence coming through her Solo, and looking at the Christmas card with its undisturbed snow like thick coagulated paint on the eaves and trees and roads. She took off her winter boots, using one foot against the heel, and then the other.

"May I ask you a personal question?"

"About Mr. Johnson again? Or about my views on law-and-order?"

"You know anything about mental breakdowns?"

"Who having one?"

"Can you tell?"

"There're books. But there're lots of signs."

"Is falling asleep, one?"

"Could be. Could be not."

"Can I tell you something?" Before she told it, she took her pantyhose off. The room was hot. Her skin was itching. Her upper arms and legs. "Nothing."

"Nothing? You just said."

She rubbed her upper arms with the Solo. The cord needed unwrapping.

"It's nothing."

Lee began to laugh. Lee's voice with the laughter in it was deep and suggestive. The telephone cord was untangled now, and she started to rub her legs with her left hand. Her skin felt warm. But the itching was disappearing.

Lee was still laughing her suggestive laugh; and she continued to pass her hand up and down her legs. She was beginning to feel warmer. It was a strange sensation. She had never rubbed her legs this way before. And the pleasant sensation went all through her body as if it was her own blood surging; as blood would surge and pump life and vigor through the system after a long run, or after a strong rubbing with Limacol, or after pushups, or after orgasm. Her hand was now rubbing her other leg.

"Are you there?"

The sensation of pleasure was turning to one of satisfaction and excitement. She had never done this rubbing to herself before. She raised her dress above her knees, following the itchiness that travelled like a contagion. She looked at her legs. They were strong.

And the hair there was thick and black and strong. She could still hear Lee's breathing through the receiver. The excitement from her rubbing, her blood which she could almost feel circulating freely throughout her legs, was getting hot now. The delicate pure cotton that had protected her from such extravagances was now damp, and fragile; barely able to withstand the force and the passion of her fingers moving up and down rapidly strong and sure like white-head bush bleaching stains and spots away; determined to get rid of the blemish.

There was no way of telling now, of telling at all, if her breathing was her own. Or Lee's. Silence fell. The line that joined them seemed dead. The cord, the breathing, the silence and caressing became one compelling, encompassing activity. Falling outside the basement were thick pieces of white feathers. Flakes falling off a tree that was being shaken. She was barely aware of their falling. And she remembered airing pillow cases in the backyard, near the white-limbed trees that gave too much shade to her tomatoes in the summer, and always, in winter and summer, seeing the feathers fall out of the two pillows, and carried away immediately in the wind. And she remembered hearing the howling of the wind through the branches of the white-limbed trees. Cedars? Maples? Those with white limbs. And next door now, someone turned on a stereo, and the booming of heavy music, steel and voice, tore through the thin wall. Her back was resting on this wall, leaning to be more comfortable; to be relaxed; to be free to commit her act; to be more accommodating to the demand of her body.

The music pouring through the sand, the poured concrete and the plastic of the barricade dividing her from the laughter next door, was slow and full and thick, just like the music she listened to, in better moments. The falling pieces of feathers by her front window passed before her eyes in the time and rhythm almost, of the music. The wind was splattering snow against the glass; and that was the only sound that was breaking the flow of her fingers as they rubbed her skin, covered partially by the one hundred percent cotton; and the falling snow was, too, the only soft relief from the pounding of the reggae music next door.

"May I ask you a personal question, Lee?"

A dog is scratching the outer door of the basement entrance.

"That dog again! That blasted dog and those sinners next door!" She laughed aloud, and deep; and there was more than a sense of sensuality in her laughter. "The personal question I was going to ask you. Being alone, Lee. Being alone all the time and doing things like taking off all my clothes with the lights turned out, even though there's not a living soul here, but me. And those people next door playing all this tuk-music., I am sure you can year it coming through the telephone. Listen. You hear it? Deafening me all hours o' the night. Sometimes, I swear that if I don't cover myself in total darkness whilst I dress and undress, I might see one o' those bastards' eyes spying through a knot-hole in the wall, spying at me as I dress and undress. I can never, never, after all these years living alone, undress with the lights on. Is something wrong with me? There's that dog scratching at my door, again! God, no, Lee! I can't do *that*. Poison a dog? No, man. That isn't Christian. I know you've told me many times to do that, and I myself threaten to do the same, but I couldn't bring myself to that final action. How would it look for me to see my name in the *Toronto Star*, or on the ten o'clock CBC *Journal*, arrested and charged and in front of a judge? Oh God, no, Lee! And to be put in prison with a lotta women, wickers all of them, 'cause I heard one of the doctors at the hospital saying that the condition in prison breeds lesbian women who are wickers. And he said you can never tell what dirtiness women in prison are proned to do, and what would happen in those circumstances? But listen to me, now. If I was to put just a lil ground-up glass bottle on a bone and feed it to this blasted animal,

I wonder what would happen. Perhaps, up in Scarborough where you live, people does behave so. But down here, in this ghetto, where there's all this crime, with people unemploy', undecentness to make a sinner *croil* in shame, rapes every day, they would swear there's a connection between the colour of my skin and the extremity of my action. Not me, darling. There's that dog, again."

The dog was scratching against the metal frame of the storm door.

Without asking Lee to hold, she placed her Solo on the bed; unrolled the hem of her dress; pulled her winter coat back on over her shoulders; and went to the front door. The dog smelled her kindness. And it began scratching more vigorously, and started to yelp. Before she could open the door more than an inch, the dog was squeezing itself through the crack of space. She watched the animal do dances of happiness on the linoleum and scatter rugs, leaving trails and puddles, as she remained holding the door, now with a large enough space. But the savage was already inside. And the opened door brought in the wind and the cold which ripped the cloth protecting her legs, and made her legs seem like paper. Her legs were no longer itching. But the cold drilled a thin icicle of pain through her breasts. The dog was still dancing a dance of happiness. Prints from its paws, and puddles marked its circular frantic progress over the floor.

She closed the outer door. She closed the inner door. She applied the three bolts, and turned the key, and locked out the cold and the night.

"Imagine those Eskimos and explorers in the olden days!"

"What Eskimos?" Lee asked her. She was surprised that she was still on the phone.

"Let me give this blasted dog some milk."

"Without warming it?"

"That never crossed my mind."

"Warm it, and call me back.'

The telephone went dead.

The dog was quieter now. It sprawled itself on the linoleum. It followed her movements with its eyes and its tail that moved like darts and a snake.

She opened her small, white, chipped fridge, which was packed with food. In the shelves in the door were wedges of cheese in yellow plastic wrapping; bottles of soda water "for gas," tomatoes and apples wrapped in cellophane paper; milk in cartons, one carton of homogenized, and one of two percent fat; pieces of ginger bought months ago in the Kensington Market, and looking not like human fingers, deformed and amputated above the wrist, and tins of marmalade and jams from Jamaica, which she had never visited. And in the fridge itself, on its three wire shelves, were plastic containers of food: rice, peas, rice-and-peas, roast beef, roast lamb, roast pork; and bottles of tomato paste, bottles of grapefruit juice, and five containers of yogurt, "for losing weight." One of these days, soon, she said, talking to the dog, I have to get rid of this food. You could eat this? Tummuch food for one person! And at the front of the top shelf, was her bottle of five-star Hennessy brandy.

The two-burner stove whose elements were like two staring eyes, standing beside the fridge, made of white enamel and chipped in as many places as the fridge was, had two saucepans on the elements. The saucepans were made of enamel. She had bought them at a fifty-percent sale at Honest Ed's. She cleaned them and made them shine as if they were made of precious metal, as if they were silver. In them was split-peas and rice, and a thick, rich, dark-brown stew of braising beef, chunks of pig tail, carrots, onions and mushrooms. When she lifted the lid, the dog scampered on its legs, wagged its tail as if it had seen a stranger it liked. She could never tell with dogs. They danced whether it was a friend or a foe, except that this one did not growl. The noise it made told her it was trying to speak. The smell of the stew was making it salivate. But she gave it milk. In a Pyrex bowl. Cold milk. "Not my stew, you brute-beast!" she told the dog, oblivious of her words and her presence now, and consumed in the taste of the milk, wagging its tail in a different meaning and excitement. "Waste my food on you, a blasted stray-dog!"

She stooped and ran her hands over the wet fur of the dog, taking from its coat the accumulation of snow and icicles; and probably fleas, from the wet, grey hairs. Her hands touched more bone than flesh.

She poured herself a Hennessy. A large one. "This cold weather," she told the dog. And all the time she sipped, and the dog lapped, she could feel eyes from behind the wall spying on her. The next-door eyes, the eyes she was sure watched her undressing every night. "The ghost of Satan watching me," she told the dog. And she made the double shot of Hennessy the strong justification of her indulgence.

She began to undress. And stopped. And turned the lights off. The Pyrex bowl moved as the dog tried to find its food. She turned the lights back on. And stood in front of the looking glass on the bureau, and tried to see her whole back, from the neck to the bottom of her spine. The dog was bending itself into a hairpin, using its fangs to bite into its wet, itching fur. And she stopped undressing and watched the dog and wished she herself had double joint, was supple and young still, like this dog, so that she might see herself from every angle, just as the dog was doing. She looked at herself long, and critical, and then, as if with a sudden pang of self-consciousness, or of shame, for the dog was staring up at her, she chose a new nightgown. She was no longer cold, and she did not have to select a flannelette. She pulled the long black silk nightgown over her head, adjusted her left breast which had slipped out, holding it with tenderness, and fitted it inside the bodice of the delicate, shiny material, all the while allowing her hand to hold its weight for a longer moment than the adjustment required. "Cancer, boy," she told the dog. She looked at the dog. The dog was on its high legs. A small, pointed, pink-coloured thing came up and out from under the dog's belly. The dog was looking square into her eyes. And it continued standing on its hind leg, and then rushed to her, and grabbed her right leg with its front paws and started its motion. "Are you trying to foop me, dog? Is this what you carries on with, next door?" She swallowed all the Hennessy in one gulp. The dog was still on her leg, making its motions. "Is this the kind o' dog you are? Did those bastards next door train you to foop people?" She threw the dog aside with the fling of her leg, and her slipper slid across the linoleum. She dragged the long telephone cord with the Solo from the living room area, said something to the dog to get it to leave her leg, and it did not, and then she screamed, "Git! Git!" It sat on the linoleum, wagging its tail. She put the television on to bring more people into the room, to protect her. The dog turned its attention to an American woman who was spraining her brain to name the Prime Minister of Canada. "Is it Church? Winston Churchill?" she asked the host.

She lay on her back on the soft, large bed, and its accommodating springs took all of her weight and her exhaustion, her heaviness of spirit and of body, in the middle of its soft trough. The springs cried out a little, as she moved, making herself comfortable as she dialed her third friend for the night. These same bed springs had once been crushed by the weight of two bodies, hers and *his*, the one heavier than the other, long, long ago, on nights when their two desires were as loud as the music pumping from next door. The body of the man she was married to had left its mark on the damaged springs, and on her attitude to men ever since. It is five years since she has had a man in this bed; and she doesn't really know how she has withstood the abstinence, and the foopless nights, her

Bible and her Christianity having nothing at all to do with it; and the dog in its own way of knowing things, using its smell in place of human intelligence must have sensed it, and acted.

"Last January the second, is five years, to the day," she said, with the dog appearing to listen, turning its head away from the correct answer to the question about the Prime Minister of Canada. "Of course!" the woman on television said, purple with shame. She spread her legs, passing her hand across her nightgown to make room for the spread of her legs, and the dog jumped into that space.

"You *dirty* son of a bitch!"

Her scream was more of terror than of shock. She held the dog by the collar and in one movement which encompassed her jumping up from the bed while holding the dog, and opening the door, and then the other door, she slammed the dog into the snow on the steps, on the concrete perhaps, closing and rebolting the door in the same action. She could feel the pain in the dog's moaning even with the door shut tight. The cruelty of it, but the same of it, too. She tried to shut it out, but it seeped through, nevertheless.

She dialed Ruby.

The voice was moaning. Her own voice reflected the passing of time and of shame and of the Hennessy. And at last, there was one final moan.

She had killed the dog.

She dropped the Solo.

She gave out a sound that was high and chilling and terrible. Like the painful joy of giving birth. But higher and with more pain.

She dialed again. And there was a busy tone. Ruby had taken her telephone off the hook. It was now past midnight. The passing of time and of shame and the working of the Hennessy collapsed her into a shape on the bed, with her legs drawn up to her breasts and with her arms wrapped round her body. Her body was cold.

Three days have passed now, and have found her flat on her back, unable to move, too weak and too weakened; too tormented and afraid that should she move from beneath the three thick blankets, the thing on her mind, the death of the dog, its murder would be exposed to the world, and bring her continuing bad luck. Her world is the world of her three best friends.

Her Solo has been ringing and ringing, and left unanswered. Once, she counted the ringing for thirty-nine times. That would be Ruby, who was persistent. And it rang at intervals which were irregular, but on account of her state, it seemed it was ringing with an annoying persistence, as if the caller could, like the bastards next door who owned the dog, see her and know she was home. Her silence and pretense, and the stiff body of the dog, fortunate in its cold undug grave and not yet attracting flies and other things and worms that would devour its body from the inside, burst its bulge and make the tightened skin pop, and give off the smell she had walked beside on the hot tarred roads, under the sun that was no friend of weak bodies and things, she was glad for once that she was living in this cold, cold place.

This cold, this bitter cold, this cold she had cursed more than she had blessed it, was now a preserver of rot and decay, a concealer of murder. Inside the cold basement apartment, cut off from her outside world, by her deed and by her own wish, the body of the dead dog grew into a proportion as serious as the murder of her friend Mr. Johnson by the policeman, and turned her action into a sin, which she had not quite faced, nor prepared an explanation for. And worst of all, she suffered the chill and the scandal that it would come out in her church. To her pastor. And to the congregation of West Indians, mostly women, always willing to receive rumours about members in their community of the church and of the home; and more telling than that, even in their Christian manner and righteousness, to make those rumours grow, like the quantity of rice in a saucepan with water, expands.

"You hear?"

"'Bout the dog?"

"No, man! Not one dog, was *three*. I hear it was three. Maybe four."

"What a thing, eh?"

"This city does this to women."

"Appears the only thing that stop her from killing the owners of the six dogs was that . . ."

"My God! Only God could save her now."

"Providing her soul in order for that salvation."

"We have to pray for she, man!"

And give it their own broad interpretation of sorrow, misfortune, wickedness and damnation.

She lay for three days and three nights still dressed in her light blue hospital uniform, and did not even change her underwear, did not bathe and did not brush her teeth, as she changed her position on the sheets getting warm and sweaty from her body, as if she had a fever, and was coming out of it, with the fever's heat pouring into the cotton of the sheets; and she lay on her back, deliberately, because looking into the ceiling of the basement bedroom, she was at the same time looking into the heavens, to God, where she knew her release and her absolution would come from, and was, at the same time, giving the pain in her left side an ease. In the three days, and the three nights which were longer, she knew by heart every formation of cobwebs, every spot on the ceiling where the sun touched it, at the exact time of day, she could remember the reflection there when a car passed, and the larger reflection when a truck lumbered by in the thick snow; and she knew and learned to live with the shadows, which she accepted as ghost and spirits, frolicking about on the ceiling. She got to know the movements of the bastards next door: learned their habits, could hear the toilet flushing and hear the slam of the cover, and know whether it was a man or a woman doing his business; and she could almost see, so sharp was her concentration, the man and the woman as they came down the stairs, as they shouted to each other, as they prepared their daily routine of reprimand and abuse. And of course, she heard no dog barking.

And she knew what hour the postman came; something as small as this, as ordinary, which she had never know for the five years since she was working in the hospital. The postman came between eleven-thirty and twelve-thirty. Not more punctual than that, since his time was measured not in footsteps but in the number of bills he delivered. And she got to know how many people knocked on her basement door, and some on the window, and then stood for the time of decency, and then in disgust pushed paper and brochures, and other material which she had no use for, through the letter box. And she knew for the first time, that any of these unseen people could have broken into her home while she was working on the ward.

And in the three days, moving from the bed only to visit the bathroom to pee and to "number two," she read her Bible. Parts in it which she thought she had grasped through her intelligence, through her love of literature, and because of her critical mind: the parting of the sea; the flight of the Israelites which she compared to her own plight in this city, on the hospital ward and in this basement and beginning back in Barbados; how many people spoke as if they were Israelites, and most of them had never seen a Jew; the covetousness of King David and the beauty and sexuality of Bathsheba; and her own favourite passage in the whole Bible, the story of Jonah in the belly of the whale.

She was close to this miracle, this example of the power of God. For she had been born on an island, and whales and sharks and barracudas thronged the waters, and came close enough to shore for her to see them, and witness, that Good Friday morning at two o'clock, a shark bites a fisherman's foot, clean, clean, off; and the salt in it could not soften the pain, nor clot the blood. The fins and the gaping mouths, and the big humps on their backs, and the fountain of water rising majestically to the heavens, from the back . . . was it the back, or the mouth, or the side? . . . of the whale. And she realized that it was not a whale at all, for there were no whales off Barbados; and she was confusing her memory of her school books in Standard Seven with something else. It was sharks. She had seen sharks. Their fins, and their cavernous mouths. In the sea. And on the land, dead. And when they got on the land, it was for dinner: fried shark steaks with lots of black pepper in the channels cut into the pink flesh, with fresh thyme and fresh parsley and fresh eschalots and fresh red pepper rubbed into the flesh; with a deep covering of floor and dropped into the buck pot, and fried until they became golden and tender and with juice oozing from them. She knew sharks. But it was the whale and Jonah . . .

She read the passage two times each morning before the time when she would just lie and do absolutely nothing, not even think, although she could not prevent her mind turning, just lying there, and allowing the life to remain in her body and leave it, as she wanted it to do, if it was God's wish and judgement; for she had no more interest in life. And after this time, perhaps in the hiatus of meditation, perhaps in a kind of half death, or half sleep, she would read the passage two times more, and wait for night to come, meaning the darkness from outside, to come into the bedroom which remained in its on darkness, because in the three days and three night she did not turn the lights on.

She experienced and worshipped the independence she had, for if she was not free, if there was someone in the basement with her, if she still had *him* bothering out her life, or if her child had lived, she could not subject herself so completely to this thinking. In the midst of the darkness there was light, and the light is that she could be here, on the bed, waiting for the sign, the sign to end this heavy burden, this indolent motionless, this seemingly interminable waiting.

The telephone would ring at the same hour each morning. Lee? At the time that someone who expected her to be at a certain place, and did not see her arrive, and had given her the period of speculation, and then had called. Ruby? The same time every morning, and every night. And then, after the first day, the telephone would ring every half hour. It seemed to her, lying on her back and listening to it, sometimes urging it to ring to let her know there was someone out in the city, alive; at other times, willing it to stop ringing, as it seemed that the person calling was transferring her anxiety into the high, piercing and disturbing ring of the instrument. It seemed sometimes as if the telephone's ringing was its eyes, and that it could see her there. It was so persistent sometimes. Yes, those half-hour trials were obviously Millicent trying to reach her, trying to understand what was happening to her, wondering if she had killed herself.

"Kill myself?"

People never cared for you: friends, husband, wife, children, relations, and, of course, your hospital and your head nurse, when you were a part of the order of things, and were where you were supposed to be at the specified hour. But when you did not turn up, and were not heard from, the first thing they wondered was, "I wonder if she killed herself?" Even before they wondered if she was sick. Or broke. Or had money for bus fare.

"Me?"

On the first day, which began three hours or so after she had flung the dog's body out to hit the hard frozen cement steps, counting from that time, it was painful, it was terrifying, it was full of darkness. The weight was sitting full upon her. The heaviness of the act, growing with time, with the silence of the dog; and the blame and the guilt; and the feeling that caused her body to go numb, that the entire world saw her in that act, that nothing else about her counted, that if there was a question, "Who is this woman?" the answer would be, "She is the one who committed murder." It was so encompassing. So amplified. So total.

And it was easy in a way, for the weight rendered her incapable of undressing, or preparing for bed, for reading her Bible, for making dinner. And for calling anybody on her Solo. They would all have to respect her privacy. She was so dead in spirit the first day that the lights were left on; and the *Journal* became a white, speckled, shimmering screen; and the radio played on the same Buffalo station throughout the night and into the next day, all day. And the first few calls at the appointed time when normally she and Millicent would be setting the world right with gossip and laughter and woman-talk, were long.

It was very hard, and sad.

On the second day, things became worse. She could feel her body get heavy, and hot, as if she was carrying a temperature; but she knew it was the burden of her deed. The deed was raw now. Exposed. At its height of infection. And painful. There was no cure, save waiting for the scab that brought on the healing to form, and spread. And the body outside the basement door to begin to swell.

It was on the second day that she read Jonah, the first chapter. She read it so often she knew it by heart, all the commas and semicolons. It was on this day that she began to notice the regulation of the postman's visit, the dropping of advertising materials through her letter box, the routine of the noise and footsteps and the growling between man and woman coming through the tin wall that divided her from next door. Above her head, she could make out no definition in *their* lives: it was one heavy thud as if they walked in winter boots. And she knew, would bet her bottom dollar on it, that all the calls that came, persistent and long, were from Millicent.

The light-blue uniform became creased, and stuck between her thighs. Four of the buttons down its front were off, ripped off as she turned in her sleep, and as she changed positions, in the fits of depression during the day. Her brassiere remained fastened at the back, and her breasts were sometimes in the cup, and sometimes both of them were squeezed out. Mostly it was one that had slipped out. And her hair, which she normally wore combed out and reaching her ears, with two braid on each side of her face, and worked into a hairstyle like a diadem of ebony, sparkled by beads of red, black and green, was now uncombed, flat at the back where the weight of her head had matted it, and at the sides, when she slept on her right or on her left. But at the top, it stood as if it was hair of wire. She did not worry about her appearance because she did not look at herself in the looking glass above the toilet bowl, nor into the one over her bureau, in these first two days of her retreat.

She could feel herself getting weaker; getting smaller and thinner, and at the same time, getting stronger because her heart had less to work with. Always, from the morning of the second day, there was a taste of mild bitterness in her mouth. A dryness. As if sandpaper was being passed over the bridge of her mouth. And in all this, she remained calm, punishing herself, expiating her body and hoping that her mind would be cleansed also, and that she would not go mad alone in this basement, and was not able to prove she was not mad.

On the third day, she panicked. Suppose, she thought. Just suppose. Suppose her body could no longer take this punishment, and she stopped breathing; suppose her mind could no longer withstand the torment, and her mind snapped, and she became mad, insane, gone off the head. If any of these things happened, there was no one in the whole world, meaning no one in this city, who could find her. Who would come and rescue her? And put her into the ambulance? And if she died, no one to notify anybody. There was no mother now, in Barbados. Her father had died a long time ago. And there were no cousins, third or fourth even, and removed. Her only known relation was a second cousin living somewhere in Brooklyn or New York. "Why have I lived like this? Cut off, cut off, cut off!"

More than once, as these fears broke in upon her concentration on the Bible, she thought of eating her pride, if she had strength to do so, breaking her fast of penitence and absolution, and calling Millicent, or Lee, or Ruby, and telling them where she was, where she lived.

Strange, how in more than three years, in this close, sincere friendship with Millicent; in two with Lee, and one with Ruby, she had not given any of them her address. Is there somewhere she could be found, traced and tracked down through her telephone number? And Millicent, with whom she spent so much time on the Solo every night, and with whom she could express the most personal and intimate fears, aspirations and things, and never once, not once did Millicent express the desire to visit her and see where she lived. And of course, neither did she. If something should happen to her, Millicent wouldn't know how to find her.

Twice, on the second day, she had lifted the receiver and dialed Millicent at work, and had dropped the receiver when she heard Millicent's voice.

On the evening of the third day, which was the ending of the third night, she felt the full force of her withdrawal. Three days and three nights. She did not miss the biblical significance in the number. Three days were given to reply to some legal matters; men took three days to make certain decisions; and *three*, she always said, was a "damn female number." So, on the third day . . . What did God, in the creating of the world, finish doing on the third day? The Bible doesn't say nothing about a third day! . . . on the evening of the third day, she had read Jonah, chapters two and three. She felt something was happening to her. She was no longer borne down by the act. And the act did not, like her mouth, taste so bitter. Not that she had driven it from her mind, nor forgiven herself. It was no longer the totality of her thinking and her living, though she would be the last person to define her time spent beneath the three thick blankets, as living. It was not that. She could feel the lifting from her soul of the heaviness. Yes, her soul. And she was starting to feel the lightness of expiation. But she was not strong enough physically to take off her dress; did not want to; was not strong enough to use her toothbrush; was not strong enough to go to the bathroom and take her bath; not that she did not smell herself, and turned up her own nostrils as she smelled the accumulation of smells, the funkiness, as her second cousin in Brooklyn or New York would say. That kind of energy did not come to her. But she began to sin.

The day thou gavest, Lord
Is ending
The darkness falls
At thy behest . . .

My God! I am singing a burial hymn! Don't let my time come, not yet. I don't want to die in this city. So, she went back to reading Jonah. The Bible, like her light-blue hospital uniform, was rumpled, its leaves turned into dog-ears, its black leather cover coming apart from the body of the leaves, trimmed in gold; she had slept on it for her pillow; and the gold itself became tarnished and fading, as she rolled over it in her sleep, trampling it; using it sometimes as her pillow and her backrest; and in her hysteria the second day and night, kicking it with her feet, while she struggled and broke down the palisades of a nightmare.

The whole of the first day and night she studied Jonah, all seventeen verses of the first chapter. She pictured herself as Jonah; and imagined herself in the ship and in the cabin and in the bowels of trouble.

The whole of the second day she had studied Chapter two, all ten verses, until she knew them by heart, including the previous seventeen. She was certain now that she, like Jonah, was a castout, a castaway, an outcast.

And the third chapter, with its ten verses which seemed to have been written with her in mind, gave her the most trouble to read and digest, for its message of supplication was one that was too close to her act.

She disregarded the fourth chapter. She had found what she wanted in the first three, especially in Chapter two, the first three verses. There was something about these verses that touched her, something that made her own act bigger in importance, as if it was being immortalized, as if it was accorded the notoriety of being in a book of records. And it was, perhaps more so, that she was human in her faith in the Bible; was human in her Christian belief, for here was a sinner, a man who had done the wrong thing according to God, and who was punished, and had repented openly, to his God. She felt as if she had come to the end of her three-day wearing of sackcloth and ashes.

It was surprising when it happened. That she had seen the light; and had satisfied herself through her spirit, that she had spent the proper amount of time, and in the proper attitude, going over and over, in and out, every iota as she said, of the act. And it happened because she knew it could only happen with the help of the Bible. It was surprising how the words came to her. And she knew all along that the word would come from no other source.

"*And Jonah said,*" she said to the Bible, her eyes now tired and weary, hardly able to focus on the fine print, "*Jonah said, I cried by reason of mine affliction unto the Lord, and he heard me; out of the belly of hell cried I, and thou heardest my voice . . ."*

She was in a fish's belly. The basement where she had been lying, flat on her back, was like the bowels of the sea, she could feel the encirclement there, the hollowness there, the darkness there; and the rumbling of the furnace, like the organs in a stomach digesting and resisting matter. And she felt during that time that she was lost in darkness. Not one item, not one article to which she was so accustomed, before it happened, nothing, not even her teddy bear, her lotions, her hallowed Christmas card with the snow and the message about Mr. Johnson on it, none of these things could hold her attention, to remind her that she was not lost, that she was not in the belly of hell. And she put the Bible aside and got up and went into the bathroom and turned the water on in the tub, and touched it for the correct heat, and poured the remaining liquid from the Limacol into it, and went back to her collection of bottles with pills and took up her bottle of Hennessy; for she was bright enough, was educated enough to understand the metaphor of belly, of hell, and of belly of fish; but she was determined in her torment, which at times it seemed she enjoyed if she was asked about it by Millicent, or if Mr. Johnson was alive and had asked her, that she enjoyed suffering; but still she knew that the belly was her lot. She poured a large glass that had flowers painted on to it body full of the Hennessy, and she unscrewed the cap of the bottle of pills, and held her head back just a little, and tossed in one pill, and took one mouthful, large enough to wash the pill down. She did this four times. Each toss of the head was the swallowing of two pills. She was not sure, as she did not read the label, if they were aspirins or something more potent. But there was no taste. There was no fear. There was no dread. There was, judging from her attitude, no premeditation, either. She had come from under the three thick blankets which had swallowed her in a different kind of hell and belly, renouncing all her objects in the bedroom, did not see them now, and had remained under the darkness of the blankets, covered from head to foot, with the Bible sometimes between her thighs, sometimes under her foot, and at other times under her body, as if it was a hot water bottle, as she remained buried this way; and now, she could feel the passing of time and of life, and the meaning of the Hennessy with the pills; and she got into the warm water as if she were taking a soak in the sea early in the morning when it is fresh and peaceful and has no wave or movement, dressed in her clothes which became heavy and helped the weight of the brandy to lower her down; and was convinced at the first going down that she was in the belly of a wave in the sea.

A SHORT DRIVE

This Saturday afternoon at three, with the first real light, and the first cleansed skies washed so blue after the rains, there was a constant breeze and upon the breeze came the coolness and the strong smell of patchouli and summer flowers. It was tantalizing as the smell of saltness and of fresh fish brought out of the sea on a beach in Barbados. Gwen was a woman with a touch of this saltiness on her breath. And the woman back in Toronto, on Lascelles Boulevard, she too carried a trace of that smell; but her real smell was of Lavender.

Calvin sat nobly and like an emperor, stiff, with the pride of new ownership, behind the steering wheel reduced to the size of a toy wheel against his imposing size, of the Volkswagen which he had just bought, "hot," he said, for seventy-five dollars. He called it his "Nazi bug." And he too looked clean as the skies. His skin, on his arms up to his elbows; his neck, right into the V of the black dashiki; his legs from below the knee and down to his toes, all this flesh was "oiled, Jack," he said. He had shampooed his round-shaped Afro, and it was glistening although he had used Duke Greaseless Hairdressing for Men. He had given me some, but my hair did not accept the same shine as his. He looked clean. And he looked like a choice piece of pork seasoned and ready for the greased pan and the oven. He would not like this comparison. But I have to say he looked clean.

His legs were thin and had no calves. This was the first time I had seen Calvin dressed in anything but grey-green plaid trousers and blue blazer. Today, he was in cut-down jeans, which gave me the first glimpse of his legs. I could not believe his long stories, over beer in frosted mugs and Polish sausages, about playing running back for the college football team. The black dashiki, with its V-neck and sleeves trimmed in black, red and green, tempered somewhat the informality of his casual dress.

"Pass the paper bag. Glove compartment. Take a sip, brother," he said, holding the steering wheel with his left hand, and a Salem in the other. "And keep your motherfucking head *down* in case the *man . . .*"

The puttering VW rollicked over the gravel road at a slow pace. Its dashboard was cluttered with additional things which Calvin had installed. Cassette tape deck and 8-track tape deck; FM-AM radio and a short-wave radio, a contraption which looked like a walkie-talkie, and two clocks. One, he said, gave the time in the north-east, and the other, the time of the South, of the city of Birmingham, Alabama, where we were, and had been together since the beginning of the summer semester. Looking at this dashboard, I was reminded of the glimpse of the cockpit of the plane in which I had travelled two months earlier from Toronto to teach the summer course, in which Calvin was an auditor. I had never heard that term before. But Calvin was my student. And as the lonely heavy southern nights spun themselves out into greater monotony, he became my guide to where the action was, and almost my friend. The noisy VW moved slowly over the rutted road, and I could see in the distance the sights and substance and large properties, the grace and the southern architecture in the residential exclusive district we were passing on our right hand. We were driving so slow that I thought it was a mistake, that Calvin lived in this district, and that we would turn into one of the magnificent gates any minute now. One of these mansions I had passed, in the dark last night, searching in vain for Gwen's apartment. I now could see the structure I had mistaken for the house. It is a white-painted gazebo with Grecian pillars. And in the gazebo is a child's swing and a white-painted iron chair and iron table. There is no child in the swing.

"Ripple," Calvin said, after a large gulp, and wiping away the evidence with the hand that held the Salem, just in case. "This is the real shit." Last night, at the bar with the frosted beer mugs and huge Polish sausages, Calvin ordered two gigantic T-bone steaks and two bottles of Mommesin red wine, both of which I paid for. This Ripple wine, which cut into my throat like a razor blade dipped in molasses, must have been a ritualistic thing to go with his cut-down jeans and the dashiki. Or it might have been cultural. I took a second swig at the bottle hardly concealed in the brown paper bag, and squeezed my eyes shut, and shook my head. "This is the real shit," he said, disagreeing with my reaction.

On our left hand, I was passing men, slow, as if a shutter speed were set to afford a sense of the whiz of movement, men bent almost in the shape of hairpins, doubled-up, close to the grass which was so green it looked blue. And from the short distance I was, these men resembled gigantic mushrooms painted onto the sprawling lawns, and wearing broad-brimmed hats necessary to protect them against the brutal heat of the sun, and the exhaustion that the humidity seemed to sap from their bodies. I could see them move their hands as if they were playing with the grass, but at the completion of each piston-like action, the effort in their movements appearing slowed-down by the encompassing grandeur of the afternoon, when this act of slashing the blades of grass was complete, a shower of grass lifted itself on impact, a blade of steel flashed like lightning and the grass was scattered harmlessly over the lawn.

"Mexicans," Calvin said as if he didn't like Mexicans, and with some bitterness; and as if he was pronouncing a sentence not only on them, but also upon their labour.

They were soaked to their backs; and their shapeless clothes made them look Indian to me. But the formlessness of their shirts and pants was, to me, the designer's label and trademark of hard labour. They could have been Chinese standing up to their ankles in water and growing rice.

"Amerrikah! Home of the motherfucking *free*, Jack!" Calvin said. "This South's shaped my personality, and this university's fucked it up, with the result that I don't know *who* I am. I was happier in Atlanta on 'Fayette Street in the black area." I did not know what he was talking about. I was admiring the Mexicans. They looked now like figures in a tableau, painted against the blue-grass lawns. And the manner in which they had thrown out the commercial proficiency of the power mower and the precision of mechanization by the bare power of their hands made me deaf to Calvin's protestations. And it seemed that they were showing the superiority of their knowledge about nature and things and their own past in this temporary but scorching menialness of labour; and expressing their own protest, as Calvin was with words, with the violence of their muscular arms.

Calvin was now slouched behind the steering wheel, as if the Ripple had suddenly changed the composition of the blood in his veins. His right arm was extended so that his fingers just touched the steering wheel, as if he wanted no closer association with it. As if he was despising the wheel, the VW, along with the statement he had just made about rejection. "What the fuck am I getting a college education for? And writing academic papers on Reductionism for?" I still did not understand what he was talking about. But he brought the VW to an uncertain stop. We were under a tree. Calvin had told me the name of this tree. They were all over the South; and they cluttered the path through a woods to the building on the campus where convocations were held. The first time Calvin told me the name of this tree, he told me about a woman named Billie

Holiday. I did not know who he was talking about. But he started to sing the words of a song, "Strange Fruit"; and we were inhaling the sweet smell of the magnolia trees and the wind was unforgiving in bringing the strong Southern smell to our nostrils. I would have trouble remembering the name of the woman who sang this song; and more often the title of the song slipped my memory. But I remembered one line, only one line of the song about Southern trees. *Blood on the leaves, and blood at the root.* Calvin had sung the entire song from memory. His voice was off-key. But that afternoon I looked up into the thick branches of the trees under which we were walking to the place which served beer in frosted glasses and huge Polish sausages, and only the raindrops accumulated on the leaves after the downpour dropped into my face. And now, this afternoon, the VW stopped uncertainly, because he had never accumulated the thirty dollars to fix the brakes, we were stopped under a tree.

"What kind of tree is that? I don't think we have these trees in Toronto."

"The size, or the name?" Calvin asked.

The mouth of the Ripple bottle was in his mouth. A little of the wine escaped his lips, and it ran slowly down into his beard, but I could still see the rich colour of red, like blood.

"The same."

"Poplar. This be a poplar tree."

We were shaded by the tree. And I was beginning to feel great relief from the humidity which embraced me like a tight-fitting shirt.

"Southern trees bear strange fruit."

Calvin's voice had not improved in the month I had first heard it. I smiled at his rendition.

"Black bodies hanging in the Southern breeze."

We remained in the shade, and I could feel the breeze making my body cool, as if I was being dipped slowly into sea water. I was comfortable. But Calvin was not: sadness appeared in hi eyes. His lips formed themselves into a sneer. He moved his body, and the bottle of Ripple became heavy and caused the seat and the leather to cry out. The leather in the seats of the VW was the most valuable feature of the old rumbling automobile. He moved his body in the small space we shared, and I could smell his perspiration, and his breath laden with the menthol from the Salems, and the sickening sweetness of the Ripple.

"Dualism, my brother," he said. He leaned over, took the bottle from me and drained it dry. "What the fuck? I've seen the ass-whuppings in Selma, 'Bama, and Little Rock."

The breeze stopped. The languor of the afternoon was heavy, and we were once more lumbering over the road which turned to hard, dried, uncared-for dirt. It was sad. The sadness was like the sudden fall of dust under the low-hanging trees, when the scent of magnolia rises like shimmering ZZZs you see, if you kneel down, rising from a hot tarred road.

"What do you want to be then¿ What do you want to make of your life, if not a scholar?"

"Miles!"

"Away from Birmingham?"

"Miles Davis!"

I did not know what to say to this; and so Calvin continued to let his feelings and fantasies come out of his thin body, and the coming out made him large, and grand and strong as the running back he always boasted he was when he played for his college football team.

"As Barry White says, bro, *let the music play.* Let the music play on. Let the motherfucking music *play,* Jack! I be Miles. I am Miles. Or I am Coltrane. Trane. I am Otis. I'm Nina Simone. And I am 'Retha! And I am on a stage at the biggest theatre in the South, but not the Opry, and *thousands* are out there in the dark, screaming my name. My toon. My voice. My riffs. My trumpet. My tenor-horn. It's the same fucking thing, Jack. Let the music *play*."

The smell of Calvin's Salems, the old odour that had settled inside the VW, filled my nostrils; and with these smells was the smell of cloths that are wet, and drying in the back seat. I could also smell the oiliness of southern-fried chicken from Chicken Box Number Two. We had eaten chicken many times in the VW, as if we were still suffering from that segregation of accommodation, although it was our manner of checking out the beautiful women coming out of the women's residence in their pink shorts, and white shorts and blue shorts.

We were by ourselves on this road of dried mud, in a field that was growing something I could not recognize. Corn came to my mind, as this place was in the same part of geography as that island where I came from; so corn came naturally to my mind; but there was not the lusciousness in the endless spread of green that made me feel we were adrift on the sea. We were alone, although far to the right I could see the smudged whiteness of the pillars and other parts of the architecture from colonial times. And on our right, not with that distance, some small houses, and from them sentinels of rising white smoke that turned blue as it reached high above our heads. And still the sun was shining.

And then in the distance, like the call of my mother's voice, miles away, but only a few yards from the make-shift cricket pitch we had gouged out of our own mud to play the game, my mother's voice calling me home for dinner: rice cooked with few split peas because there was a War on, and served with salt fish from the Grand Banks of Newfoundland, thin and flat and full of bones but transformed by the improvised wisdom in these things by my mother, and soaked in lard oil, tangy from the cheap Australian butter, it was said, we imported from Australia, to us in a commonwealth of nations, friends; and tomatoes picked from our backyard; that welcoming call that wrenched me from my friends and playmates, disappointed that I had not hit the ball for six, or four, or even a single in the hot, hot-competing afternoon. So, did this sound come to me, unanchored in this vastness of living thriving green, in the rickety VW with a stranger, drinking Ripple concealed in a brown paper bag, from the eyes of the sheriff.

In the blue-white distance I heard the heavy rumbling of a train. A freight train. I followed the train as it wriggled its way like a worm through the greenness on the land, as it moved like a large worm, and in my mind, through the history its approach was unravelling and through the myths of trains: men on the run travelled on them; men fleeing women and wives and child payment hid on them; and men in chains and those who escaped from chain-gangs were placed on them. And the best blues were written about them. The rumbling of this train, like the rumbling of that train in the cowboy movies of the Old West, seemed interminable as a toothache that comes at sunset and that lasts throughout the groaning night, like a string pulled by a magician from the palm of one hand, like the worm you pull from the soft late grass-covered ground that does not end, and that makes you late to go fishing. I heard a siren. Or a whistle? There were so many sirens I was hearing this summer in Birmingham because of civil rights and fights with sheriffs, that I mistook the name of the sound. I heard a siren. The siren ended the train.

"Police cruiser?" I asked Calvin. "Or ambulance?"

"In this neighbourhood, could be either. Both. Chitlins and hogmaws. One goes with the other."

"Cops coming through the grass?" I still did not know what was planted in the growing vastness surrounding me.

Calvin lit another Salem. The VW was immediately filled with smoke. This lasted for one moment. Then it was filled with a tingling, sweet and bitter smell. It was not the Salem that Calvin had lit. It was not a Salem. But he filled his lungs with the smoke and then shot two unbroken, thin and fierce jets of white from his nostrils, making him look in that moment like a walrus. Speaking through smoke and coughing at the same time as if his thinness meant tuberculosis, and with his breath held, he said, "What can we in the South do with this dualism-thing? Before it fucks us up?"

"Education could never be so destructive."

"Spoken like a true West Indian who knows nothing about the South, and Amerrikah."

"Education is freedom."

"Spoken like a man who's never lived in Birmingham, or in any city in the South."

"You need education."

"We need a black thang. We don't need no education, brother. A black thang. And a black conclusion."

"And what about your seminar on Reductionism?"

"Shit! Can you see me discussing that at my mother's Sunday dinner table? She be calling the cops, thinking this nigger's crazy!"

The VW became quiet, and filled with the strange smoke. The words Calvin was using were larger than the capacity of the small "bug," too bulging with the possibility of explosion and violence. I went back to the Mexicans on the lawns. I began to have the sensation of being rocked from side to side. But it could have been the vibration of the freight train, which had not yet come to its end from within the tunnel created by the endless fields of growing things. Looking outside through the steam of smoke from Calvin's fag, I saw cement and concrete, and paper blowing along the narrow sidewalks and into the street. The light here was harsh. There were no flowers. There were no poplar trees. The trees were stubby but they did not shade the blinding, shimmering waves that came off the surface of the sidewalk. I wished, at that moment, that I was back in Toronto among the red brick, the dirty red brick and cobblestones, passing shops that sold the *New York Times* and the *Times Literary Supplement*, and that sold Condor and Erinmore pipe tobacco and French cigarettes and French leathers or "letters" – I never knew which was the proper term – things I was accustomed to and knew how to handle, among the buildings that were not so imposing, and the short streets. Space there was more manageable. I wished for the softness of streets shaded by small trees, and lined with cars, many of which belonged to students and were broken into; with garbage pails of green and other wrecks; and I wanted the softness of the northern seductive and betraying nights; and to be amongst the unthreateningness of broken-down homes with cloth at their windows and with unpainted boards nailed across the windows and the doors, derelicts from the nights of rioting in the cities in the North – Detroit, New York, Washington, D.C., and Toronto.

Calvin must have been buried in similar thoughts of wanting to be elsewhere, must have come to a conclusion of similar importance, or to some agreeable compromise with his thoughts about education, for he straightened his back, and the vigor and youth of his years came back into his body. His eyes were bright again, and the whiteness in them shone. The dashiki he was wearing made him look noble and like an emperor; stiff and with the pride of knowing where he was.

"This is the very last time I be laying this paranoid shit on you, brother. You are my guest here in this city. I am a Southerner, and we Southerners're hospitable people. I'm gonna show y'all some real southern shit now, y'all!"

He had lit a Salem before he had spoken. He was the kind of man who could not make a serious statement before he had first lit a Salem. Smoke streamed through his nostrils, and he looked like a walrus again.

"I'm Amerrikan. This is my motherfucking country."

"You were born here, man."

"I'm a Southerner. So, let's have some Ripple. Let's drink this shit."

It was a long road. There were no streetlights. Dust swirled round the tires of the VW as it pierced its single weak headlamp through the oncoming darkness. "If the man don't get me for this Ripple, he's sure's shit gonna get me for this light!" The moon was a dark sliver of lead, far off to the right. Calvin was still in his cut-down jeans and dashiki. But I had changed. I was in white. White Levis and a white dashiki, bought from the Soul Brother Store. When I went into the store, dark and musty and smelling of old cigars, the owner greeted me, "Brother, come in, brother!" He charged me twenty dollars more than the price I had seen on the same clothes in two other white stores on the same integrated street. But I did not divulge this to Calvin.

"Lay it on me, brother!" Calvin had said in admiration and in approval when he picked me up.

"Be cool, man," he had told him, trying hard to be cool.

"Gwen opened your nose!"

"Shee-it!" I said, hoping it came out right, and heavy, and properly Southern.

"Shit!" Calvin said. His speech was like a crisp bullet in my chest.

Now, driving along this road, in the middle, there was no dividing line, and if there was we could not see it; in the swirling flour of this thin road, cramped in the VW, with the smell of smoke, a trace of leather, and the acrid languor from the fumes of Ripple, making less speed than the rattle of the muffler suggested, and hitting stones in the middle of the road, the two of us, rebellious and drinking in our joy, like escaped prisoners; but I, like a man redeemed, Gwen had said when I was at the door like a gentleman, "Shee-it, you ain't leaving here to walk those dark street at this hour, man. This is the South," saying it with a pronounced West Indian accent; we were screaming and hollering as if we were both born in the ecstasy of mad Southern Saturday nights, in Birmingham.

Calvin slapped an 8-track tape into the player. "My Favorite Things" came out. The hymn coiled around the jazz solo, reminded me of matins at St. Matthias Anglican Church in Barbados; and especially evensong and service. I could picture myself walking in that peaceful sacred light, one hour after the sun had gone down behind the tall casaurinas, when there was a slice of a moon, like this one in Birmingham, and walking between thick green sugar canes in my black John Whites that kicked up almost as much dust as the tires of this old VW. And each time Coltrane repeated the main statement of the tune, I could hear and recall the monotony of the tolling bells. There, my mother walked beside me, in contented sloth of age, of sickness and of Christianity. Here, I bent my neck to the charmed pull of the music.

Calvin is silent beside me. This music is his. I have heard this music before, probably, all the places and things and colours that the music is showing me I have faced in Toronto. The tape is scratched badly.

In the distance, pointed out to us by the weak left headlamp, is a barn, or a factory; perhaps something that was once used as a portable camp for soldiers. Soldiers are always on mind in Birmingham this summer. The Civil War, which a magazine swears in its cover story, is about to be fought again: white people versus black people. Soldiers with muskets, vertical straps of leather aslant their soldiers, fighting for the other cause. And the flag of their confederation, with its own two vertical blue slashes across its broad, bloodied shoulder, signifying something different. This building in the shortening distance sits in a square stubbornness in the middle of the single headlamp, with no grace of architecture like the white-painted gazebo. From this distance it is black. It soon looks brown. Light from inside the building is being forced through small windows that are covered by blinds made of sacks of sugar, not for Bohemian style but from economy. And as we get nearer still, the truth of its dimension, size and colour, are exposed to us.

The saxophone reminds me of the singing of old women, repeating the verse of the hymn as if their age has crippled their recollection of succeeding verses. So, I begin to think again of my mother, leading the song at the Mother's Union service, going over it again. "Rock of Ages." This saxophone is not speaking of such desperation, though.

We are approaching Gwen's wooden house.

Calvin stops the VW, for no reason. And I realize he's always doing this, but this time he parks it, and it rocks forward and backward just before the engine dies. We are now bathed in the light from the naked fluorescent bulb on Gwen's porch. I did not see this light the night of the party. The rain was too heavy that night.

"You're really into Trane playing 'Love Supreme!'" he said.

"Not 'My Favorite Things?'"

"'Love Supreme,' brother."

How many other things in this city of Birmingham, this South in this culture, in this short time here, had I got wrong? I had heard a train, but was there a train rolling through the green fields like a lawn mower? I had seen a moon, but now that we were stopped, there was no moon.

"A love supreme, a love supreme, a love supreme," Calvin said. "Nineteen times Trane chants it." I can see movement in Gwen's house, at the side; for the bedrooms are at the side.

Calvin got out, leaving me in the car, slammed the door shut and stood beside the car. A splattering of water hits the gravel. I imagine steam rising. I can smell the sting of the water. And then I too get out and shake my legs, each one to straighten the seams of my tight-fitting jeans. Calvin is still peeing and shaking. Some men can pee as long as horses. But it looks more as if he is being shaken by the peeing, in short spasms of delight and relief. Each time I think that Calvin is finished, he shakes again. I was wrong about the name of the tune on the 8-track. I am wrong about my mother. It was not "Rock of Ages." It was not even the walk through the country lane going to St. Matthias Anglican Church for evensong and service that had pulled those memories from me. It was I myself. As a chorister in the St. Michael's Cathedral, singing a song of praise. Was it Easter I was thinking about? Easter? Or Christmas? Rogations Day? Quinquagesima Sunday? Could it have been Lent? *O, all ye beasts of the sea praise ye, the Lord. O, all you fish of the sea, praise ye, the Lord?* Could it have been that? Yes. That was the comparison of the repetition which the beauty of the saxophone ought to have brought back.

"Every time I hear Trane playing 'Love Supreme' I gotta have me at least *one* smoke, and—" He seemed short of breath all of a sudden. His words were cut short. Nevertheless, there was a lingering, a drawing-out of the enunciation of his words. His words would be cut off. In mid-sentence. As if he were struggling. For breath. And trying. To talk at the same time. The middle door on the porch opened and light flowed weakly out, and I could see Calvin's eyes, now red and fierce, and at the same time peaceful, and filled with water. But he was not in tears. He was happy.

"Want a joint? Can you handle this shit, brother?"

"I'm cool, man."

"Shit'll kill you. It's a motherfucker. It kills the black arts, and the black musician."

"I'm cool, man."

"Know something? Let's not waste time with these chicks. Forget Gwen." I was wondering what kind of a man Calvin was. "Let's talk, brother. You're going back up to Toronto next week, and when you're gone, ain't nobody I can talk to, nobody on this campus, in this city, in this fucking country. Let's talk. And I gonna cut out all these 'motherfuckers' and 'shits' in my speech, and just talk." I was sure he was reading my mind. But I 'Love Supreme' brings back memories of something my grandmother used to hum, just after she lit the kerosene lamps every evening. Some white folks calls this shit a canticle. Took me years to stop confusing canticle with cuticle. Heh-Hey! But, anyhow. This canticle thing has a Latin name. Man! I kicked more ass, I was superior to everybody in my class in Latin in high school. Hate the thing now, though. But I know it all by heart. Had to learn it by heart. Been learning it by heart from hearing my grandmother, singing it for years. Listen, *O, all ye works of the lord, bless ye the Lord; praise him, and magnify him forever.* Want to hear more?"

"Didn't know you were Anglican."

"Baptist! To the bone. But I read that shit in a book that had words like *works, nights, days, whales, water,* etcetera, etcetera, and all were spelled with a capital letter. Isn't that something? The English be strange motherfuckers. Strange people. In the South, right here in this city of Birmingham, we worship the English, culturally I mean. The English use colons like Coltrane uses the E-flat! Baptist to the bone! Baptist to the bone. And anti-English, except culturally." He threw the marijuana cigarette, now smaller than his fingernail, through the window. The VW's engine started as if the whole car was about to explode. It stuttered, and finally it turned over. "Life is better without chicks around. Sometimes. We're going to the Stallions Club where there's the best rib sandwiches and fried chicken in the whole city of Birmingham! If not in the whole South!"

Pandemonium, sweet as pecan pie and ice cream, struck me full in the face the moment the door of the Stallion Club was opened, when Calvin pushed me inside, first. The room was dark. Bodies were moving. The laughter was loud and sweet and black and jocular and exaggerated. Smoke was rising and swirling. And above the lighter darkness of the bodies in the room, the smoke remained there like halos. The music was climbing the walls. Music such as this I had never heard. It was like a baptism, a final submergence into the hidden, secret beauty of the South. Loud and full, enunciating each vowel, each nuance possible of behaviour, each instrument, each riff. I heard a voice pleading, *"Didn't I do it, baby? Didn't I? Didn't I do it, baby?"* and I looked toward the stage, in the deeper darkness there, through the large, slow-moving dancers, expecting to see Aretha Franklin in the flesh. What a victory it would be, to know her, in this thick-fleshed Southern, warm night! I was overcome by the music. I could feel my entire body relax. I could smell the odours around me. I could feel my blood. I could feel the difference, and the meaning of my presence in the South. The fried chicken. The barbecued ribs. The tingling, sweet nausea of burnt hair. The cosmetics and lotions in the glassy, bushy "pompadoo," as Calvin called it, on the fat, healthy jowls of the men and women dancing. I could feel my own body give off a stifled exhaust of smell. I could feel the sweat and the excitement under my armpits. A housefly was in the room. It came and rested on my top lip, and I did not brush it away. I was, for the first time, at home in the noise, the smells, the fragrance, the sounds and the voice of this city of Birmingham. And they all made me nervous, as they made me feel good. *"Didn't I do, it baby? Didn't I . . ."* I was like a man drowning in this foam of a wave that one moment ago had been wafting me in its freshness; I was moving towards the front of the swaying crowd that was coupled in its own sweetness. I looked into their faces. And those faces that were not buried into the necks and shoulders of men and women, wore flat expressions. Masks. No one was smiling. No one was grinning. No one was laughing as he danced. No teeth showed in this relaxed, coagulating, heavy and soft coupling of the music with the voice. It was as if the voice was giving them a message they all knew and desired. I could feel and taste the powerfulness in the large room. It was like a country. A country of men and women, all of the same colour, the same breathing. And this became my baptism: I had never imagined it was possible to be in a room so large with only black people. Never in Toronto. Never even in Barbados. I looked around to see, just in case. And there was none, not one white person. It was a beautiful sensation, and it frightened me. This is why I thought of power-fulness. And now I knew what it meant. I could feel it in my blood. Two large women, heavy in their thighs, heavy in their bosom, heavy in their arms, heavy in their waists, each one about fifty-five years old, were tied together in the slow almost unmoving dance; their breasts pressed against each other, thighs glued together beneath their mini skirts, looking like logs of mahogany polished to a high magnificent sheen, arms lassoed to arms like tentacles, or in a Boston Crab, and with the weight of their waists pressed together, begrudging space and denying any man's hand from forc-ing itself between their impenetrable love, close as if they were Siamese; love for the music and for the voice that pumped this love from one into the other, blood through veins, these two women moved in their heaviness like oil on shining glass, oblivious to the fact that there were hundreds dancing along with them. They moved as if they were on ice. They moved only because I had seen them leave one spot small as a dime, and occupy another dime's area, not that they themselves could ever know that they had moved. They were close to me now, and I stood for a moment and watched them. I watched them grinding out their satisfaction and their ageless joy in this heavy, segregated world, in this black section of this city, safe amongst numbers, and amongst blackness created through the dance. *"Didn't I do it, baby"*? A black world and a black poem which the dance itself had formed and had drawn a circle around. "This is a black world," Calvin said, having to shout.

I was now only three paces from the stage. I stood. I had to stand, for the bodies were not moving now. They were grinding. I was the only one who moved. I was the only one out of the rhythm. Inching to the stage, I was the only one out of place.

"Didn't I do it, baby?"

The face of the singer was bathed in black perspiration. It was like the water of baptism and of revival. And it was growing out of the body, like strength. Not dripping like an exertion. The thin, tight body looked as if it was being tormented. I could see this through the slits of space in the crowd as the dancers moved. I could see it as a slice of a fish; a slice of a human being; slithering in the shimmering sequins on the long dress that was like an extra skin. She was bathed in the white material of the dress, like a dolphin. *"Didn't I do it, baby?"*

"This sister can whup Aretha's ass any . . ." And Calvin's voice was blocked out for a moment by the passing of the two women between us, "any mother . . . any day!" Here in this room, I needed space even to hear. The song came to a perspiring end. It was a soft end. And it was followed by an explosion of applause. Handkerchiefs, fingers and Kleenexes came out to repair the cheeks, and wipe away the beads that had damaged the neckline and the collar, and the forehead for the duration of that love-making rendition. And before the women and men had completed the renovation of their cosmetics, the mermaid of a woman on the stage began another song. *"A midnight train to Georgia..."* Without warning, without even a desire to join in this dance and in this circle, for I was out of place, inarticulate, foreign, without speech and gesticulation, one of the fat ladies took me into her arms. It was like a mother knowing before the expression of pain is made taking her child in the safety of her breast and bosom. I sank deep and comfortable in the billow of her love, as her arms wrapped my smaller body in embrace so much like my mother's, that I felt I could fall off into a sweet slumber and surrender myself to her; except that the song was raging through the magnolia and pine and poplar woods of a land that held such frightening memories. And Calvin was there to witness my surrender, and , perhaps, in a seminar on black behaviour, live to tell the story. But she held me close. She held me tight. She held her left arm round my waist, and her right hand on the softness of my bottom. I began to travel all those miles between the never-ending rails of steel, going from one place I did not know to a place which was even farther removed from my present; but to a place which was identifiable, as I was able to *know* where I am now. And so, I buried myself in her flesh, her perfume acting as a mild chloroform, and I found that Gwen and the woman in Toronto climbed into the sweet delirium along with the woman holding me, and I paid no regard to those two encumbrances, and allowed myself to be moved so very slowly by her; by her body that was guiding me, and by her blood which I thought I could taste. But that would have been, in addition to the unseemly unnatural acts, incest. I was dancing with my mother. The smell of her body, and the strength in her legs which were tightened round my left leg, was like the tightness of a thick towel after a bath deep in winter. I could hardly breathe. But I could just as easily have died in her arms.

The housefly I had seen earlier returned and lighted on the woman's mouth. She pursed her lips, unwilling to release one hand and let got of my body; and the fly fled. It probably had learned, through its ugly leaden antennae, what thunderous violence her anger would give rise to, in the slap the woman would have used.

Her lips were roughed in a deep red. Like the blood inside her body which I felt I could feel and taste. But I was not entirely passive in my enjoyment. My eight fingers were pressed deeply into her soft flesh. With difficulty I tried to move to the music, in my own slow, sweet time. It was like poetry; and I thought of poetry. And green and golden I was huntsman and herdsman . . .

"Are you screwing me, nigger?" she asked. And then laughed. A breath of Jack Daniels came to my nostrils when she spoke. I could feel her weight. I had made a wrong step, and her weight fell upon me. I wondered what it would be like, if by accident, I went to make another wrong step, and she were to fall on top of me. "You want me?" She whispered this into my ear. I smelled her lipstick. "You're screwing me, ain't you?" Her mouth was at my ear. I smelled her perfume, and the cosmetics and the treatment in her processed hair. She tightened her grip on me. She tightened her grip more. My breathing became more difficult. And then she groaned, in a short spasm. "You like me, don't you, small-island man?"

Whatever Georgia was, whatever was the ruggedness of the landscape, whether of rocks or of stones, green fields of sugar cane or of cotton and corn, the concluding journey was before me. The singer was washed in perspiration, pouring out of her body with a sensual righteousness; the sequins in her dress moved as the breathed, from her ankles to her covered arms, like pistons on the very train that was pulling into George, long after midnight. *"Oh, as I was young and easy in the mercy of her means, time held me green and dying though I sang in my chains like the sea."*

"I want you, nigger. I have to have you."

I could feel it. I could feel the soft inside of her thighs. I was hard. The singer was coming home. Two sequined arms dropped at her side, in victory like that which concludes exhaustion of the flesh. And sudden so, the strong feeling thundered down. The rain had arrived.

"You want me, don't ya? I want *you*."

"No, I don't want you," I said.

"Well, fuck it! Nigger, you're *mine*."

"Clovis!" It was Calvin, like a referee forcing himself between two locked boxers. "Clovis! Take your motherfucking hands off the brother! The brother's with me, motherfucker!" And Calvin ripped at Clovis's head, as if he was delivering a jab to the face. And when Calvin's hand returned from the face, in it was the wig which had contained such allure and fragrance of Duke Greaseless Hair Dressing for Women. His head was shaven bald, and was shining, and he was shaking with anger; and he said in a huskier voice, "Shit, Cal! I thought the nigger was mine!"

"Motherfucker!" Calvin pushed him off.

A few men and women danced close to us, looked at me and danced away. I stood looking at Clovis's shining head.

"Motherfucker, this is a Yale professor!"

"I could've *swear*, Cal, honey, the nigger was mine. I am very sorry, sir, I am very sorry," Clovis said, offering me his hands. I remember his hands were very soft. But by this time I was feeling the eruption in my stomach. And Calvin, sensing this, and intent upon freeing me from this assault, this offence, and knowing that I had lusted after the wrong person, was easing me with some force through the thick of the crowd, to the entrance. On my way out, I barely recognized Clovis's voice, as he stood where he was, saying, "I knew the nigger looked strange, as if he didn't belong here, weren't one of us, weren't from the South, so what the fuck was I supposed to think?"

I could not wait until I was on the gravel patch in front of the entrance of the Stallion Club before the vomit spewed down on my white dashiki, onto my white cotton Levis, into my shoes, with the noise and the slime and the bad taste, and Calving talking and talking.

"Shit, brother, couldn't you *tell?*"

"How?"

"Didn't you see the motherfucker didn't have no breasts? Couldn't you see?"

"How? I was mesmerized by the woman singing 'Midnight Train to Georgia.'"

"That motherfucker was a man, too, brother!" The vomit punctuated whatever else he was about to say. It was coming out with pain and with violence, as if I was trying to rip something awful, something vile, some sin, some hurt, clean from my insides.

"I was in love with the woman singing 'Midnight Train.'"

"The woman singing is also a man," Calvin said. Pity and disappointment in me, registered in his explanation. "The woman is a motherfucking man, brother! This be the South. Birmingham. In the South, it be so fucked up you can't tell one motherfucker from the next."

"I thought the man was a woman."

"It's a motherfucking *man*, Jack! A *man!*"

He lit a Salem. "Sure's hell ain't Toronto, Jack!"

NAKED

There was no resistance to the turn of the key when I put it into the lock at the front door that morning at about two o'clock, stomping from one foot to the next, my movement arrested by this encumbrance, my head spinning from a few drinks, on the point of exploding; and anxious to get into the house, along the short hallway which seemed longer now; and into the restroom, not to rest but to relieve myself of the pressure on my bladder after the full night's drinking at Eglon's restaurant with friends I had not seen in twenty-five years; and whom I had toasted in the wet, tear-stained, red welcome, with wine at the welcome party, each one of the five boyhood friends lost to my confidence in the hot sun for all those years in Barbados, four times each; and found out on this night, that after all that time, in the cold of this city that almost wrenched the life from out of our bodies; afterwards, after toasts and replies, and the late dinner at Eglon's when we had to wrench Eglon from a waitress's arms and legs and have him without her, re-light the gas burners; take the joint out of the freezer, and wait until it warmed up and his desire cooled off; again and wait some more; in all this waiting drinking time I had a presentiment gnawing at me, that someone was opening my front door, a fear like the naked feeling I once had when I felt that someone was opening my mail. I should have come home and foregone all their invitations to go back home to Barbados; "'cause it's warmer there, man." I should have restricted those toasts and come home and take out Tuesday's garbage; wash the dishes left to rot in the sink three days now; put the heavy crystal stopper back into the brandy decanter; and number the pages of the paper I had been working on; or write the fourth page of a letter I had begun complaining to a woman in Miami four pages ago, in stating my position clearly, and without diplomacy: she was a married woman; and get some sleep after I had peed. I was freezing. Eglon did not turn the furnace back on.

I made a note in my mind, as I pulled the key out and pulled the door shut behind me, already unzipping my trousers, to take a good look in the morning at the front lock. And I ran the short distance down the narrow hallway, and rushed into the small bathroom on the first floor, leaving the door open. And exhaled. And allowed the relief to pour itself noisily and with splatter crudely into the white porcelain bowl. And I listened to the drop of my water falling from the short resounding precipice, making two different noises in the hollow empty bowl and in the room and the house, rejoicing in my freedom that I could make all this noise in a house though joined to another on my east side, as if I were siamesed to the neighbour who I can hear break wind and breathe as she comes down the story-telling stairs; and independent because there is no cat no dog no pet and no animal. So, I could shake in a spasm that made my entire body shake with this freedom. It made me warm as if I were back in Barbados. I stared at the looking glass above the white wash basin – was there a sale of razors at Shoppers? – and in it, in addition to myself, was the picture on the wall. My back was facing it. I needed a shave. In the morning I shall use the new gold-painted razor the woman from Miami had sent the day before; and try on the silver ring from Mexico I had been give by the Miami woman when she was in Mexico learning to speak Castilliano from the Spanish boys on the beach, where the silver is real and cheap, and sold at prices tourists from American found "cheap." And I would come back into this same small bathroom, with the life-size looking glass, and take a photograph of myself with my Canon camera, which I had bought at a yard sale in a mansion the Miami woman had taken me to, and send it back to her in Miami to let her see that it works. I could pick out the dot on my silk tie made from the sauce of the jerked pork I had eaten three hours before. The button at my neck was undone. The smell of my breath was close to that smell rising from the swirling porcelain bowl. I flushed the toilet. No cat no dog no pet no animal called companion, only the breathing of the woman on the stairs next door. I was far from the nighttime inhabitants on Yonge Street, and from the skinheads and punks and punks in hairstyle, "kids" whose youth terrorizes me as they lean out of cars and greet me with names that should be bleeped or deleted from anyone's lexicon; and from women of the night who stand at Church and Gerrard, and stare and model goods and flesh and kind in glimpses, and whose smiles do not tell me how much it shall cost, because the cops are vigilant and want their share. The water gurgled and swirled and disappeared and replaced itself in a different colour of blue. I looked into the looking glass. I ran my thumb and two fingers over the fine sandpaper of the skin around my mouth. Was there a sale at Shoppers Drug Mart? I flicked the switch and the breathing vent in the ceiling, and the sharp light died. I was now in total alarming darkness.

Outside the small bathroom which smelled of Dial soap that was blue, the house was in darkness. I remembered years ago in another house, in similar palpable darkness when my mother would touch my hand, less terrified than her, and soft and trembling, trying to put the man back into my terror. But I know every corner, every article, every cup and broken saucer, every crystal glass, end of chair and counter, and tops of picture frames with dust, as if I see with a white cane; and can, with that vision, finger any one of them, in even the thicker darkness of that other house;

retrieve the last tea bag from the cupboard above the stove, with my eyes closed. I know where each picture and painting on the walls hangs. In the few seconds that I am standing in the darkness outside the sweet-smelling bathroom, I am seeing the same tune with my surroundings tied to me like twine. I was safe in this darkness. Under the fluorescence in the kitchen that could pinpoint a rice grain against a damask tablecloth, I noticed the trim on the door that led to the back garden. It was leaning inwards. Towards me. At an angle. Torn away from the frame. And leaning inwards, so deliberately I was able to pause and think of Pythagoras and measure the angle of its collapse. And I said the words to myself, perhaps not to myself, but spoke the words, that it was leaning at an angle of forty-five degrees. I noticed this. I began to search for other disarrangements. I would see one large, black wood ant crawling, and would follow the journey it had made up to this point of my discovery, and discover the lurking, destructive soldiers six inches away, concealed under a piece of wood. So, sharpened by the shock, I noticed the inner door and the screen. The screen was punched out. All of a sudden I felt the cold wind of the cold morning. It undressed me and I stood bare in its disrobing power. The inside wooden door was open, too. I turned on the spotlight to the garden. Its weak light played over the backyard. In it the things I knew by heart, for years, the railroad ties, whitened tomato plants, shrivelled roses all white in the light and in the weak time of November, were undisturbed. The snow was clear. I became scared that someone was watching me, someone was closer to me than I knew, red-handed and light-fingered, someone in the same room with me; someone like Eglon caught with his pants down, and uncertain of his next move. I was back alone, along that road with no street lamps, narrow as a path the width of my feet, walking in the middle of its cool wind, afraid to touch the blades of sugar cane which could sever my eyeballs from my head. I was missing most of them because the torchlight in my hand shook through my fright and was weak, because the batteries did not respond to the two large brown pennies I had inserted between them to lengthen their natural short life. The spotlight showed me the untouched snow on the patio; and the same snow in the unblemished garden beds which did not give much last summer because the squirrels were loved and harboured by the woman on my other side who came from the Soo, where humans loved animals and kissed dogs and kissed cats and placed the plate and the saucer with leftover food on the floor for them to gurgle in and lap up, and which I tried to kill, since I could not murder my animal-loving neighbour; and none of whom I managed to maim, or kill, or disfigure. The unmarked whiteness of the walks round the lower square of bricks now buried beneath a coat of thin but concealing fresh snow. All my flowerbeds were blooming in their barren, cold whiteness. *How did he enter?* I turned the spotlight off. It had given me no greater vision than the darkness of a pointing white stick.

Back inside the kitchen, the walls were unmolested. Pictures and paintings of landscapes of trees and grass and food, apples and pears, were untouched. Pots and pans, serving spoons and enamel saucepans, in which I had cooked sauces with red wine left back in glasses after parties and collected in one large decanter, were as I had left them, untouched; dead in the motionless of a photograph taken by my memory. I had a real photograph of them upstairs. But that was for milking the insurance company, in case of burglary. I opened the six doors of the cupboard, and without counting took another picture and inventory of their contents and arrangement, against the last memory of having seen them, hours before. *How did he get in?* Crystal glasses and silver cutlery, valued by their age and their use, were left sparkling. But someone had entered, light-fingered; and was caught with his pants down. Had Eglon thawed out the rage in his loins?

The absence of tracks now buried under snow; the tools for entry used and undiscovered, made me think of the wind, invisible everywhere: like a mosquito at the ear at the lake. And then I remembered another photograph taken of my habit of leaving the light to the basement turned off. The light in the basement is burning now. It was never left burning. I hate my basement. I have all basements. I have no one living with me, cat or dog, pet and animals, perhaps a few unwelcome mice; but I do not need the basement; and I went down into it, two times a month, to drop my jockey shorts into the wheel-of-fortune washer; and before the washer made its first revolution, I would be out like a light.

Fear struck me naked. I forgot to fill out the coupon for cheap lessons in karate. I do not know a trigger from a barrel from a pin. In Barbados, there are no machetes. Fear and my inability to track the progress through my home of the unknown, unseen, undetected light fingers, were joined together, like twins. Someone's hands had touched the cup I used to drink my tea, ten times a day; had touched the crystal tumbler I raised to my lips with the two ice cubes and rum in it. St. James Rum from Martinique, a place I never visited but which could be imagined in a tour anywhere in Quebec where they spoke the same language; someone had rubbed his unwashed fingers over and had washed his lips on the lid I had put to my lips; and that this could have happened . . .

It was yesterday, at the dining table, not ten inches from this very trim broken off at forty-five angles from the rest of the door frame, that I had opened the *Globe* and followed the path of its words along the road fifteen houses on the ease side of me, about a man down the street, found dead in his red bed with blood covering him like a comforter, with his throat cut from left ear to right ear, as he slept in his basement without a cat, dog or mouse to bark; and the *Globe & Mail* said the warmest bedroom in the house was his basement. There was a smaller column, on the same local page of news about this city, about a woman; and it was so sad and so brutal, and her pet, a black cat she had found half-dead on Yonge Street buried in the deep garbage of papers and pop bottles and French letters late into Tuesday night before, and had weaned back to health and to love her, was the only witness when he was found sleeping on the woman's breast in her pool of warm milk that was red. And this city was becoming so unredeeming in its brutality against women that I could not finish my tea nor read to the end of the three frightening columns to see who had saved the poor cat from being taken back to Yonge Street, to be Scott-missioned like the beautiful white girl, twenty years into her life, sitting on a sleeping bag, to find another lover of cats or a bed at noon. Nobody was worried about the young white girl lying in her own fortune and kindness. Before I could step out of the house to go to court at College Park to give a verdict on a man caught stealing a box of crackers in a supermarket on Jarvis Street, I drank two strong brandies, and hoped to stay awake to hear the man's plea of defence, and to steady my nerves more important than the man's words, to give sober justice; and I prayed that the man who would be before me, it was a man, I think, but I prayed that he would not be before me for any kind of assault. If I had a woman living in this house with me, cat or dog, pet and animal . . .

I moved through each room touching things, backs of chairs, shades of floor lamps, an ashtray, a frame of a framed photograph, straightening a pile of books so that they were the same limpid size, making sure they were there, that I owned them, that I had not imagined my possession of them, and as if I myself was the thief, evaluating the look I had in mind to make any easy fencing sale of; and barter for a bottle of wine, or for a package of cigarettes, or for a plastic container of stuff that looked like flour but tasted sweet as sugar and addiction. The first article in the *Globe & Mail* that morning explained the bartering of stolen property. You want a sewing machine, so you steal a vacuum cleaner, and run your finger down the column in the community paper, which was free, until you found a nice housewife with six children and an unemployed husband, whose parlour was piled high with dust and dirt because her husband had sold the vacuum cleaner to buy canned peas, instant mashed potatoes and minced meat, and afterwards was himself minced in her wounds. You didn't have to linger on dark street corners around Jarvis or Sherbourne or Church or Parliament like women of the night to wait for the fence: those corners were now inhabited by prostitutes who dealt in a different kind of currency and wholesome property, cutting out policemen, pimps and middlemen. So I continued touching the backs of things and chairs, and books left on tables, remembering how each one had been placed; was that crystal ashtray left so close to the edge of the drum table? Did I, thinking of the sentence of this man charged with theft, strike three matches to light one Davidoff cigarette, whose stub is now sitting with the three burned matchsticks? And the radio; was the radio left playing rock and roll music when I myself always had it turned to CBC-FM? And then into the next room, the sitting room, which my mother told me twenty years ago, talking about other things, was the "one room in a house where you can tell if the person have *class*." In this room I first saw it, the indication that *he* had walked over the Istanbul carpet, and had considered rolling it up, to barter it for a rolled cigarette in his fleeting light-fingered time; "it takes five minutes only to trash a house" with greater efficiency than any crew of Tippet Richardon's of my possessions I like and were valuable and had not paid for yet. The door of the cabinet that contained valuable pipes, Meerschaums and Petersons, was left open. Was I on the front steps, fumbling with keys, while he was still fumbling with his decision and his choice? It was last Christmas that I had paid three hundred dollars for one of the Petersons; and the one that cost four hundred dollars was given to me by her. And at an auction at Waddington's, imitating the wealthy and disregarding the breath and health of the previous owner, I had bid four hundred on the Meerschaum, and had got it, and had vowed never to put it in my mouth, but would put it on display in a cabinet; and the moment I got home, I had searched in my library and had found a rare book on Meerschaums and Sherlock Holmes, and a silver cigarette case, with initials that were not mine, that sent the price sky-high, bought at the same auction with the pipes. The cabinet had been looked into, and forsaken, and left askew; and the Meerschaum was left on the top of my antique desk, at the wrong angle. My cigarettes were not to the thief's taste. He probably wanted cigarettes of a different strength. I searched the top of the desk for fingerprints, not knowing how to look for them, but knowing, even without the knowledge of Sherlock Holmes, that fingerprints are always searched for, and are always left. The desk needed dusting. If I had a woman, or a maid, cat, dog or companion animal . . . Weeks before, I had drawn lines with my forefinger across the thick film of neglected housekeeping, and had thought of animal companion, dog, cat, maid or woman; and wife, in the stifling allergy-giving dust. The three parallel lines I had drawn at that time lasted three weeks less three days. *The thief had been in the house.*

A silver cigarette box. A crystal ashtray. Three oil paintings and one watercolour. They had not seen the thief. *What did he like? And want?* And suddenly I remembered whatever I owned that was of value was upstairs. Perhaps *he* still was upstairs. My entire body had become paralyzed, deadened by the clear picture I would face in the emptiness of the three rooms above my head. Study, library and bedroom. I thought of women: of women arriving home in the dead of winter, dead tired because they chose no man's company and despised every man's love, deciding to live alone, and discovering that their practice and philosophy of independence is now violated by the presence of a man whom they cannot see but whose violence their gender can imagine; and if they had carried their view of the newspaper articles about women, nothing in their purse, a whistle, a knife, even a gun, nothing could wipe away that first raw effrontery of molestation; and if it was so with me, how curdling, how cruel, how chauvinistical, using their own words for us men, could it be? The fear, the paralyzing fear made me feel weak, made me begin to choose my weapon and my manner of facing this situation; making me silly in the face of the unknown but knowing danger, of this disgrace. My limbs refused to function. There was no weapon. There was a shoe. There was a broom. There was an iron pipe taken down from holding up the suits in a spare closet. But it was in the cupboard in one of the three rooms above my head, and I could not remember which. The fatigue and the confusion about counting books, of remembering their exact number, as if I was making an inventory before selling them, and there were more than two thousand of them; the possibility of replacing many of them, rare and first editions; and many signed by their authors, most of whom were already dead; and my private and confidential files of correspondence in which, not anticipating theft and burglary, I had been expansive with risks about the truth and candor about women friends; and frank about men and women whose privacy and confidence were the conditions in which many of the letters had been written to me, signed in the boldness of their affairs and gifts: flesh, kindness and kind; and the small photograph of a woman framed in a silver oval frame who did not come from Mexico, and which I had bought the week before, at the most expensive store in this city that specialized in silver. And one photograph of a woman, somewhere now, framed in a brass frame which I had bought the day before from an Indian store near the Bloor subway station that specialized in junk from Canada that was not completely destroyed nor disfigured in fires, in the surplus stock garnered after billowing flames had engulfed the merchandise. The woman in this brass frame was the wife of a second-hand dealer. Suppose the thief, not knowing, and not knowing value and irony from villainy, mistaking brass for gold, should fence the frame in the same second-hand dealer's store, and see the autograph of his wife, and trace the hand-writing to my door! This frame was priced at one dollar and ninety cents. All this raged through my mind like the waves of fire that had licked the merchandise in the vast warehouses in the cold suburbs of Scarborough and Pickering, where the warehouses are larger and from where the oval pure-brass frame had been rescued; all this occurred in two uncounted seconds of complete cowardice and fear that I would face this exposed nakedness slipped away by a thief who mistook brass for gold, and despised pure silver. Perhaps *his* hands were dirty. Perhaps his fingernails had crescents of squirrel's droppings under them. Perhaps. He was a complete stranger. And he would be dressed in blue jeans. His jeans were no longer blue. They were faded in the crotch. In the ass. And at the knees. And the back of the knees. They had walked through manure, and in the paths passed and trodden over by squirrels, and now the cow manure I had placed in the garden, not reckoning with the squir-rels. And if *he* had scaled the fence before the snow fell, he would have touched the same plants as the squirrels had eaten; and had jumped and had scampered out of the range of my water-pistol gun filled with ink and poison; for those squirrels had tormented me all summer long, leaving behind their almost indistinguishable tracks in the beds they had devastated. In the garden, in the snow left undisturbed, and lying on its white blanket are the leaves of the maple tree, not rotting on that part of the raised patio, which looks like a thick, uneven carpet.

And throughout the house, over the Persian carpets, *he* has walked, has touched and evaluated with his smeared hands, all this done in the privacy of *his* treasured intrusion is the smell of his desecration. The man had probably kept his battered Adidas for speed for escape with agility and lack of detection. He was free to evaluate the arrangement of the life he smiled on, as he planned and carried out his robbery of my privacy. So, I continued up the short flight of stairs to the first room on the second floor, to face this man of whatever size, whatever colour, whatever arms, whatever age, and with no weapon in my hand. I was prepared to die.

"Don't play hero and get yourself killed protecting money in a till that doesn't belong to you," the policeman said.

"Don't make the mistake of disturbing a burglar in the act and get shot. It can be replaced," the bank manager said.

"Your life is worth more than a few possessions," the woman in Miami would say.

"Your home," the policeman said, "is your goddamn castle. If a man breaks in, you can kill him, and ask questions after. But kill him first."

At the top of the stairs, I waited. I listened. And I panicked. *The thief is still in the house.* I heard a car speed by. I wished I was outside to hail the car and bring the driver in. And I heard the slush of snow pelted against the tires as it sprinkled the sides of the car, and splash back onto the road. And then I heard the night, and its lateness, and the noise of sirens at the corner of the street, patrolled after hours by prostitutes in pairs; and I could feel the darkness outside come right into the house, just as the thief had done, and it changed the nature of everything around me. I grabbed the balustrade firmly, to steady my consternation and my fright, and I remembered once more the four warnings against disturbing thieves, including the advice and determination to kill him first. Was this thief a woman? Is a woman ever a thief?

But with what? What would I use? What piece of wood, stick, chair-round, could I dislodge in time, in defence, in offence, and strike the fucker down? In my pocket was the small metal implement I used for cleaning Peterson pipes, and peeling Mac-Intosh apples. It has a knife with no sharpness to its blade, and a pick that can drive a very small hole into a cube of ice. I hear footsteps. Slow, creeping, cautious, casing footsteps. Thieves, I was told, are tougher than ice. And cooler, too. And then I knew. I knew where the footsteps were coming from: the neighbour on my left was too cheap to pour pink insulation into the wall between us, to keep out her groans and moans and ecstasy from her cat, dog, pet and animal, companions . . .

I fixed my eyes on the man coming towards me. Dundas Street is filled with women going for dim sum for lunch on payday. He is dressed in faded jeans. The jeans are no longer blue. There is a hole in the ass. He has just turned against the wind to light a cigarette. There are holes at the knees. He wears running shoes. And from the short investigating distance, I can see Adidas printed in the battered, shapeless shoes barely recognizable. He is walking as if he is about to jump and dump a ball into a basket. He wears a lightweight windbreaker over his pale blue V-necked sweater. His hair is long and stringy, and I want to believe it is dirty. And his hands move nervously. "You can tell a thief is a thief," my mother always said, with the conviction of a judge, "by his fingers and his hands. A thief is a light-finger son of a bitch, so the hands and fingers of a thief are always moving, looking for something to take up. That's how you can pick out a thief from out of *any* crowd." This man is thin. His arms are long, and as he walks they do not swing in the natural rhythm of his walking. And his hands are shaped and carried in that manner I knew and came to recognize from my mother's certainty, a deduction more popular and more applauded in a land of thieves where I was born: thieves and politicians, more popular than Sherlock Holmes, knowing a thief by the way he holds his hands. This is *my* man. My thief. The man who entered my house. So, I accused this young man of the theft, although I did not know him, had never seen him before: but he walked with his hands in *that* way my mother told me about.

And my accusation turned to dislike, to hatred, to profound animosity, to discrimination for all the men I saw on the street who were wearing jeans and sneakers and long hair. I remembered the hippies, and the blame they bore for the way they dressed. I remembered the flower children, for I was old enough to have seen them on the streets, in the fields and in the clover of rock concerts, and had smelled the flowers they carried in their hands that had painted circles with "love" advertised in their palms and on their chests. But I hated this man's long hair most. And I was sure that every man on this crowded street, so dressed, this afternoon, was a thief. I wondered how much this man had felt when he had touched, when he ran his fingers over the things in my home that afternoon? I wondered if he had wiped that act out of his mind the moment he had fenced the things he took. I had not discovered one item that he took. But I knew that he must have taken something. So, was the theft committed in the afternoon? At the moment I was raising the third glass of wine to my lips and welcoming my friends of twenty-five years past? Was it in the daytime? Or in the darkness of night? The snow left no clue of his movements. His entry into my house was like an undressing of a person against his will; against her will, and he had stripped this person naked, of his privacy and of her privilege; and he was the only living being in this city who could break the husband's heart that his wife's photograph was in the arms of another man he did not know, framed behind glass that had no glaze, in an oval frame that had escaped the tongue of fire and matrimonial conflagration.

I walked faster, caught up to this man and walked behind him, like a detective on the positive point of identification and arrest.

The man stopped. And I stopped too, looking foolish, feeling foolish, as his shadow. He crossed the light. And I crossed too. If I had a gun, even though this man was not inside my castle, he would be dead. But all that happened was that I almost bumped into him. I was feeling foolish.

"I beg your pardon," I told the man.

The man did not respond, say sorry, or it's no problem. My mother always told me that a thief has no blasted manners. The man had not turned, had no acknowledged the excuse, did not apparently want to show his face. For he knew me from my photographs in my home; but did not know that I knew. I was looking also at his fingers. Yes, it was like an undressing of a woman without her consent. It was done with distaste. He had stripped her naked, ripped away her privacy and her silk panties, molested her private parts and her privacy. He had smudged her innocence. And had thrown the sacredness of her privilege, to keep her body within her power of consent and of disapproval, out through the window. I was sure this was the man. I walked behind him, shadowing him. The wind came and smoke curled from my Peterson, and the bright lunchtime afternoon turned to London, and I became Sherlock Holmes in a fog of thickened London crime, tracking down my man.

The man quickened his step. I quickened mine. The man slid between the slower moving pedestrians. I tried the same thing, and when I did I was blocked and barricaded by a group of Chinese men carrying cameras, looking like tourists, looking for sights to take a snap, and moving and not looking. One tourist caught me in his sights. The man melted into the crowd.

And I was now tense and angry, and I pushed innocent people out of my way, including some Chinese who were not carrying cameras.

"Hey!" a woman shouted at me. "You purse-snatcher! Hey!" she screamed, over and over.

I slackened my pace of pursuit, and tried to look innocent and not like a purse-snatcher. And then I saw the man, standing at the corner, waiting for the lights to change, talking to another man, sharing a secret; and then he handed the man something he had taken from his pocket. He turned his back towards the man, sharing his secret; and the man bent over, cupped his bands, and the thief cupped his too, and when I draw abreast of the two of them, the man had borrowed a cigarette from the stranger who was lighting it.

"You're late for your class in Psych," the older man was saying.

"Yeah," the thief replied, "that's why I'm breaking my ass to get there." And he moved away in the direction of the downtown campus of Ryerson Polytechnical. Students could be thieves, I said. Graduate students can be even better thieves.

I stood and watched him fade into the thickness of the Chinese carrying cameras, and other pedestrians with purses and handbags over their shoulders, who were moving slowly, watching this man move like a cat in his Adidas, watching the grind of his tight faded jeans which had two holes in the seat, watching him move his fingers round the cigarette in that way and precise manner my mother had warned me about thieves, and other light-fingered people.

I was reluctant to return to my home. Cowardly against possibilities. I was fearful that in my absence the thief had, like lightning, struck twice. And it made me numb. But more than this feeling of despair mixed with resignation, was my relief at having succeeded in releasing myself from the burden of possessions, breaking the former tie of ownership and the responsibility that goes with it, and I became uncaring about either the damage or the loss of things I had left in my home. "Your life is more valuable." I heard it over and over, this good germ of advice. But then I reasoned that if all is taken, if another thief, the man who had given the cigarette, were to behave uncharacteristically like lightning, would I not have to spend time, which I could not afford, replacing these things? And how was I going to repeat the comfort and the job, duplicate them, and put back the sense of acquaintanceship I had had with all the possessions which adorned my home? I was in two minds. Because I could see the sense of regarding possessions as objects, things, burdens, appendages; and placing upon them, with the sense of possessiveness, the seal of value and the elixir of beauty. It was not so much what the price of the object was, as the pleasure and the aesthetic meaning of that object. I was still standing. And the crowds of Chinese tourists moved around me, as if I was a statue in the island of flowers on University Avenue, as if I was a stone in a stream and the water was going around it, to get to the mouth, and leaving in the detour an accumulation of weeds and straw and moss; and then ignoring my encumbrance and going about its way, as if there was no encumbrance at all; and not all of them were Chinese and not all of them carried purses and handbags on their shoulders. I was at the junction of the area called Chinatown and Bay. More young men wearing jeans that have lost their blueness, and in running shoes which slopped from the fashion of beating the newness out of them to make them look old and fashionable, were in the street. How many of these? Which of these? Any of these? I needed a drink. I felt weak. I needed two drinks. I needed to clear my head, and drown my anxiety about thieves in a few dry martinis, straight up, and with four olives, for nourishment.

I entered a neighbourhood bar. It was not my neighbourhood. It was not my bar. My neighbourhood has no bar. It was not the bar I usually drank at, on the penthouse floor or roof of a hotel in the less light-fingered section of the city. So, in this bar I was uncertain where to sit: whether to perch on a stool at the long black-topped shiny bar where the waiter had false teeth and false hair, the two of them protuberant and conspicuous; or take a seat at a table off the bar and large enough for four persons, and whether the waiter would feel he was out by three potential tippers; and whether he could see his reflection in the bottles lined like toy soldiers in front of the mirror, and notice that his hair was on wrong. I was experiencing a loss of self-esteem, a bout of uncertainty about things I used to be sure of, that the break-in of my home was causing; I was feeling that I was a marked man, that anyone on the street was able to look at me and see a mark on my forehead which said, here is a man who is to be stolen from, who is to be molested, and who can and should be molested again, since he has already been molested, whenever and by whoever chooses to molest him. I could imagine the mark on my forehead. It was seen by everyone but myself. I felt like a refugee must feel: bearing his heart and his history of his own country with forked words of persecution, in order to convince complete strangers who do not know his country and have never read his history and who sit in judgement on his claim that his brothers were torturing bastards. This man seeking refuge has to do two things. He has to paint of picture of degradation of almost all his native institutions, including his brothers and sisters. And he has to hope that this portrait of his country given to unschooled judges does not engulf him himself into the same pit and picture he has painted of his country, and that they might not see him separate from the degradation of the place he lives. But I did not think that this was the case with me. I was simply a marked man. A hit.

After the first scotch, the barman had no olives in his bar, I was aware of the lightness of my spirit. I spun my stool and faced the stores in the College Park indoor shopping plaza, and saw a woman getting her fingers painted red and made longer with false nails, and a woman with a white apron, which covered most of his body, was squinting her eyes as the shampoo dropped into her eyes which were closed, after her hair was aged with the white soapiness and fell in strands of dreadlocks. And inside the bar itself, the other tables were filling up with men and women after work, drinking beer. The man beside me smelled of perspiration and after-shave lotion. It could have been one of these two smells, the sweat or the lotion that I found offensive to my allergies. It could have been my own odour, the sweat from shadowing. The man beside me was dressed in a crimpolene suit of royal blue. His shirt was striped in broad lines of blue and white. His tie was stained at the knot. It was striped in thicker splashes of blue and white. He had not shaved since yesterday. He was talking to the man on the other side of me. I was the sandwich of their conversation. He leaned over each time he had something to say to the other man. He released from his mouth, as he did so, small, white, thick balls which evaporated before they reached the shiny black arborite counter of the bar. The waiter remained standing in front of the three of us, making circles with the wet cloth on the polished counter. He did not miss one drop. The man on the other side of me was dressed in a white T-shirt and a blue cardigan sweater and black trousers. I thought of moving one stool to my right to allow these two friends to carry on their conversation without having the spit from one of them fall into the second scotch before me, and to allow the waiter a cleaner sweep and larger circles with his cloth.

"Said he'd be here," said the man in the cardigan, "in fifteen minutes. We've been here more than fifteen minutes."

"Long as that?" said the man in the striped tie and striped shirt. "It's only five minutes." He seemed irritated.

"That makes ten more minutes, then."

"Yes, ten."

"And in ten he should be here, then."

"Five from fifteen."

"I *know* that!"

"Thought you'd forgot."

"Why're you talking to me as if . . ."

At this point I thought it best to get out of the sandwich. "Would you mind?" I told the man in stripes.

"Go ahead," he said.

"Sure thing," the other said.

I was already buried deep in thought, in a dream, trying to remember when I had had the dream, picking the pieces up from my bed which was lumpy and which did not take my body that night in any restfulness; putting these pieces together as if the snatches from the dream I was trying to recall were the cardboard snippets in a puzzle; recalling now a chair that was ornamental and shaped like a peacock or a nightingale, and made of metal that looked green in the dream, the colour of some precious stone, and moving this chair from its leaning position on a wall, to discover it had no legs; but when I stood it upright, legs grew into place as if they were there from the moment of manufacture; and when I went to place the chair amongst the other furniture in the room, all of a sudden the floor disappeared. The floor had been there when I discovered the nightingale chair. But the floor disappeared when I held the chair in my hands. I began to stir the four cubes in my third scotch. Dreams are dreams, I said to the cubes. Are just damn puzzles to make your life miserable, and cause you to see things that are not there. But I really did not believe what I was thinking.

"How much you say he got?"

"Well, from what he said . . ."

"Jackpot?"

"He had a damn good picture of the place."

"One o' those fancy places, weren't it?"

"Not far from here, neither."

"Townhouse job."

"You shouldda seen the *things* in that joint, he says to me. Christ! Like a museum, he says to me. And what does he *take*?"

"Don't say it."

"Like hell, don't say it!"

"Paintings. Pictures. Silverware. Things galore. And books."

"We're not in the book business, Ted."

"Sure, sure! But the things!"

"Ain't it funny? When you do a job like this, the things you know about the person!"

"*And* the place."

"You could get to know the person. If you had time. And if you didn't have to get out so goddamn quick."

"A helluva thing. The things you find out."

"You could maybe draw a picture of the owner. Sometimes even blackmail the bastard."

"With a quick eye," the man in stripes said, "you know his personality from the things you touch and select to take."

I had been taking the pieces of the dream from the assembled interpretation, and was dissatisfied by the easy assembly; and I was taking them apart again when I found myself, against my better sense of decency, eavesdropping on their conversation. I was taken in by their language, more than by what they were saying, and I tried to place them in their status, in the houses they lived in, and in the context of their existence. But I could not. This city was too democratic. And all it took to give an impression was the right-looking clothes. If you had the money, you had the class. It could be bought at certain cheap places and prices in this city.

"Frinstance!" the man in stripes was saying. "He says to me, he says he's sure it was a black house."

"What you mean?"

"A black."

"Colour?"

"The owner. He says he knew this from something. You know what?"

168

"Photograph!"

"Too simple. For Chrissakes, a blind man won't need eyes to know from a photo, *that*!"

"Clothes?"

"Don't be a goddamn—"

"What's so silly about clothes?"

"Don't you live in this city? Don't you see that you can't hardly tell from clothes if it's a man or a goddamn woman?"

"Yeah, they wear some weird clothes in this city! Some weird colours and weirder cuts!"

"Is there anything you can think of? *Anything?* That you can tell between them and us? Any goddamn thing at all?"

"I won't name the obvious."

"No."

"Anything, you say. Now, lemme think. Any thing. Anything. *Any* thing. Colour!"

"You mean, like, they're black. And we white? Now, that's dumb. Of course, we are white! And they're black."

"But I'm talking about *nobody* in a goddamn house, and you'll still know who the goddamn person is."

"Black? Or white? Well, shit, I said so, didn't I? A photo could tell you *that*!"

"There's no goddamn photo! Don't you understand? There is no goddamn photo in the place! Want another beer?"

"Sure. No photo."

"Two beers!"

"I got it. I just got it. Size o' shoes!"

"Drink the goddamn beer, will ya!"

"Thanks."

"Hair."

"Here? Here where?"

"Hair! Hair! Like on your head."

"But you said there wasn't no photograph!"

"For Chrissakes! There was two Afro combs in the second-floor bathroom. Here's our man now."

"Ten minutes."

"Yeah, it took him ten minutes."

"What took you so long?"

"I had a class. In psychology. I missed the last two Fridays. And I didn't want the prof to . . ."

He was dressed in faded jeans. The jeans were no longer blue. There was a hole in the ass. He was wearing running shoes. And from the short distance I was, I could see Adidas barely visible and recognizable in the battered shapeless shoes. He had on a light-weight windbreaker over his pale blue V-necked sweater. His hair was long and stringy. And his hands moved nervously. You can tell a thief is a thief, my mother always said, by his fingers and his hands. This young man who joined the one in the cardigan and the one in the stripes, moved his hands and his ten fingers, touching and wiping them, as if he were rubbing dice, caressing them before a throw.

"Mike here's been telling me what an easy . . ."

"Piece o' cake! Gimme a sip of your beer. Got a cigarette? Piece of cake. Thanks. Snow was on the ground. So I had to be damn careful, so I jump over the fence adjoining, and nobody seen me. Shit, and I landed right on the step, the back step of the back door. And it was so easy, so I put a little weight on the back door and Jees! you shoudda seen how it sent in, and all I could think of."

"But you got the stuff!"

"I have the money."

"And the only mistake I think I made—"

"No goddamn mistakes, now!"

"Man, we don't want to hear none!"

"A little mistake. I forgot to nail back the beading on the back door. Left it leaning at an angle, forty-five degrees."

"Why an angle?" the man in stripes said.

"Why forty-five? For Chrissakes, why not thirty-five, or fifty-five? For Chrissakes!"

It was not the same man I had been shadowing in Chinatown, near Bay.

"Did you expect me to take out a pair o' compasses and measure the goddamn angle, for Chrissakes?"

SOMETIMES,
A MOTHERLESS CHILD

She went back on her knees beside the bed. But the words did not come. "I can't commune with you this morning, Lord." She got up, rubbed the circulation back into her knees, pulled the pyjamas leg from sticking to her body, passed her hands over her hips, promised to eat less food so late at night, touched her breasts for cancer, and said, "Lord, another day, another dollars." She walked out of the bedroom and into the cold hallway, four paces long, passed through the living room, which served also as a dining room and kitchen, and into the tiny bathroom, colder than the short hallway. She looked up at the colour print of a man with a red beard grown into two points, strong piercing eyes, thin face and sallow complexion. The man's heart was not only bare, but outside. Something like a diadem, or a crown made of two strands of branches, thick and plaited with thorns sticking into the man's head, was causing drops of blood to fall from his skull. The colour print was above the sink. "Father God," she said. She closed her eyes and continued to pee. The man's hand was raised, the right hand, in a salute like that made by a boy scout, or like a gesturing giving benediction. It was this gesture which made her say, "Thank you." And with that, she felt better. But the words they were saying, and the words written about the Jamaican; and the sad memories that the snapshot of her husband brought back; and the drying up of her own words so necessary to begin the morning with; and the snoring behind the wall, all these worries passed from her mind and made her step light and carefree as she stepped into the shower. She hated showers. But they were quick. And this morning, in her hurry to be happy, she pulled out the new-fashioned circular knob, and the water, cold as winter, pounded against her body as if it contained small pellets of ice. She shrieked.

And before the scream died down, she was on the telephone to her landlord, who lived above her head. She hated that more than she hated showers.

"*Mister* Petrochuck!"

"Yes, my dear?"

"Am I paying you rent for this place? And I can't take a proper bath in peace without the water turning cold, cold, cold as Niagara Falls, and freezing my blasted body?"

Through the receiver she heard his hearty laugh and words in some foreign language, which she hated next to having to take showers, which, after five years she still did not know the origin of; and when his laughter abated, and her angered lowered, she heard Mr. Petrochuck explaining the difficulty.

"I tell you two times now, Mrs. Jones, he was saying, no longer with laughter in his voice, for in a way he both feared and respected her. "Two times I explain it now. You turn knob to left for the cold. And you turn knob to the right for the hot. And you turn before you pull out knob."

She felt ashamed to have to be told these explanations again. "So, how the hell am I to know that? Where I come from, you turn to the left for the hot. *To the left!*" She tried to imitate his accent, to diffuse both her frustration and her anger. "And you turn the knob to the right for the cold."

"That's right."

It was her time now to laugh, and to laugh and talk as she teased him.

"Thanks, Mister."

"Thank you, Mrs. J."

"Sometimes, I feel like a motherless child . . ." She was already in the shower, and the water was warm, and her voice was beautiful and clear above the sound of the water which came out in jets, as if it was mixed with marbles that had been taken from a furnace and mixed in cold water. *"Sometimes I feel like a motherless child . . ."*

When she was dressed, she started to prepare a sandwich, using Wonder Bread and canned salmon. She put a slice of tomato and a leaf of lettuce between the soft white slices. She wrapped it in a large white napkin, then into greaseproof paper, then into plastic. She dropped it into a brown paper bag. She placed a five-dollar note on the paper bag, and secured it with a paperclip.

She pushed the door of the small room behind the wall where she was standing in the kitchen, and looked at the large body curled in the shape of an embryo, on his left side, breathing heavily through his mouth. And she admired his smooth black body, muscular in the places where men his age are muscular; and with his hair cut in that odd style which she never liked, with two things that looked like lightning marks shaved deep into his short hair; and after she had taken in all this, as she does every morning during the week, she turned the light on.

"You!" she shouted.

This is the way she greeted him every morning; the way she chose to rouse him from his sleep. There was a smile in her shout, as she stood by the door, blocking it, sturdy as if she was a prison guard. "You!"

Her voice penetrated the sleep that he had been embracing, and it might have penetrated also the nightmare that his sleep had wrapped him into, for with the second call he sprung upright, and started to tremble in terror. She noticed that he had a hard-on. But she was his mother.

"Don't shoot, don't shoot!" There was terror in his pleading.

"Who shooting you? Boy, who are shooting you?"

"Sorry Mom."

"Is somebody shooting you? Look, fix yourself in front of me, do."

He pulled the sheet up, and covered his nakedness.

"School isn't this morning?"

"Yes, Mom."

"Well, get up, you!"

"Thanks, Mom."

And she laughed and hugged him tight, as if it was a farewell of love. He wrapped his strong black arms round her body, and she could feel his heart, and she was sure she could feel his blood. Then, she released him. She turned the light off. She closed the door. She shook her head from side to side in profound satisfaction at the way he was getting along, making plans for him and for herself, but more than anything else, making plans for his future. She was so proud of him. So proud. And he was growing so well. She gathered up her purse. She selected a large bag. She folded it and put it into the leather bag in which she carried her purse and other things. She turned the lights off in the rest of the apartment. But she was worried about something. Why would he say, "Don't shoot, don't shoot?" But just as soon, she put it out of her mind. He was such an obedient boy. She began to hum, and before she closed the front door, and before the clock on the mantelpiece chimed seven times, she heard him say, "Bye, Mom. Have a good day."

Her shower this morning was warm and embracing, and the water soaked her body as if she was still bathing in the waves of the sea. She was feeling better. She would manage her work today, and not complain. She would even change her mind about taking showers.

"Life is so good!" she said, turning the key in the lock.

When she walked down the short path, covered with snow with ice beneath, her steps went gingerly, and she didn't mind the winter. *"Some-times, I feel, like a mother-less child . . ."*

"BJ! BJ! Hey, man! It's Marco, man! BJ!" He waited as usual, until he was sure, until the caller had identified himself by name, before he even moved from the chair where he was reading a book, *The Autobiography of Malcolm X.* He wanted to be sure. He had to be sure that he was opening his mother's door to the right person.

"Hey, BJ! It's Marco, man!"

Years ago, when he skipped school on the smallest pretext, and felt he was clever in doing so, his mother got the landlord, Mr. Petrochuck, to check on him; and Mr. Petrochuck asked her how he could check on her son, and she told him how. "He can't fool me, Mr. P, so don't let him fool you. Just look along the alleyway between my place and the house next door, and see if you see if my son left. Make a note of the footprints in the snow, and I sure, Mr. P, that a man with your experience in the Second World War, as you always telling me you was in the Alpine Battalion with skis and a gun on your shoulder, that you would know what time may son passed through the alleyway on his way to school." The landlord's laugher, and hers, and his remark that she was a better spy than any he had faced in the Russian Army, lasted throughout the rest of the conversation that ended with her giving him her number at work, with the instruction to call her back. She spent that morning with her hands in the rich foamy water in the double sink, washing crystal glasses from the party the night before. But her laughter turned to anger and violence when she heard Mr. P's report; and when she got home at seven o'clock that night, she was tired and blue with fuming, but her energy came back to her, just as she was revived from the morning shower, and she stood over him, ten years old on that cold Monday night, and she counted twenty-one times that the leather slipper was raised and landed on his back, and she stopped counting, and did not hear her words as she drove the slipper across his back, ripping away one of the thongs, and shouting and muttering and screaming as she flogged him. "Let me tell you something, you hear me? Let me tell you something, young man. If you don't want to go to school, I will take you myself, to the nearest police station, and let them lock you up, you hear me?" And it went on that way, the sharp blows from the slipper rising in their unsatisfied anger, and her voice piercing the peace of her place which she kept clean and in which she made no noise, careful to be decent and respectable. ". . . And, and-and, living in this place with all the things happening to black people, to men and boys like you, and you wanting to turn out like them?" And it stopped only when there was a pause in her energy, and in her anger, and she heard the pounding at the door. At first she thought it was the police. And she got scared. And then she felt grateful that they had come to take her son away. "Serve you damn right!" And then she was terrified. She saw herself in handcuffs, taken out to the police cruiser and placed in the back seat, with the road of neighbours watching, and led into the station, the same police station she was going to take him to, and have her fingers placed on the ink pad, and in ten small spaces, printed as a criminal, and the charge of assault, or bodily harm, or violent assault, whichever charge they wanted to lay on her. And then she recognized Mr. Petrochuck's voice. "Are you going to kill this boy?" And the relief, and the protection his presence brought, as if he was still in the Alpine Battalion and had rescued a detachment of his men ambushed and encircled by their own loss of control and nerves. She did not lower the broken leather slipper again but held it in her right hand, as her eyes filled up with tears. And she embraced Mr. Petrochuck, and she asked him to sit with her for a while, and she remained silent and heavy with her grief which shook her body in spasms from time to time. That morning when they had spied on him, as he explained it to Marco on the telephone, hours later, the snow had betrayed him. It had remained firm and pure, clean and like innocence itself, without a blemish, because he had remained in his room all day, listening to music. Marco had supplied the school principal with a note of excuse, with his mother's signature forged on it. But he learned his lesson and deceived the landlord who continued to report his activities to his mother; and excelled in class through his brilliance, and because he was bright he had more time to do the things he wanted to do. So, this morning, when he heard her leave, as he has been doing for years, he put his coat, a fur-lined jeanjacket over his pyjamas, put on his sneakers, and walked from the back door, his private entrance, through the deep snow, right to the alleyway, and through the alleyway to the front of the house. Then carefully, he walked backwards, placing the sneakers exactly into the footprints going away from the back door, retracing his steps, right back into the house. He had been doing this so often that he no longer regarded it as a skill. Or as deceit. It was like brushing his teeth as the first activity after getting out of bed. He took off his sneakers, brushed them off on the mat covered with a copy of yesterday's *Star*. He dusted the snow off his jacket, as he had brushed the low-hanging branches of the tree in the alleyway, and put it back into the cupboard where he kept his stereo and CD player and his clothes, and which he had covered with a piece of cloth he had bought from the Third World Books & Crafts store on Bathurst Street. The cloth was Kente cloth. He had read somewhere in his voracious appetite for books that Malcolm X was married in Kente cloth.

"It's Marco, man."

He closed the book, after putting a bookmark between the pages; the bookmark was a sliver of Kente cloth; and replaced it into the shelves, which took up two complete walls in his small room. The shelves were crammed with books. All the books were paperbacks. All the books dealt with black people, and were written on black subjects, in fiction, philosophy, religion, art, culture and his favourite, biography. He kept his school texts under the bed, on the floor.

"BJ! Man, it's Marco!"

He was not impressed by the impatience in the voice, and before he went to the door he rested the Gaulois cigarette into an ashtray, he lit some incense, and he turned down the volume of John Coltrane playing "A Love Supreme." He put his housecoat on, and went to the door. The ashtray was a square crystal one, which his father had bought eight Christmases ago and had never used. His father did not smoke.

"Fuck, man!" Marco said, stomping one foot after the other, on the worn coconut-husk mat. "It's fucking cold out here, man!"

BJ looked at Marco sternly.

"Sorry, man."

A trace of a smile came over his thin lips as Marco remembered his aversion to foul language. So, he opened the door wider, and Marco squeezed between the post and him, and went in, and stomped one foot after the other, although his sneakers were already wiped clean on the mat. He hunched his shoulders, and pushed his hands into his jeans side pockets and said, "It's fucking cold, man!" Under his arm were newspapers.

"You should control your emotions better than that."

Marco looked cowed, and said, "Sorry, man. But it's all right for you, man."

The embraced, touching bodies, and slapping each other on the back three times, as if they belonged to an old fraternity of rituals and mystery. They let go of each other, and did it a second time, with their heads touching the other's shoulder. It was Italian, and it was African, and it was this that joined them in their close friendship for the past nine years. They saw each other every day, either at school or here, in BJ's room. Their parents never met. And did not know of their sons' deep friendship. And it never occurred to either of them that they should bring their parents into their strong bond of friendship. BJ's mother went to every school event that required a parent's presence. And Marco's mother and father attended them too. But they never met.

BJ went to the small square table in a corner with an African print covering it, and on which he had put a large leather-bound copy of the Holy Qur'an. Two glasses and a bottle of vodka were on the table. Ice was already in the glasses. He had been expecting Marco. The ice was already melting.

"Punctuality," he told Marco, "is also not an Italian characteristic, although *we* are blamed for inventing CPT."

"Fuck, man! Gimme the drink!"

And BJ poured two strong vodkas. He had not forgotten the orange juice, but he could not risk taking it earlier out of his mother's fridge, just in case. He did this now, and when he returned, Marco was sitting in a straight-back chair with his drink already at his lips. He poured each of them some orange juice.

Coltrane was at the stage in his song, chanting "a love supreme," over and over. Marco joined in the chanting. His voice was deep for his age, eighteen, similar to a bass.

"A love su-preme, a love sup-preme," he chanted. "Nineteen times, fuck, you say he does that. Sometimes, you don't know, BJ, but I feel he's gonna sing it maybe twenty times, or eighteen times! Fuck!"

"Unless your concentration diminishes, Coltrane won't."

"Fuck!"

BJ went back to the table, brushed a piece of ice from it, and ran his hands over the cover of the Qur'an. It was covered in brown paper, cut from a bag from the Liquor Control Board of Ontario weeks ago, when he went to pick up his weekly supply of vodka. He was seventeen then. But he looked older. He always looked older. This did not fool the manager at the LCBO store around the corner from his home, and he knew it; so to save the embarrassment, he used forged identification, including a schoolmate's birth certificate. He felt guilty about doing this, on the first three occasions; but it was the style of the times. Only last week he read in the *Star* that the police had caught five immigrants working illegally under false names and with forged social insurance numbers. It was the way of the times. And he was a born Canadian, so, "Fuck!" Marco consoled him, and himself. On the brown paper cover he had printed HOLY BIBLE. On the bedside table, beside his single bed that had an iron bedstead, he had placed the Bible, just in case. He read the Bible, too. His mother had given him the Bible. But he devoted his devotions to the Holy Qur'an. Coltrane was now into the second part of his song. The music came out at them with equal balance and power, even though he had turned down the volume, out of the four speakers. The speakers were four feet tall and more than one foot in width. He had built them himself. The other components in the stereo, he and Marco had reconditioned from spare parts and odds and ends thrown out by neighbours up in North York. Every piece but the CD player they had reconditioned themselves.

"Did you check out the things for me?"

"Yeah, man," Marco said. He was almost perfect in the speech of black people. It came out easy and almost natural. "I got me the Form, man."

"Well, let's spend a few moments scrutinizing the entries, and adding to our fortune."

"All these books. Fuck. Man, you's something else! All these books!" Marco would busy himself by taking out a book, flipping its pages, replacing and repeating this until he had touched almost every book in the shelves. And he did this to allow BJ to concentrate on the Racing Form. "You're like, like a walking 'cyclopedia, man. And also a genius at the track. Fuck!"

"All it takes is concentration, Marco. I've been telling you this for years. Concentration. *And* dedication."

"I gonna give you something Italian to read. You know anything about Italian classics? Man, I gonna lay some Italian literature on you one o' these days. Like Dante, man."

"Third shelf, sixth book from the right. Second bookcase."

The book Marco picked out was *Seven Systems of Dante's Hell.*

"Fuck! I didn't know he wrote this, too!""

"Imamu Baraka wrote that, Marco. That's a different inferno," BJ said. "My mother is fine. She didn't ask for you this morning."

"Fuck!"

"This morning she pushed my door and greeted me in her usual way, 'You!' I pretended I was sleeping, but all the time I could see her face and the worry in it, and the worry in her body about her work, and I was pretending I was sleeping. I was up all night, reading."

"This black power shit?"

"As a matter of fact, Marco, I was reading Shakespeare." Marco got up from his chair and went to the bookcase. He knew this one. This one was, in a way, his favourite bookcase for it contained books he too liked. The bookcase was made from unpainted dealboard, sawed and cut by him and BJ; and it occupied the space in the wall between a window and a cupboard. It ran from the floor to the ceiling. BJ liked everything in his room to run from the floor to the ceiling. It had something to do with perspective, he said.

Marco did not understand, and said, "Fuck!" to show his sentiments. If his room were larger, BJ knew that they would have built the speakers from the floor to the ceiling. In this shelf in the bookcase were books by Shakespeare, which Marco liked and did well in, in school, preferring *Romeo and Juliet* – "Fuck! Not because I'm Italian, man!" – and *As You Like It* and *The Merchant of Venice*, which they stopped studying in school the term before he reached that grade. BJ preferred *Henry IV* and *Othello*, "because you're black, right? Fuck!" But BJ told him, "because it contains the best and, perhaps, the most noble of Shakespeare's noble poetry. I don't even like the character Othello. Iago is a more realistic character. I see Iagos every day in class." And to all this, all Marco said, years ago when they had this conversation the first time, was "Fuck!" They have had this same conversation many times since. And Marco uses the same single word to express his sentiment.

"Today is the last day. I suggest we go out with a bang. But how many classes would you miss if we got there for the first?"

"Lemme see. Biology? Physics? English? And basketball practice."

"I will do your Biology and Physics assignments for you. Or we can do them together at the track."

"Fuck!" Marco said. He rubbed his hands as if he was cold. He poured himself another vodka and orange juice.

For young men, for eighteen-year-old boys, really, they had an enormous prodigity for alcohol, which is the term BJ used laughingly, when they would sit in his small room and consume half of a twenty-six ounce bottle of imported Absolut Vodka; and if his mother had returned home and had seen them, she would shake her head in pleasure at their hearty living for orange juice. "You two boys don't know how good I feel to see you drinking orange juice instead of all this damn Coke and Pepsi!" And after these long bouts, their speech was not even slurred.

"Did you remember the *Globe?*" BJ read the *Globe* everyday. He read the racing tips first. He read the sports section second, the editorial third, and the foreign news section fourth. He read nothing else in this newspaper.

"Woodbine, here we come!" Marco said. "*They're at the post!* Fuck!"

"Should we invest a hundred each? What is your opinion, Marco?"

"A hundred bucks? Fuck! Why not, man? I deposited yesterday's winnings in my account. Those tellers're *weird*, man. She look at me with all that bread as if I was a drug dealer! Fuck, man!"

"Today's the last day, man," BJ said. Marco noticed the tone of his voice.

"You all right, man?"

"You have to do something with the money in your bank account. Something. *Some* thing. And we have to think about the car, too."

"Today is the last day, man. So if we lose . . ."

"Don't say it!"

"Sorry, man."

BJ went to his dresser, a narrow, tall piece of furniture which his mother had bought at the Goodwill Store on Jarvis Street, to save money, and when he had stained to make it look like mahogany. It looked like a mahogany antique piece of Georgian furniture, although he did not know that. It had five drawers. In the top drawer, under his handkerchiefs which his mother starched and ironed and folded into four, he kept his cash, arranged in denominations in ascending order, inside a box that contained cheques from the bank. He opened this drawer now, and took from it a metal box that had a key. He brought the box to the bed and unlocked it. There were four boxes that used to contain cheques in the metal box. They were full of bank notes. No note was smaller than a ten. He did not count his money every night, but his memory was good, and he knew that with the withdrawals and the deposits into his private "safe," that he had five thousand, three hundred and five dollars in it. He could not tell his mother about this. He could not offer to lend her money, not even when he saw her moaning and crying and cursing his father for having abandoned them; not even when her rent of four hundred dollars a month was in arrears. And sadly, not even when she had to postpone her registration for one month, and never caught up, in the Practical Nursing course at George Brown College. She would kill him to learn that he had so much money, in her house, in all the time she was seeing misery, in all those days when she had to cut and contrive. But he had prepared for her. At such a young age, it seemed ominous, too adult, too final a thing this preparation by someone so young. He had opened a savings account in her name, at a different bank from the one she used. Marco put his winnings in a chequing account. But he kept his in cash.

"Here's twenty tens, Marco. I'll take twenty, too. This is the last day, so I'm staking you. What we win, we keep. What we lose, well . . ."

"Fifty percent of our winnings should still go in the kitty, man. Fuck!" It was their business arrangement. And they stuck to this code, like members of a gang. "And look for a long shot, man!"

"There's no such thing, Marco. No such thing. My father went to the races every day. Faking illness from work. And family crises and emergencies. He had to be there. In summer and winter. He even walked there, once. Not to mention the times he *had* to walk home. And he bet on long shots because he was a gambler. He was a gambler. And was greedy. He was a fool. A damn fool. He thought he could get rich from the track. We are different. We are investors. Don't ever let me see you betting on a long shot! Long shots are for racetrack touts."

"Why can't we use the car?"

"How many times do I have to tell you it's not safe to be driving that kind of car in Toronto? It's safer to drive it in Montreal."

"Oh man! What's the point of having the wheels and not using it? Fuck!"

"Have you told your parents you own a white BMW? Or more correctly, a fifty percent share in a 1992 white BMW?"

"Well, fuck no, man! For them to execute me?"

"Exactly! My mother doesn't even know I can drive. As long as our friend respects our confidence, the car will remain parked in her underground garage in Scarborough. Now, I have to make my *salats*."

"Make your salads, man. Make your salads. Fuck."

"Are you going to respect my religious principles? Or are you leaving?"

"I'll respect your salads, man. I'll respect your praying, man."

The Timex watch on BJ's write began to buzz. It was the hour for prayer. Marco poured himself a vodka quickly, wanting to stop the racket of the ice cubes in his glass and the sound of the vodka pouring out of the bottle, now almost empty, before BJ began his prayers.

BJ pulled a cheap Persian rug from under his bed, unrolled it, and placed it in front of the table on which were the Absolut Vodka, and the Holy Qur'an. He placed the Qur'an on the floor in front of him, and he placed his hands before his heart in the demeanor of prayer and concentration.

All this time, Marco was looking into the pages of *Plutarch's Lives*, which he had taken from the bottom shelf of the narrow, unpainted bookcase that contained only classical literature. And he sucked on the vodka, straining it through his teeth and the melting pieces of ice cubes, as his friend *ommmmmmmed* and *ommmm-mmed* and intoned *"alla hack-bar"* which is how Marco understood the pronunciation of the Muslim prayers. Fuck, he said to himself, this motherfucker is real serious. If I didn't know he was serious, fuck! It was nine o'clock. The morning was crisp and cold and clean.

The boy flung the newspaper, aiming for a different spot, and it banged against the window where she was with her hands in the thick, white dishwater, foaming like the waves that banged against the rocks near the Esplanade, and then retreated back into the calm, blue sea. She was thinking of home. She had seen him. "You little bastard!" And the boy jumped back on his bicycle and sped out of the circular driveway over the crunching snow. It was ten o'clock. The morning was cold. When she had got off the subway and was walking to this mansion, the wind ripped into her body, and made her think of going back home the moment she made herself into a woman, meaning when she had money; and it made her feel as if she was naked. The wind had the same brutal touch as *his* fingers on her backside that day when she was bending over the vacuum cleaner. He had not touched her. She imagined it was his intention. And imagining it, it made it real. The wind swept up her legs, right between her thighs, clawing at her pantyhose with such force that she thought she had left home without putting on her underwear. "I should have been born a man," she said, to the boy disappearing over the smashed snow, but really not for his ears. Men didn't know how lucky they are, she said, continuing her thoughts; they don't know how damn lucky they are to be wearing pants to get more greater protection from this damn cold. "And in other things, too!" Her thoughts went back to her son. For she had seen the photograph of the Jamaican family on the front page of the *Star* newspaper many weeks ago, and now this morning, when that damn boy pelted the paper that almost broke the window where she was, here was another one. She wiped her hands in her apron, and studied the newspaper. It said that the young man was seventeen, and it said that he was living with his mother in a big house in the suburbs, and it said he was in the car with another young man about his same age, and it said that he was not going very fast and that the traffic policeman didn't have to follow him with the sirens on, and it said he was shot in the back of his head. She felt sad. And wanted to cry. She was leaving her own son at home so often, by himself, before the dawn broke, in bed, and she wondered if he was safe. "But praise God, he doesn't have a car. A car is the surest thing to make a police shoot a black man dead. Praise God for that!" And she wanted to take up a cause, and hold a piece of stick with cardboard stapled on to it, and a message written on the cardboard, in thick black letters: THIS COUNTRY RACIST. THE POLICE TOO! "Yes! And put an exclamation mark after it, too!" She wanted to cry. She wanted to scream. But who would listen to her? A simple woman like her? That's why, she said to herself, a man has it better, for "I am the least amongst the apostles."

The young man's face, and the face of his mother, wringing her body in tears, filled the space of the double sinks as she returned to her work. Her employers were having a party at five. And when the image of the mother and the son evaporated like the foam of soap from the two sinks, in their place were the faces of her own son, and his no-good father. She pulled the plug in the second sink out with force, and the face of that bastard disappeared. She began to hum, *"Sometimes I feel like a motherless . . ."*

BJ got out casually and with self-assurance from the taxi, at the front of the tall apartment building somewhere in Scarborough; and as he walked across the lawn, he passed a blue car in which two men were sitting. The men were watching the same entrance BJ took. They had been there for the past three hours; and they had started watching the door since last Sunday. BJ paid no attention to the blue car. He walked straight to the panel of names, and pressed one of the buzzers. It was a buzzer beside the name G. Harewood. He did not know G. Harewood. He could have pressed any buzzer. It was only two o'clock, and his school friend, who allowed him to use the underground parking, without her mother's approval and knowledge, was still in school. This was the only way to retrieve the car.

"Who's it?" a woman's voice, mangled by the malfunction in the speaker system, cried out. The voice came through louder than he expected, and he made a start. It stirred him more than that. "Who's it?" The voice was not irritable. "Is it George?"

"Yeah!" BJ said, trying to change his voice to George's voice without knowing George's voice.

"Come on up!" the woman's voice screamed. It was less irritable. "Come on up!"

And when BJ entered the lobby, he could still hear the voice saying, "Come on up!" and the buzzer on the door to let him in was still being pressed.

He pressed the button in the elevator to P2, and went down into the bowels of the building. Three women were in the elevator with him. The three women stared at him. When the three women were tired staring at him, they stared at the floor. Pools of water from melted ice were on the floor. When the three women were tired of staring at the floor, they stared at the illuminated numbers on the panel in the elevator. When it came to P2, the three women stood where they were. It seemed to BJ that they were standing in such a way to suggest that they had taken the wrong elevator. BJ got out. He walked straight to a corner of the large dimly lit underground parking area. Glimmering in the bad light of the dull fluorescent bulbs was the white BMW. He stood beside it. He looked at the front tires. He looked at the hood. He looked at the windshield. The elevator door was still open. The three women were watching him. He went round to the front of the BMW and looked at the bumper. He looked at the cap which covered the hole to the gas tank. He screwed it tight. It was already tight. It was locked. One of the three women got off the elevator when it reached the main floor and walked straight to a door marked "Superintendent."

BJ looked at the licence plate. He passed his hand over it. He was about to brush the dust from the plate onto his trousers, but he remembered in time. He was wearing expensive clothes. His trousers were black. They were full in the leg, and narrow at the ankle. His socks were white. And the shirt and jacket fitted him as if they were three or four sizes larger than his weight and size. He took a handkerchief from his pocket. The handkerchief was white, and folded into quarters. He wiped his hand, and then he passed the handkerchief slowly over each letter of the car licence. When he was done, the licence plate was glimmering almost as much as the BMW itself. The licence plate was BLUE. His beeper was beeping. So, he got into the car, with the doors locked, and the engine still turned off, and he checked the beeper. It was Marco.

He turned the engine on. Gradually, the interior of the black leather got warmer and warmer until he felt he was as comfortable sitting in it as he was in his room surrounded by all his solid-state stereo and CD equipment and books. In this car he had installed an equally expensive system. John Coltrane was playing. He had left the cassette in the tape. "A Love Supreme."

The car was warm. BJ's two large eyes filled up the rear-view mirror, and he could barely see, in periphery, the elevator door open and a man and three women; and the women were pointing in his direction as they talked to the man; but the BMW was warmed up, and it moved without noise over the caked ice in some parts of the underground parking; and he manoeuvred it through spaces left by bad and careless drivers, past large concrete pillars, and mounted the incline to the exit door, in no hurry, and all the time speaking to Marco on the telephone, and he had to repeat himself two times, for the aerial struck the top of the last exit door, and finally he emerged into the brilliance of the winter afternoon, bright in the sun but still cold. The women had just told the super-intendent, "I'm sure he looks like one of those drug dealers, and I feel he is, not because he's . . ."

The two men in the blue car saw the white BMW. And the two men made a note of it. And they registered BLUE in a notebook. And they made a check on their computer. And they began to talk on the telephone. BJ was heading for Victoria Park and Kingston Road to pick up Marco at the subway station. He was in a good mood. The last racing day was something else, "Fuck!" as Marco put it. They had won and won and won . . .

Facing her now were the most magnificent slender white sculptures of branches on the trees in the backyard. She had seen these trees change their form for three years now, and she still did not know the name of one of them. But this afternoon, around three, with the clear light and the brilliance of the sun which gave no heat, she marvelled at the beauty of thought of men travelling in olden times, over this kind of landscape, walking in shoes made from skins; and following in the tracks of wild animals they had to kill to stay alive. It was as if an artist had applied pearls and other kinds of jewels, with precision, on the branches of the trees. But she was not happy inside herself. Something was bothering her. And she picked up the telephone and called her landlord.

"Did you really see him?"

"Yes, I tell you, Mrs. J."

"Go out, dressed? In his school clothes? In time for school?"

"Everything."

"You sure it was my son? You didn't mistake somebody else for him?"

"Sure."

"Well, thank you then." And to herself, she said, "I don't know why I am in this mood."

She had selected the crystals and the silvers and the plates, and all she had now to do was choose the serving dishes, and put the place mats on the shining mahogany table. She checked the roast beef in the oven, and shook her head at the amount of food she cooked, with most of it being thrown away the next morning, since neither husband nor wife liked to eat leftover food; and with all this damn food wasting day in and day out, and so many people on the streets of this city starving with nothing to warm their stomachs, and that blasted boy I gave birth to, refusing this good rich food, saying he is a Muslim. What a Muslim is? Is a good Muslim a person who doesn't have common sense inside his head, that he would refuse all this richness? And she laughed to herself. It was a joyous laugh. A hearty laugh. A laugh from the bottom of her belly. She looked round to see if anyone was close by, to mistake her for a fool, that she was going out of her head, laughing and talking to herself like this. "And come telling me that he is fasting. *Fasting?* And all this food, all this food going to waste. I wish I knew somebody on my street, without foolish pride that I could leave a plastic container full of this food!" And she began to hum. *"Some-times, I feel like . . ."*

As BJ pulled off from the curb in front of the subway station in the east end, with Marco strapped in beside him, and laughing and turning up the volume of the saxophone solo, the BMW was so loud with the music contained within it that Marco himself felt his head was about to explode; and BJ himself was becoming nervous that perhaps the BMW would become conspicuous with the two of them in it with so much noise. The windows were rolled up. The BMW took the first entrance on the 401 West doing 80. BJ settled behind the wheel, with a Gaulois unfiltered cigarette at the corner of his mouth, one eye closed against the smoke, and he put the car into fourth gear, and the car still had some more power, and moved like a jungle animal measuring its prey, and receiving additional power because of the certainty of devouring its prey. The prey in this case was their destination. But they did not have any anxiety of time and distance to reach that destination. It was simply that BJ liked to drive fast. That was why he convinced Marco to buy the BMW instead of the Thunderbird. And that was why he got it with standard transmission. They had won the money at the racetrack one afternoon when Marco made the mistake of buying the three horses in a triactor race for ten dollars, instead of five, which was the custom. The name of the horse that won, that went off at 50 to 1 odds, was Blue. BJ knew he could not keep all that money in his room; and he knew that he could not open an account without questions asked. He knew he could not give it to his mother, even with the explanation that he had won it at the track. What would he be doing at the track? Why was he at the track on a school day? So, he bought a white BMW. He paid a friend of his, a real estate salesman, three hundred dollars to cover for him. Real estate was at rock bottom at that time, and the salesman was more than happy to keep his mouth shut, and to pocket this unearned commission. But BJ knew all the time that he had to be careful, and that a time might come when the real estate salesman, still at the bottom of the unsold houses on the market, would need more help in keeping his mouth closed. He had to be careful.

He turned the music down a little more, and he reduced his speed to 80. As these thoughts entered his head, he had been doing 150. He had just spotted a marked police cruiser with 52 painted on its white side, parked alongside the 401. But he did not know that as soon as he had pulled off from the subway station in the east end that at that precise moment a blue sedan with two men in it had pulled off too, and had followed him until he entered the 401 going west. The marked cruiser was expecting him. And as he had swooshed by, the traffic policeman was on the radio to another one, somewhere farther west along the 401. Conversation passed between the policemen in their cars. "Drug dealers for sure!" And through another system came "Question of being armed and dangerous." And the two policemen in the parked blue car up in the suburbs of Scarborough added their contribution, "We were hoping for a red Camaro, but you never know with these drug dealers. They have the money to change cars . . ." And Coltrane was playing his ass off, as Marco would say, still fond of the way he thought BJ talked, and should talk. "'Trane's playing his ass off!" he said eventually. He said it three more times. BJ grunted something. In his rear-view mirror he saw the police cruiser pull into the same lane as his, tailing him. He knew this stretch of the 401 like the palm of his hand. He was west of the Allen Road, approaching on the highway a little north, the area in the city known as the habitat of drugs and guns and gangs and called by two names, one the name of a woman, a whore: the other name of a bird, which may also be a woman and a whore. Jane-Finch. He knew this stretch of road well. He knew he could get into the express lane within twenty kilometres. The cruiser was gaining on him. Marco was oblivious to this, as he listened to Coltrane. The cruiser's red light was still not on. But BJ surmised that any time now, it would be. And the siren would start. The lanes ahead of him were crowded with slow drivers who had themselves seen the cruiser. All four lanes heading west were crowded. But that was what he wanted. He put the BMW into third. He was gearing down to stop; and the car was not so noisy with the music, and that was when Marco had commented about Coltrane's mastery of "Love Supreme," when BJ changed his mind about stopping, to face the consequences. For how would he know the cruiser was following *him?* Of the thousands of cars on the highway, why should a police cruiser pick him out because he was driving an expensive car and was a young black man? He told himself he must not be fooled by the logic of a man, or of a woman, or of a time, a better time than was taking place in this city; he remembered that logic had absolutely nothing to do with it. He was intelligent in the ways of the hunter, and in this case, the hunted. He was relying upon his instincts. Somewhere in his vast reading he had come across something about this. He was not quite sure, nor could he remember the exact quotation; but it had something to do with instinct and emotion and gut feeling. His mother lived by her emotion. So, he geared up to third, and the BMWEZ lurched forward. Marco said, "Fuck!" and tightened his seat belt. "Let her ride, let her ride!" It was already in fourth. And in and out of traffic, from the slow lane to the middle, to the fast lane, and when the fast lane was not fast enough, and the entire width of the four-lane highway seemed to be creeping, the white BMW swerved like a top spinning near the end of its revolutions. "Fuck!" Marco said when they were safe, for the time being, in a secondary road somewhere near Dufferin. "What the fuck was that all about?"

BJ smiled. He turned Coltrane up. The car was filled once more with the beauty of the music, with the pulse of emotion and the feeling of the time; and they remained quiet in the waves of the melodious tune they both liked so much, and argued about. BJ insisted, because of his new religion, that it was a religious chant. Marco, equally insistent said it was a love song.

"A love supreme," he began chanting. *"A love supreme.* Nineteen times the brother says *a love supreme!* Nineteen times, BJ!" He never lacked enthusiasm about this aspect of the song. "Fuck!"

"Nineteen times," BJ said. And he turned the music up even louder. They were cruising along Eglinton Avenue, passing record stores from which reggae and dancehall blared out upon them, past barber shops and restaurants and shops which sold curry goat and fish and oxtail and peas and rice, and they felt they could smell and taste the food even in this breathless afternoon so cold, and so un-certain. Young men, some younger than either of them, walked with a patience that came close to loitering along the lively street, stopping now and then to place their hands on the parking meters, as if reassuring themselves and the ugly pieces of metal that life was still going on, even in this cold afternoon when it was difficult to breathe; in this heart of West Indian life, when there was no atten-tion paid to the depth of the fall in the coldness and where life remained constant: the laughter and the lightness of dress and manner. "What about lunch?"

"Yeah."

"Curry goat? Or oxtail?"

"Fuck! Goat *and* oxtail."

BJ and Marco were driving around. Listening to Coltrane and taking in the sights. It was about four in the afternoon. The white BMW had just been washed at the car wash on the corner of Bath-urst and St. Clair. And the music was sounding better, it seemed, now that the car was spotless. As they handed in their chit, the four car washers, who were polishing another car, paused in their work to admire the white BMW. And they looked long at the car and then longer at the two teenagers, and said something with their eyes and said something to themselves, and went back pol-ishing an old black Pontiac. BJ was accustomed to people looking at him and then at the BMW. And when Marco was with him, if it was in the parking lot of a supermarket or in a mill, they would go through the order of looking and staring, a second time in reverse.

They were cruising along Bathurst now. It was Friday afternoon, about five. And the traffic was heavy. And BJ was driving within the speed limit. And as he turned left into the street before Dupont, to tack back on to Dupont because there was no left turn there, from under a low-hanging tree came a police cruiser. BJ and Marco were alone on this stretch of road. And the cruiser came close to them, and BJ understood fast enough, and pulled over and stopped.

"Get out! Get out!"

"Yes, officer."

"You too! Get the fuck out!"

"Yeah, officer."

The policeman was out of the cruiser, and he had his hand on the T-shaped nightstick. His other hand moved to his gun to make sure, it seemed, that it was still there.

"Out!"

They were already out.

"Okay, okay!"

"Who're you talking to like that? Eh? Eh? Who're you fucking talking to, like that? Eh? Eh?"

And with each "Eh?" he poked his T-shaped stick into Marco's ribs.

"Up against the car! Up against the fucking car! Both o' youse!"

It seemed that in his training, his lecturer had had a hearing problem and he had to repeat each answer two times; for he was now saying the same thing two times, as if it was his normal way of speech. Or as if he was also accustomed to talking to fools or immigrants who didn't understand English, and he had to speak in these short, truncated, double sentences.

"Spread your legs! Spread your legs! Come! Open up! Come! Open up!"

And they obeyed him. BJ could feel the dust from the side of the cruiser, which needed a wash, going into his nostrils. He could feel the policeman's stick moving around his legs, round his crotch, up and down, up and down. He could feel the policeman's hands, tough and personal, strong as ten pieces of bone, feel his thighs, his chest, under his arms, between his legs, and feel his penis and his testicles; and then the ten pieces of bone spun him round, so that he now faced the policeman. BJ stood silent and calm as the policeman did the same thing to Marco. He thought the policeman was treating Marco more severely.

"Where you get this goddamn car?"

Before BJ could answer, the policeman was talking again.

"Where you get this goddamn car?"

BJ was about to say something when the policeman cut him off.

"You steal this car? You steal this car?"

Marco opened his mouth to speak, and thought better of it.

"Who owns this fucking car? Who owns this fucking car?"

BJ put his hand into the breast pocket of his suede windbreaker, and was about to pull out his driver's licence, when the policeman came at him. His hand was on his gun. His gun was in his hand. The policeman seemed to see red. The policeman seemed to feel his life was being threatened. The policeman was behaving as if BJ had taken out, or was about to take out, a dangerous weapon. The policeman turned red. He came at BJ with great force, as if he was tackling a running full back, and when he hit him, he had him flat onto the side of the cruiser. Dust rose from the side of the cruiser. The cruiser leaned for a short time off its tires. Marco was about to intervene when BJ raised his hand to stop him.

"Come on, nigger! Come on, nigger!"

And he slammed BJ into the side of the cruiser a second time.

The policeman put his hand behind his back, and when he brought it from behind his back, he was holding handcuffs. He snapped them on BJ's wrists. He poked the T-shaped stick into Marco's side and ordered him into the cruiser. And he pushed BJ towards the cruiser, and threw him into the back seat beside Marco.

He drove off. Voices of other policemen and of a dispatcher babbled on the radio. He seemed impervious to the racket of the other voices. He drove south on Spadina and turned right at Bloor; and left on Brunswick, and into a few short one-way streets, and then he was back on Spadina going south of College; and then he turned east onto Dundas. BJ recognized the Ontario College of Art and the Royal Ontario Museum. He visited the ROM twice a month on Saturdays, to study African cultures and art. And Marco went along with him on many occasions. They had been doing this for three years now. BJ recognized Division 52 police station. And his heart sank. He had heard about Division 52. Wasn't it a police officer from 52 who shot a Jamaican, many years ago? The policeman moved on to University Avenue and turned left, and took them northwards on University. Apart from the crackling of voices from the other invisible policemen and dispatchers, the cruiser was quiet. It was six o'clock and the winter light was fading fast into night. And if night should catch them in this cruiser, alone with this policeman, oh my God! The policeman had not spoken in all this time. He had smoked two cigarettes. They came to Queen's Park, and took the roundabout and were beside Trinity College, and back onto Spadina. Marco had a cousin who was attending Trinity College; and he took BJ there, one Friday night at dinner, and they ate fish without pepper sauce. BJ loved the huge oil paintings, and the black gowns the students wore. In all this time, BJ said nothing. And Marco said nothing. Marco was slapping his trousers' legs. BJ sat with his eyes closed, his teeth pressed down tight, and if you were sitting in Marco's place, you would have seen the slight movement in BJ's jaws.

"Get the fuck out! Get the fuck out!"

It took them a while to realize who had spoken to them. It took them a while to recognize where they were. The policeman came round and unlocked the cuffs from BJ's wrists.

"Get-outta-here! Get-outta-here!"

He had let them off beside the white BMW.

His mother remembered it was a big day on Saturday, a wedding she had to go to, and she rushed from work to get to the hairdresser before he closed. There were many women there, some of them had been there since early afternoon. It seemed that every woman in the place had an important church service on Sunday. Or an important dance date. Or a wedding to go to. She was tired, too tired from a long day, and she dozed off as she sat in the chair. She could barely hear pieces of conversation around her.

"I know a Jamaican man that the cops kill."

"But that was five years ago, child!"

"And in Montreal, too. Not here. As a matter o' fact, this partic-ular Jamaican had a daughter who went to school with me, in . . ."

"I mean the Jamaican man. The Jamaican who get killed and brutalized by the police. Those ladies you was having the discussion with, do they know the Jamaican man?"

When she opened her eyes, she realized that the hairdresser, Mr. Azan, who was rubbing the grease into her hair, had been talking too. He turned now towards the ladies who were still with their heads over the square sinks, and to the others under dryers. But he did not say anything to them.

"How long is this going to take? I have to get home and see that boy."

"How the boy?"

"Bright as anything. Doing well in school. Someday he going-crown my head with pride and glory. Praise God. But apart from that, sir, he's a boy. And that means he has his ways. How long?"

"Well, let's see. It's going on seven now. Comb. Folding. Gimme a few minutes. You'll be done in no time! No problem. Not to worry. Yeah, man. You'll be out in no time."

And when his mother left, a new woman, years taken from her appearance, years taken from her gait, years taken from her attitude to herself; and with her hair a bright mauve, and shining, and smelling of the lotions and the smell of the hairdressing salon, it was eight o'clock. But she was beautiful and looking young; and feeling sprightly and full of life. And that was what she wanted for the wedding on Saturday afternoon.

The yellow police cruiser was stopped a few yards ahead of her. It was a dark night. She had looked up into the heavens a few moments, a few yards father back, and smiled as she wondered and remembered that in this city you don't see stars as you see stars back home, when you can become dizzy counting more than three hundred in one raised head and spinning eyes. But when she saw the police cruiser, she became tense and the feeling of paranoia, which came to her every time she saw a police cruiser, came to her now. The black-clad police officers always brought a tense, angry tightness into her chest. And the tightness moved swiftly into her guts. And without knowing, she always felt that it was a black man, or a black woman, but more frequently a black man who was stopped by the policeman. In all the time she has been living in this city, she never saw a white man stopped by a policeman. But then, of course, there had to be some white men stopped by the police. All couldn't be so much more better than black people, she said. And she always felt the black man was innocent. She assumed that. He had to be innocent, she figured, because he was black. And she always thought that the policeman stopped him for no reason at all that he was not breaking the law; but that the police was merely testing him, and anticipating that he would break the law, showing the black man who had power and pull. And the way she always saw the police hold his truncheon, as if it was a long penis, in an everlasting erection, as if he was telling the black man, "Mine is more bigger and more harder than yours!" This is the way she always felt whenever she saw a police cruiser stop a black man in a car.

The night was darker now. She was walking on Davenport Road going towards Bloor Street, and the cruiser was still too far from her for her to see clearly. But she was sure that the man held inside the cruiser was black. She hurried her steps. And when she drew almost abreast of the cruiser, it was still too dark for her to see the man's face. The roof light inside the cruiser was not on. But she would bet her bottom dollar that it was a black man, a black youth, a black child. Her stomach became tight. There were two policemen. She remembered the argument in the hairdressing salon. Two? Or three? There were two. And they were standing beside a car. It was a lovely car. She had seen cars like this one all over the ravine where she worked in a mansion. It was a beautiful car. Many times, standing at the cold, large, picture window, looking out into the blank, white afternoons, with the rhythm and blues music from the Buffalo radio station behind her, she had admired those beautiful cars coming and going along the street in front of the large house. This was a beautiful car like those. It was gleaming. It was white. And it blended well with the snow that was now falling. And she wondered why the licence number plate did not contain numbers like other licence plates. All it said was BLUE. What a strange licence to have! BLUE? And she was feeling so good just a few moments ago. She understood blues. But what was this blue? He must be in a blue mood. What a strange licence to have! BLUE? But she laughed to herself: she herself liked the blues. Rhythm and blues. She was sure there was someone in the back of the cruiser. She had just passed the show window of Mercedes-Benz, when the bright colour of mauve in her hair was reflected back to her and showed her bathed and professionally coiffeured, and hennaed. It startled her. The colour did. For the instant of the reflection, she could not move. She looked at herself in the reflection. She leaned her head slightly to the right, and then to the left; stood erect before the show window and could see not only her reflection but also a salesman in the window looking at her, with his right thumb raised in approval. He had smiled and she had smiled. And then she had moved on after having stolen a last glance at herself. This was before she saw the police cruiser. And when she saw it, all that gaiety in the reflection of the show window evaporated. She was beside the cruiser now.

The two policemen were walking away from the cruiser, going to the white BMW; and she caught up with them. She stopped three feet from the policemen.

"Keep moving, ma'am."

She wondered who was in the dark back seat of the cruiser. And she thought of the Jamaican man, the poor man and his two fatherless girl-children. They said that when the policemen had burst into the house that Sunday afternoon, just before the peas and rice were dished and served, and the shot was fired, his head burst open just like when you drop a ripe watermelon from a certain height. They said his head burst open, clean clean clean.

"Why you-all always bothering black people? Why you-all don't go and try to catch real criminals, them who molesting children? And women."

"None o' your business, ma'am."

"Who say it isn't none of my business? I pays taxes. I obey the law. I have a right to ask you this question, young man."

"Move on, lady. Or I arrest you for obstruction."

"Obstruction? Who I obstructing?"

"What did you say?"

She stood her ground. But she was not so stupid to repeat what she had said.

"Lord, look at this," she said under her breath. She felt she dared not pray, appeal nor talk to her God aloud with the policemen to hear. And the policeman who spoke to her was about to forget about her, when she started up again. "I hope you're not taking advantage of that poor boy you got locked up in that cruiser and I hope you read him his rights and I hope he has a good lawyer to defend him, oh God, for if it was my son I would surely lodge a complaint against the two o' you with the Human Rights commission and complain and tell this policeman to please kiss my—"

"Lady!"

The policeman knew there was something said, although he did not quite know what was said. He knew there was this bond and agreement which he could not break. And he became uncomfortable, and nervous, and felt threatened, as if somebody, this woman standing in front of him with nothing in her hands, save her handbag and a plastic bag full of leftover roast beef, was going to take his life from him. And he rested his hand on the side of his waist where he had his gun.

She took a last glance at the beautiful car, and shook her head with some disappointment that she could not see through the heavy tint of the glass to make out the person inside, and satisfy her prejudice that it had to be a young black man. But she was not going to give up so easily. So, she leaned over the bonnet of the car, being careful not to smear its sheen, almost feeling the cold of the glass, as she peered through the obstructing glass. Inside, on the passenger's side was a young man. She could see that much easily enough. But she wanted to be sure, to be certain that this tinted glass was not playing tricks to the young man's colour. Perhaps, he was black, and this tint was changing his colour. She could touch the glass now and feel the coldness of it, and, at the same time, the comforting heat from the engine, even though it was turned off. She stared, and saw him. It was a young man. A young white man. And the man inside the car, feeling his own shame for his predicament, held his head aside, as if he thought his profile would hide the identity of his face from this malicious woman whom had seen five minutes before. He did not know her, could not remember ever seeing a woman with her hair dyed mauve, and sticking up in the air as this woman's hair was doing in the tricky changing light caused by the passing cars. He held his face in a profile against her staring eyes. And felt the curiosity in her eyes, and thought he could feel the love and the sadness in her manner. If he was not handcuffed behind his back, he would push the door open and invite her in. But what would he say to her? Perhaps, he would call out for help. She moved away, walking backwards for the first few steps, and the smallness of his space, and the fit of the manacles made the car seat large, and it became larger and embraced him in the growing space of his temporary imprisonment. She was walking backwards to get a last glimpse of the licence plate, BLUE, which still made her smile at its eccentricity. And when he walked past the police cruiser, her body flinched, and the tightness that she sometimes deliberately put her body into, to prevent the cold from climbing all over her bones, came to her as she moved beside the cruiser. She could smell no similar smell of polish as she had done standing beside the beautiful car. She could sense no powerful fragrance of leather in the interior, as she had surmised with the white car, named BLUE. And she could feel no warmth from the engine of the police cruiser, as she relished in that short moment when her curiosity challenged her wisdom. The police cruiser was cruel, and ugly and tense, and made her feel guilty. And in this shame, in this surrender of self-control, she walked away not being able to tell, should she be asked, what was the colour of the cruiser. But she made a note of the writing on its side. Division 52. She would never forget that number. And she amused herself, heading to the next bus stop, and if no bus came to rescue her from the gnawing cold, the subway station at Bay, that if she was a gambling woman, she would play combinations of 52 in tomorrow's Lotto 6/49.

Time, and not the consequences nor the cause of his presence here, this evening where he was, was heavy upon BJ's nerves. He paced up and down, with various thoughts entering his head, and his panic and isolation made the space much much larger, so that he was buried in its vastness, and the time and the consequences, what they could be, and the cause became real and he could see his life, his entire life in three short hours that had passed. All these things passed through his mind, and for each of them he had no solution. He paced up and down, not having enough length in the square space to make his pacing more dramatic, and less of pathos. And when he again realized the restriction of the square space, his mind bounded backwards to a time, which he had almost wiped from his memory, recalling a time when he had spent four hours in this same police station, in another cell, alone and not knowing really why he had been locked up, not having had a charge laid against him, not having had a policeman enter the warm cell and interrogate him about the alleged theft of a kid's bicycle that afternoon in August when he and three other kids were horsing around and pretending to be bagmen – they did not play with girls – near the corner grocery store, trying to beg enough quarters to buy ice cream, when his mother was at work down in the ravine, this other kid came wobbly on his bicycle, his first, a present *his* mother had given him for Christmas past; and one of the other three kids took the bike playfully from the little kid and the little kid started to cry and ran home with tears in his eyes and told his mother, and his father returned with sunburnt arms bristling with black hairs and chest like a barrel covered with the skin of an animal, with the black hairs punching from under a nylon undershirt and with his underpants showing just above the waist of his green trousers, when the kid pointed at the coloured fella, dad; the coloured fella is who took my bike; and all hell broke loose with *mama mias* spewn all over the road in white vomit, and as if it was still Christmas and hail was falling, and the cops came screaming down the avenue going against the pointing of the white arrow, two carloads of them, to solve this ghetto delinquency, that began as a small neighbourhood kid's prank, "I didn't mean nothing," and slam! into the cruiser, nigger; into the goddamn cruiser, you goddamn nigger, *mama mia* Hail Marys and BG not understanding the various languages and accents being vomited against him, no explanation in the eyes of the man who owned the peddling grocery store, no explanation from his three friends who did not know Italian and Greek and were no longer within earshot and speaking distance to translate this crime, no understanding from the father with his chest buried in black hairs ripping the air with gestures which BJ thought at first were karate chops, but later knew their meaning even though he knew no Italian and no Greek, and no understanding from the four cops who descended armed and sunburnt like the father to solve this serious crime, git, goddammit, git! into the goddamn cruiser! no, not in the goddamn front seat, in the fucking back, where youse belong; and they took him down, and did not book him, and put him in a nice large warm cell, large through his age, bigger, goddammit nigger warmer than the piss-small room you and your goddamn mother lives in! you fucking West Indians! and they left him there to stew and to mend his thieving ways, and then, hours later, when the time for his supper of plain rice and boiled king fish and boiled green bananas had come and gone, the truth was known, and the kind sergeant came with a Styrofoam cup of steaming coffee, have a cup, come now, have a cup; and then said, a little mistake, if you can understand what I mean, you being such a little fella to know these serious big things, a little goddamn mistake and you happened to be the goddamn unlucky one. So, beat it, kid, and don't let me lay my goddamn eyes on you again! Git!

Too young to know what he had done; not knowing what he had done; not knowing what the policeman in the cruiser had done; not knowing the exact shape of his fate this time, but wise enough to know that he was going to have some fate, BJ paced and paced. And then, perhaps because of his Black Muslim sense of destiny, he stopped walking up and down. He decided not to worry. "Let the motherfuckers come!" he said, but within his heart he was calmed by the small square space, and by his history. And then he worked it out in detail, and with a logic he was capable of, but which, in the circumstances of the steel surrounding him in the four smells of impatience and of no restraint, the smell of vomit and old urine, in the circumstances of an unclear head, he had permitted to elude and overwhelm him. But when he had worked out his plan, he lit a cigarette, all that they had left him, and in his mind, for his mind was clean and not touched by circumstances, he took out the long-playing record, could see his fingers ease it out of the jacket, and put it on his stereo, and remained standing, listening to the words of Malcolm X's speech, *The Ballot or the Bullet.* He was asleep, standing, before the introduction of Malcolm X had finished. And he was stirred from his reverie by the opening of the door, and walked out into the dark cold parking lot, to his car now buried and made invisible by the falling snow. Marco was somewhere else: in another cell, held until *his* parents could come down from North York to sign him out. Two men walked beside him. They were not in uniform. He recognized his car, for the snow had not touched the letters BLUE on the licence plate. And he made the gesture to go to it, even though he did not have the keys. And he was corrected. "We're going for a little drive . . ." And he was put into the back of the cruiser. Left alone, to himself, behind the plastic protector thick as brick, strong as steel, and with his two hands free. The blue unmarked cruiser drove off in the white pouring quiet.

From the top of the street, near Bathurst, she could see the red lights. They were whirring. They scared her each time so much just to see them, that they gave her the impression they were making great noise, and that the red lights were silencers of that noise. She could see the four police cruisers parked in the middle of the road, and one at the side. She could see the large, red, ugly vehicle of the fire department. She could see a smaller, but equally ugly white-painted ambulance. And from the distance she was, turning into the smaller street where she lived, she could see the road filled with people. People were leaving doors open and running and passing her as she walked, heading in the direction of the spinning red lights on top of the police cruisers and the fire department truck and the ambulance. She had never witnessed a fire of this bigness in this city before, and so she walked as fast as she could, in the deep sliding snow, to reach the sight.

The road became more crowded when another police vehicle, a small panel-type truck marked Tactical Squad, forced itself into the road from the other end of the street. She was sure now that someone was holding someone hostage. She had watched many of these scenes every day on the soap opera shows in the mansion down in the ravine where she worked. And tickled by the transformation of a movie into a slice of her real life, she tried to hasten her stride, but without success, for the snow was too deep. She felt the excitement the spinning red lights gave off, the curiosity of staring at these kinds of lights on a highway ahead of you, and she passed each house from one end to the next now as long as a block, her blood quickening, and not once through her mind passed the thought of "Who's sick?" and she did not once consider her neighbours nor the landlord in this absent thought of compassion. It was the excitement she was heading to. People, she could see them now, people were being kept back behind a ribbon of yellow plastic, and one policeman stood guarding the yellow plastic ribbon, which measured the area round one house, and disappeared out of sight, perhaps down a lane or the thin unwalkable space between two houses. And this ribbon reminded her of birthday parties back home, and on Christmas morning, and once, when she was no longer a child, taken by her mother to an opening of something where they had a long ribbon like this before the entrance. On that occasion, the vicar of her church but the ribbon with scissors. Her excitement was now in her blood, and with her blood hot, she was no longer recognizing things, and landmarks and the shape of the uneven concrete steps the landlord had incorrectly built to save money, and that caused her to slip even in the summer. She was forcing herself against these strangers to reach the entrance. And she could see the splotches and the drying small pools, the spots, taking some time to be registered in her excitement as blood. She could see the blood on the steps and blood along the narrow lane, and the lane became difficult to see, as it went beside the house on the left. A dog walked out as if it was drunk. And when it vomited, what came out was like grape juice.

She could see policemen inside the room, collecting things, some of which they were already bringing out. And she could see the attendants from the ambulance arranging something heavy on to a stretcher. She could see the clothes being brought out. She could see the stereo equipment, speakers, CD player, amplifier. And the books. And the small Bible. She wondered who lived here. She could see the books. Books always interested him. And then she realized she was thinking of her son. He always had his head inside a book. And one book she saw was the Holy Qur'an. She wondered if this was the wrong address.

She could see the policemen inside the room, at the back near the door to her kitchen, walking round the small space, nervous and silent. The street outside was silent too. No one was talking. But she could hear their anger and their resentment and their hatred. She was beginning to learn how to listen to this kind of silence.

And then, there was a sound. A sound very similar to surprise, or to shock, or even to the satisfaction that what you are about to see is the shock, but that you are not prepared for it.

They were bringing a body out. Two ambulance attendants carried the stretcher which had wheels like a bier of a coffin, but which had to lifted part of the journey – the short journey from the back of the house, down the two short cement steps which the landlord had not got around to fixing properly, a little way to the right of the rear door, and to the ambulance after going through the thin lane, down two more steps and up the three steps of the basement apartment front door. As they lifted it up the steps, the wind, which was cold and strong, blew the cloth off the body of the corpse. A cry went through the people. It was a young man. A boy, still with his mother's features. No more than sixteen or seventeen or eighteen. A black youth, with a close-trimmed haircut, with Zeds for patterns and an X for style, dressed in a black woollen jersey, black slacks, white socks and black shoes that could, if he was alive, help him to jump against gravity, like a basketball star. Or Michael Jordan. And when the wind had taken the blanket on it short wild curtsey to the wind and to the night, the people made that sound again, like a gigantic taking in of wind.

She could see it too, And she saw the head, and it was out of shape from something that had hit it. Disfigured. And the blood was covering the face. And the stretcher was covered in thick blood. And the black clothes the youth was dressed in were red now, more than black. The blood seemed to have its own unkind and disfiguring disposition, and it seemed to drip and mark the journey from the room at the back of the basement apartment through the room itself, through the small backyard, through the lane and out into the cold wind. It looked as if a cannon had struck the head, and the head had exploded and had been cut into pieces, like a watermelon that had slipped out of the hand. To her, it seemed as if the brains of the young man were coming through his mouth, as if his eyes were lost against the impact of the bullet. To her, it looked like a watermelon that was smashed by the wheels of a car.

It was too much. It was too cold. It was too brutal. It was too cruel. And there was too much blood. Worse than the American soap opera she had watched earlier the afternoon of this Friday night, down in the ravine.

"BJ! BJ Fuck!"

It was somebody screaming. She did not know the voice. She looked around, in this crowd of people only one of whom she knew, her landlord, and then she saw the owner of the voice. It was a young man. There were tears in the young man's eyes. He was dressed in a black jogging suit, black Adidas, and white athletic socks, and he seemed to have something wrong with his right hand or his right side, for he was doing something with his body which made it shake, as if he had a nervous habit, like a tick, hitting his right hand against his right thigh. He looked Portuguese to her. She did not know him. "BJ! BJ! Fuck!"

Questions for Discussion and Essays

Austin Clarke is the winner of the 2002 Giller Prize, the 2003 Commonwealth Writers Prize, and the 16th Annual Trillium Prize for *The Polished Hoe*, which was also long-listed for the 2004 International IMPAC Dublin Literary Award. He is the winner of the 1999 W.O. Mitchell Prize, awarded each year to a Canadian writer who has not only produced an outstanding body of work, but has been an outstanding mentor among young writers. He is the author of nine novels and six short-story collection, including *Choosing His Coffin: The Best Stories of Austin Clarke, Growing Up Stupid Under the Union Jack, The Prime Minister,* the culinary memoir, *Love and Sweet Food,* and, most recently, his new novel, *More.*

1. How important is a sense of "origin" (familial, regional, cultural, racial) in the stories of *In This City*? When are "origins" threatening or comforting, "facts" that are naked and inescapable, or "stories" that are freely imaginable?

2. In "Gift-Wrapped," the narrator uses a notably lucid voice, but in parts of stories such as "Initiation," "Trying to Kill Herself," and "A Short Drive," the narrator explores much more complex and tangled language. Why is this? What can you say about the stylistic choices that the narrator makes in different stories, and at different moments in the plot?

3. Clarke has developed a reputation for a sensitive and humourous use of dialect or vernacular in much of his fiction. Comment upon the use of dialect in stories such as "Initiation" or "I'm Running for My Life."

4. Is *In This City* about Toronto specifically – its specific neigh-bourhoods or demographics, for instance – or else about "the city," broadly speaking? How "translatable" is the collection as a portrait of modern urban life?

5. What can you say about intercultural or interracial relationships in the collection? What about the relationships between people who are together "West Indian," or "black" but, in fact, possess very different backgrounds and experiences?

6. How are gender differences depicted in the collection? Are there, in the various stories, consistent differences between women's and men's choices and their ability to get something accomplished?

7. How is sexuality and physical intimacy depicted in the collec-tion? When and how are moments of bodily feeling and satisfac-tion represented, and what, if anything, does this say about the pre-sumed "pleasures" of city life?

8. What role does music play in Clarke's stories? What can you say about the specific music that is cited, and its relationship to spe-cific plot lines or character psychologies? (e.g. What is John Col-trane doing in "Initiation," "A Short Drive," and "Sometimes a Motherless Child." What do you know about the song "Sometimes a Motherless Child" itself?)

9. Comment upon the generational rifts that are articulated in stories such as "Gift-Wrapped," "Initiation," "Letter of the Law of Black," and "Sometimes a Motherless Child."

10. Have you read some of Clarke's other books? If so, what comes to mind when reading *In This City*? Do you see continuity or differences between Clarke's books?

Related Reading

NOVELS

The Survivors of the Crossing.
　Toronto: McClelland & Stewart, 1964.

The Meeting Point.
　Toronto: Macmillan, 1967. (Republished Toronto: Vintage, 1998)

Storm of Fortune.
　Boston: Little Brown, 1973. (Republished Toronto: Vintage, 1998)

The Bigger Light.
　Boston: Little Brown, 1975. (Republished Toronto: Vintage, 1998)

The Prime Minister.
　Don Mills, Ont.: General Publishing, 1977. Toronto: Exile Editions, 1994.

Proud Empires.
　London: Gollancz, 1988.

The Origin of Waves.
　Toronto: McClelland & Stewart, 1997.

The Question.
   Toronto: McClelland & Stewart, 1999.

The Polished Hoe.
   Toronto: Thomas Allen, 2002.

More.
   Toronto: Thomas Allen, 2008

SHORT STORIES

Amongst Thistles and Thorns.
   Toronto: McClelland & Stewart, 1965.

When He Was Free and Young and He Used to Wear Silks.
   Toronto: Anansi, 1971.

When Women Rule.
   Toronto: McClelland and Stewart, 1985.

Nine Men Who Laughed.
   Toronto: Penguin, 1986.

In This City.
   Toronto: Exile Editions, 1992. (Republished Toronto: Exile, 2008)

There Are No Elders.
   Toronto: Exile Editions, 1993.

MEMOIRS

Growing Up Stupid Under the Union Jack: A Memoir.
  Toronto: McClelland & Stewart, 1980. (Republished Toronto:
  Thomas Allen, 2005)

Public Enemies: Police Violence and Black Youth.
  Toronto: HarperCollins, 1992.

A Passage Back Home: A Personal Reminiscence of Samuel Selvon.
  Toronto: Exile Editions, 1994.

Pigtails 'n' Breadfruit: The Rituals of Slave Food, A Barbadian Memoir.
  Toronto: Random House, 1999. University of Toronto Press,
  2001.

RESOURCES ON CLARKE'S WORK

The Austin Clarke Reader. (Ed. Barry Callaghan.)
  Toronto: Exile Editions, 1996.

Choosing His Coffin: The Best Stories of Austin Clarke.
  Toronto: T. Allen Publishers, 2003.

Austin C. Clarke: A Biography. (Author, Stella Algoo Baksh.)
  Toronto: ECW, 1994.

Of Interest on the Web

1. www.bookbrowse.com/biographies/index.cfm?author_
   number=907
   A "visitor's site" to browse a biography of Austin Clarke, read book summaries, excerpts and reviews, at BookBrowse.com.

2. www.library.mcmaster.ca/archives/findaids/index.html
   The McMaster University archives Web site. Direct Clarke link:
   library.mcmaster.ca/archives/findaids/fonds/c/clarke-a.htm

3. www.thomas-allen.com
   Austin Clarke's publisher website

Review - THERE ARE NO ELDERS – *EXILE CLASSICS SERIES FIVE*
by Austin Clarke
Exile Editions, issued 2007
Review by Tony O'Brien
September 2, 2008 (Volume 12, Issue 36 – *Metapsychology online reviews*)

How many of this year's crop of collections of short stories will be republished in fifteen years? Not many. A short story that reaches beyond its time is a rare thing. *There Are No Elders* was first published in 1993, and Exile Editions have done readers like myself a huge service by reissuing this collection. The book is a collection of eight stories, all focused on different aspects of life as experienced by West Indian immigrants to Toronto. It would be a mistake though, to say that the book is only about one ethnic group and the dilemmas encountered by those finding themselves in a culturally alien world. Clarke is a skilful crafter of fiction. His characters, situations and dialog reach beyond their particular circumstances and exert a universal appeal. That probably accounts for the longevity of these stories, as much as their appeal.

The book commences with the strong and disturbing "If the Bough Breaks." Five West Indian women, affluent and fashionable, are having their hair done after a hotel lunch and martinis. When they hear police sirens they immediately assume a black person is about to be arrested. A white teenager is led away, setting up an intense exchange between the women. The girl is vulnerable in the hands of the police. There have been reports in the papers. Why should they care about a white girl? What about their own daughters? The women are caught between race and gender solidarity. The conclusion of the story illustrates the humanity of the five women, but not before Clarke has forced us to confront difficult moral questions. As Norman Mailer says on the back cover of the book, there is a moment in Clarke's stories when "one realizes one has learned something new that one didn't want to know... And so on one goes, alternately congratulating and cursing Austin Clarke, while changing the workings of one's own mind."

Clarke's ear for spoken language is superb. When the girls are discussing the teenager taken away by the police one comments: "She was unfaired by the police." It's hard to imagine how that sentence would have the same impact in grammatically "correct" English. "If the Bough Breaks" becomes a little didactic when one of the women declares when discussing racism: "...it is the history and experience of each and every one of us in this room." There are a few other points too, where I felt the characters were giving voice to Clarke's thoughts rather than their own. However, the narrative is completely compelling. The twists and turns in the plot, the buildup of suspense, and resolution are terrific. Clarke includes revealing details like a master painter unobtrusively placing a small object in a larger scene, not to draw attention to itself, but to emphasize the main point of the work.

Many of the stories are set in Toronto, but they hark back to the West Indies, with scenes of family life, adolescence, and coming of age. By drawing on the West Indian background of his characters as well as on their current urban life Clarke is able to set up contrasts that give these stories energy and tension. "In an Elevator" sees Susan Cole, a young office employee recovering from a bad episode of food poisoning, shown in stark relief against the cleaners who wait for her to vacate the toilet, and the black man who enters the elevator as she's leaving work. This is no ordinary uncomfortable ride with a stranger. Someone has pressed all the buttons, probably the cleaner in an effort to exact revenge, or perhaps just assert herself. And the man is black. He's listening to a Walkman, so it's probably rap music. He wears a cap. Backwards. His hair is shaved. We're stuck with Susan and her growing anxiety as the elevator descends, floor by floor. When it stops, the man is polite and courteous. He leaves an indelible image in Susan's memory, and she tells herself her tears are caused by the cold air.

"Beggars" is a story within a story. The action takes place on a crowded commuter train, with people crammed up against each other so close their flesh touches and they can smell each other's perfume, aftershave or body odour. Each jolt of the train causes another small collision. The first person narrator is pressed against a woman whose life he imagines, or rather, invents. In this inner story the woman lives with a violent, disappointed husband. She takes meticulous care of her appearance, and she plans to leave her husband. When she gets off the train her fellow passenger follows her with his eyes, wishing he could follow her in real life. He's stalking her, but she doesn't know it. He thinks of "the fear that resides on women's faces when the man who walks close to them carries an identity they cannot penetrate." In the end the man is deterred by this fear, but deterred from what? With "Beggars" Clarke builds two levels of tension and leaves readers to sense it without relief.

The stories are poignant and moving, at times funny. There's one about a middle aged man who takes a prostitute home then spends the evening drinking with her. There are two tales of reconciliation, one welcomed, the other not. The separation of mother and child leads to another reconciliation, this time of the older woman with her own mother. Clarke is comfortable writing from both men's and women's perspectives and despite the West Indian perspective he brings to bear he's not dependent on this, and neither are the stories. Austin Clarke shines a bright light into some dark places. *There Are No Elders* is well-worth republishing.

This book is entirely printed on FSC certified paper.